Brian A. Williams is a professional writer, for whom the film and book *Blood Oath* have been a lifelong ambition. At the age of 12 he discovered the transcripts and photographs of the war crimes trials his father conducted on Ambon and Morotai. From that time on, he felt that this was a story that must be told.

Having studied law, Brian Williams has worked in video and film before obtaining a degree in Drama. He has since written a number of film, radio and television scripts, including the soon to be released film *Vanished*, and the multi award winning radio series *The Global Countdown*.

He is currently at work on a play and another feature film project.

BRIAN A. WILLIAMS

BASED ON THE SCREENPLAY BY
DENIS WHITBURN AND BRIAN A. WILLIAMS

ANGUS
& ROBERTSON

First published in Australia in 1990 by Collins/Angus & Robertson Publishers Australia

First published in the United Kingdom in 1990 by Angus & Robertson (UK)

*Collins/Angus & Robertson Publishers Australia
Unit 4, Eden Park, 31 Waterloo Road, North Ryde
NSW 2113, Australia*

*William Collins Publishers Ltd
31 View Road, Glenfield, Auckland 10, New Zealand*

*Angus & Robertson (UK)
16 Golden Square, London W1R 4BN, United Kingdom*

Copyright © Blood Oath Productions Pty Limited 1990

National Library of Australia
Cataloguing-in-Publication data:

Williams, Brian A.
  Blood oath.

  Bibliography.
  ISBN 0 207 16693 5.

  1. War crime trials - Fiction. 2. World War, 1939-1945 -
  Indonesia - Ambon Island - Atrocities - Fiction. I.
  Title.

A823.3

Typeset in Baskerville by Midland Typesetters
Printed in Australia by The Book Printer

5 4 3 2
95 94 93 92 91 90

Dedicated to my father, John Williams
Q.C. – the inspiration; my mother, Dorothy
Williams – the true believer; and Ursula
Kolbe – the catalyst.

AUTHOR'S NOTE AND ACKNOWLEDGEMENTS

This book is based on a series of war crimes trials of the Japanese on Ambon and Morotai, Indonesia, in early 1946. What follows is a dramatic synthesis of those events. It in no way purports to reveal the 'truth' of what happened. Rather, it seeks to illuminate the kinds of forces that were to shape the post war world, forces that still have direct effect on the present.

For example, there was no direct or indirect US involvement in those trials conducted by the Australian government. But it was felt important that the US policy for the reconstruction of Japan should become a focus for dramatic tension in the story because these trials were operating against a global setting. The US policy, founded on the preservation of Emperor Hirohito, is fundamental to any examination of the period.

Indeed, with the death of Emperor Hirohito in 1989, a new era of 'reflection on the past' seems to be emerging in Japan, where discussions about 'responsibility' and 'policy' can take place more openly.

Finally, the character of Captain Cooper, although based on my father's formal role as Prosecutor, is one with a life and viewpoint of his own. However his 'journey' does embody one of the most striking characteristics of the Australian courts which conducted these trials. That is, a strict application of the 'presumption of innocence', against all the cries for blood and revenge which were deeply felt at the time. The old Australian notion of a 'fair go' could not have had a more paradoxical setting.

I would like to thank my parents again. In addition, I would like to thank Denis Whitburn, Ursula Kolbe and Noel Purdon for their rigorous and constructive suggestions, Annie Bleakley, who added this to her already considerable workload as co-producer of the film, and finally my editor Kathy Metcalfe for her enthusiasm and dedication.

CHAPTER ONE

THE DIG

Mist. Tendrils, curling around the sago palms, fanning out across the dark jungle. Thickening into fingers, now concealing, now revealing the brilliant colours, the strangely distorted shapes of trees, of birds, of men.

Mist. A play of light over sombre, pallid faces lined with sweat. Apprehensive faces, very aware of other faces watching them closely. Ruddy, flushed faces, some young and open. Faces that seem as confused as the nervous ones but close up, are edged with a hardness and strength of purpose. Young warriors in a tropical gothic haze. Australian soldiers moving beside their Japanese prisoners through the jungle in an almost dreamlike march. No longer at war but not at peace.

Mist. What had it concealed during the last three years? What secrets lay beneath its shroud over the dank, rotting undergrowth? Was the mist now choosing to withdraw? Or would it remain forever? Like its island namesake—Ambon. 'Island of mist.'

For Captain Robert Cooper, this is the day when the mist would have to clear. His case must become unshakeable. Standing, concealed by the mist under a durian tree, he watches the hobbling approach of an old man, helped by his young grandson. Strange how such a case now had to rely on the memory of a frail old man, and he had heard it from an eyewitness, who had been killed by the Japanese.

Cooper feels the eyes of Jack Keenan, the guard sergeant, demanding his attention.

'Halt!' Keenan shouts.

The Japanese and the Australians stop. Keenan glares at the prisoners with barely concealed hatred, impatient with the wild-goose chase they have been on. He exchanges a glance with the Corporal next to him. Mutual frustration, relieved only by the sound of one of the Japanese pissing in his pants. Keenan sniggers.

'The Emperor didn't order you to do that, did he, Tojo?'

The Australians explode in a raucous laughter that sends flocks of hidden parrots screeching from the trees above, their frightened squawks mixing with the laughter and shame below.

Cooper is too preoccupied with the old man to notice. He moves forward slowly with him to the edge of a clearing. Cooper points across the clearing.

'Is it here?'

The old man peers around, willing himself to remember. Cooper observes the burn marks on his withered arms and legs. Probably a *Kempetai* reprisal for smuggling food to a prisoner. The Ambonese had suffered terribly under the Japanese. If they had not been so courageous in smuggling food to the prisoners, many of Cooper's potential witnesses would not have survived.

Suddenly the old man spots a small broken down hut almost concealed by a clump of trees. He starts to hurry towards it but has to slow himself as a racking cough sends him into a spasm. Cooper catches him, as he stumbles.

'Easy, easy. No rush!'

He waves Keenan to follow. Keenan snaps the guards into action.

'Righto, this is it! Quick march! Speedo!'

The Japanese are shoved forward roughly by the soldiers. They exchange terrified looks, uncertain of their fate.

Cooper gently steers the old man towards the hut. The old man stops and points to a strip of palms running away from the hut to dense jungle.

'Here,' the old man says in halting English, 'I think here. Yes.'

Cooper and the young boy lower the old man to the ground, seating him under a tree beside the hut. Cooper offers him a smoke. The old man, still wheezing, accepts gratefully.

'*Tarimo kassi.*'

Cooper strides away to the detail and halts a few metres from the palms. He nods to Keenan and turns to the young army photographer Patterson, who is out of breath, labouring under the weight of his camera gear.

'I want photos of everything.'

'Sir.'

Cooper turns to see Keenan toss a shovel to Ikeuchi, a Japanese officer who stares off into the jungle, totally oblivious to what is happening.

Ikeuchi turns to look at the shovel. It is an object of bemusement. He stares at the sergeant calmly. Keenan snaps his fingers angrily.

'Prisoner Ikeuchi. Dig!'

Ikeuchi stands his ground. Keenan grabs another shovel, steps up to Ikeuchi, his eyes boring into him, the shovel gripped like a weapon.

'Fucking dig!'

The Japanese wait, intent on Ikeuchi's next move. Finally, Ikeuchi smiles and reaches down languidly for the shovel beside him. He looks at Keenan with contempt.

'You bury us? One day we bury you.'

He starts to dig the shovel into the moist earth, tossing some dirt over Keenan's boots. Keenan jerks his head at the other Japanese who take picks and shovels from a large box opened by the Australian guards.

Cooper studies Ikeuchi's nonchalant digging. The man of stone. But stones can either be worn down slowly or they can be pulverised.

He lights a smoke and starts to walk around the dig, his boots sinking into dank earth as the Japanese are dispersed along a line into the jungle. A tap on the shoulder. Lieutenant Corbett, his assistant, removes some documents from a bulging satchel, and mops his forehead. Cooper takes them and looks them over carefully.

'Anything more?'

'That's it so far.'

'Jesus.'

Cooper hands back the statements, then studies a map that Corbett has produced. The Australian positions around the Laha Airstrip at the time of the Japanese attack are clearly marked. Sending a unit of 1100 men to defend this island against an invasion force of 35 000 Japanese, was really asking for it—Australia's Alamo, thought Cooper. Now he had to clean up the mess, with almost no Japanese records and a wall of silence from Ikeuchi and his men, he was really up against it. But if that wall was smashed, and if the hard cases like Mitchell could remember . . . if?

Cooper takes the map and walks away from Corbett.

'Bloody lawyers.'

Corbett follows him, ignoring the whispered jibe from one of the guards.

'It's long odds, sir. They could have all been killed in battle.'

Cooper nods then notices his hand agitatedly squeezing the fob watch in his right pocket. He brings it out, opens it—2.00 p.m. He studies a photo of his brother Geoff on the inside cover. It was the last Christmas gift he had received from Geoff before he was posted to Singapore. He had tried desperately to get there at the surrender, but it was too late. Changi had claimed Geoff.

If only he was prosecuting the bastards who ran Changi. But that would be handled mainly by the Brits. Ambon and Morotai, the Dutch East Indies, would be the Australian beat. But how do you prosecute a trial of nearly one hundred Japanese? Who knows?

It had never been done before. A voice of doubt.

That's not to say it can't be done, comes another voice. Too close to Geoff's?

But the Australian Government and the Australian people wanted scalps. The War Crimes Bill had been rushed through only last month. He was the guinea pig. If he delivered the goods, next stop could be Tokyo; and the prize scalp of all, the Emperor.

The heat is an enemy here, comes that first voice again, *saps your concentration, weakens your will.*

You can fight it. Geoff again?

Cooper looks at the Australian soldiers, some of

whom were also affected by the heat. He studies the face of Talbot, a young Private who had seen no action; green behind the gills and probably doesn't know one end of his rifle from the other. A real contrast to Keenan, an old pro from the Kokoda campaign; rumoured to have a nickname 'Kill 'em Keenan'; said to have honoured the Japanese code of 'no prisoners' to the letter. But now Keenan was faced with a new world. Who would adapt the better, Keenan or his enemies?

Cooper feels a strange sensation on his skin. He turns to lock eyes with Ikeuchi who is half leaning on his shovel. There was more than just an arrogance there, which usually masks inferiority. There was an ancient implacability. The personal didn't matter a damn, but how could you keep this from being 'personal'?

They are startled by a cry from one of the guards.

'Sarge. Over here.'

Keenan pushes past the Japanese to the spot. The young guard holds up a filthy, decayed foul smelling piece of cloth. Keenan takes it, spits on it and rubs it. A red and black diamond pattern emerges, 'AIF 2/21st Battalion'.

Cooper steps up to Keenan, takes it and holds it up. Keenan turns and yells at the Japanese to dig. The 'diggers', encouraged by the occasional rifle butt, resume. Cooper nods to Corbett who unrolls a tarpaulin beside the dig. Cooper steps back, intent on the insignia, as the light starts failing. The sun disappears behind thick dark clouds. Cooper exchanges an apprehensive look with Corbett and the photographer as thunder rumbles overhead.

A decayed arm is unearthed.

'Stop! Stop digging!' Keenan screams.

Cooper strides back and stands gazing at the arm. He looks around to see Talbot turn his back, retching in awful convulsive bursts. Keenan, kneeling beside the arm, looks back up at Cooper, a long challenging gaze.

Corbett kneels beside Keenan with another guard. They adjust thick protective gloves and gently prise the decayed body from the muddy earth. The face, a death mask of a silent scream.

Keenan launches himself at Ikeuchi.

'Murdering bastard!'

He grabs Ikeuchi by the neck and forces him to his knees to confront the corpse. With supreme will, Ikeuchi turns his head around, gazing up at Keenan, still defiant. Keenan, shaking with rage, spits into his face and hurls him aside.

Corbett and the guard lay the remains on the tarpaulin. The photographer stares in disbelief as he raises his camera.

The air is filled with cries from the guards as more remains are uncovered with every new shovelful. Cooper moves quickly from one end of the grave to the other, trying to take in the full horror.

Limbs tied with wire, bullet-ridden skulls, decayed photos of loved ones, decapitated torsos. Corbett and the guards frantically grabbing them before they became buried again. The photographer almost falls into the grave, tripping over the wire-bound decayed limbs. Cooper thrusts out his arm, grabs him and points him to the other end of the grave. The photographer gives a grim smile of thanks. Cooper kneels beside the long tarp, which is covered with the remains that had shattered 'the wall of silence'. Now, it was an avalanche of evidence.

Keenan, surrounded by Talbot and some of the

guards, stands beside the grave, transfixed. He is filled with an overpowering urge to strike out at the perpetrators.

Ikeuchi, smiling thinly, places a muddy skull at Keenan's feet. Without hesitating, Keenan slams back the breech on his Thompson, and places the muzzle firmly between Ikeuchi's eyes.

As one, the Australian guards raise their rifles. The Japanese glance up in terror, the moment they had long dreaded now upon them. Talbot is the only man with his rifle still shouldered.

'How does it feel, eh, Tojo? Now you're standing in it?'

Ikeuchi gazes up at Keenan, almost willing him to fire. A single drop of rain hits Ikeuchi on the forehead.

Cooper leaps to his feet, grabs the rifle barrel of the nearest soldier and pushes it to the ground. He strides towards Keenan, slapping rifle barrels down until he is face to face with him.

'Shoulder that weapon, Sergeant!' Cooper says in a harsh whisper.

Keenan, almost in a trance, turns slowly to Cooper, sizing him up. He chuckles.

'Military justice!'

'I know your feelings, but this is my show and we'll do it my way!'

Keenan laughs, almost brittle but filled with bitterness.

'Military justice? You know what military justice is, Cooper?'

Keenan looks back at the guards, some now with cheeks stained with tears of rage and grief. Keenan's laugh builds to a savage almost maniacal climax.

'You know what military justice is, boys? A bullet!'

8

Rain starts to fall, thick fingers of it, mixing with the tears of the soldiers, beating the mud from Japanese hands, softening Keenan's mask of hatred.

Keenan lowers his gun, shakes his head sharply, a silent order to the soldiers, who replace their safety catches slowly. The rain builds into a tropical downpour, drenching them. Cooper heads for the shelter of the hut, but turns to see Keenan grabbing the crucifix from around Talbot's neck.

'A bullet, Private!' screams Keenan.

Talbot's reply is lost in the thundering downpour. Keenan pushes Talbot away and shoves the Japanese back into the mass grave.

Cooper notices the old Ambonese man and his grandson standing in the rain, watching. They have been joined by other villagers, witnesses to the confrontation. The young boy has been joined by other young children, standing wide eyed, puzzled by what is happening. But the eyes of the villagers say it all.

'They probably hate me for that,' thinks Cooper. 'If they were running the show, not a single Jap would be left, and would they be wrong?'

With every new sodden shovel, more remains are unearthed. The grave is an impossible quagmire now, but Keenan's hatred drives the Japanese to even greater efforts.

Cooper watches, determined to maintain his appearance of impartiality in front of Corbett and the others. But for him also, those memories could never be washed away.

Cooper gazes back to Ikeuchi. He permits himself a small smile of satisfaction. He had the monkey. Now for the organ grinder—Takahashi.

CHAPTER TWO

PRESUMPTION OF INNOCENCE

Major Frank Roberts stands at the open window of his office, distracted. The incessant, dull chatter of typewriters and the crackling of the short wave seem far away. His vision was blurring again. Was it the sign of a recurrence of the malaria he'd caught in New Guinea in '43? If those hot needles started behind the eyes again, he'd be finished.

He strains to focus. Was it Cooper and Corbett passing the POW camp to the Legal Corps HQ? If so, he was not looking forward to it. Cooper never seemed to sleep. He was driving the case like a man possessed, a zealot. It was a whole new pressure, a personal vendetta that Roberts could well do without. But he was right in one sense—the government wanted 'results'. Kid gloves was not the policy.

Right now, however, Tokyo in winter would be infinitely preferable to this heat. But that would depend on 'results'. He must not show any signs of weakness. He would not fall off this tightrope. He'd handled the preliminary investigations with proper balance, as he had the deal with the Dutch to allow the Occupation Force to remain on Ambon for the trials. He was the man for the job. If only this weariness, this lethargy would disappear.

He turns back to see the leathery, stubbled face

of Mike Sheedy, pen poised over his notebook, his head slightly drooping, a deceptively sleepy expression. Roberts had to choose his words carefully. Sheedy was renowned for filing unflattering portraits of people and events. Admittedly, his report from Hiroshima, one of the first, was a masterpiece. But his latest piece on the mopping up campaign in the islands left a sour taste. The Australians were not stooges for the Americans. Roberts would much rather be interviewed by an army PR man. At least the facts would be presented responsibly.

'You were saying, Major, that we're here to give these people a fair trial.'

'Correct, Mr Sheedy. Revenge is not the name of the game here.'

'And justice is?'

'A presumption of innocence underpins British justice, Mr Sheedy. Whether it's civil, criminal or military law. As is the case here.'

Sheedy purses his lips and lights an Indonesian kretek, which crackles into life. He takes a long draw and rubs his ear thoughtfully. He catches the radio operator darting a glance at them, eavesdropping through his headset.

'Presumption of innocence? Yeah, it's a great concept we've got, isn't it?'

Roberts nods, as he looks down at the photo in his hand—remains from the mass grave.

'Yes. Absolutely fundamental.'

Roberts plays with his glasses, easing his gaunt frame into his chair. He knew what was next. It was signalled by Sheedy's slow exhalation of a thick cloud of clove-scented smoke.

'It's just that, well, I don't think the Australian people would agree with it in this case. Their mood . . .'

Roberts tries an indulgent smile but all he can feel is his tight lips.

'I'm well aware of this "mood", as you describe it, Mr Sheedy. Many families lost fathers, sons, brothers . . .'

Sheedy doesn't appear to hear this. His eyes are fixed on the portrait of the King above Roberts' desk. He grins lopsidedly.

'God, King and country.'

'Pardon?'

'That's your service oath, isn't it?'

Roberts suppresses his irritation with difficulty, the loathsome kretek only made it worse. The radio operator swivels around, the hissing and crackling suddenly clearing. A distinctly Southern American accent fills the room.

'Supreme Command Allied Powers HQ, Tokyo, reading you loud and clear, Ambon.'

Roberts leaps to his feet, takes the handset, and turns his back on Sheedy, quietly amused by it all.

'Tokyo, this is Major Roberts, Australian War Crimes Tribunal, Ambon. I want to leave a message with Major Tom Beckett, Chief Liaison Officer in your International Prosecution Section . . .'

He is swamped by static again. An Australian radio station blares forth the song, *The Road to Gundagai*.

'Damn!'

The radio operator frantically fiddles with the dials, to no avail. Roberts hands back the handset and turns back to Sheedy, who is flipping carefully through the photos on Roberts' desk. The man was a bloody menace.

Roberts stares at Sheedy icily. Sheedy puts down the photos, stubs out his smoke.

'Pretty conclusive evidence, wouldn't you say?'

Roberts doesn't reply but takes the photos carefully and returns them to a folder around which he ties a maroon ribbon. Sheedy rises.

'I can see you've got work to do.'

'Yes, Mr Sheedy, I have. I think we can continue this later.'

'Any time, Major. But there are deadlines, even for Ambon.'

Roberts doesn't need to be reminded.

Sheedy takes his battered hat and steps quietly to the door, pausing to adjust his rumpled, stained fatigues. He shoots Roberts a crooked smile.

'I s'pose the photos aren't for public consumption yet, Major?'

'They're classified, Mr Sheedy, permanently. Good day.'

Sheedy lingers a few moments, studying Roberts, whose head is among some documents.

'You're looking a bit pale, Major. I'd keep up the quinine if I were you.'

Roberts looks up, stunned. But Sheedy was already through the door.

Sheedy steps into a chaos of racketty typewriters, Ambonese and Australian orderlies moving files from one long table to another, a crackling short wave in the corner; this one broadcasting the cricket score in the England versus Australia match. Sheedy cocks an ear to it and looks up at the overhead fan, which hardly revolves; a creaking casualty of sabotage by the locals to reduce the comfort of the Japanese invader. Well, at least British justice was in good shape—the Poms were being thrashed on the cricket pitch.

On one wall are photos of young Australian soldiers all named and listed under four headings:

'Missing', 'Hospitalised', 'Repatriated' and 'Dead'. Sheedy turns to the opposite wall, and sees the faces of Japanese officers and men. At the head is a photograph captioned 'Vice Admiral Baron Takahashi/Ambon C-i-C'. Sheedy studies it closely and grins sombrely, silently reading names—*The Baron of the butcher shop. Smug bastard.* Beneath him, *Captain Ikeuchi/Ambon POW camp, No. 1 Bully Boy.*

Some of the Japanese officers and men are identified only by nicknames: 'The Black Bastard', 'Horse Face', 'Creeping Jesus'. Sheedy grins. The Australian genius for character description, triumphant even on Ambon.

His grin vanishes as he peers through the glare to a partition at the far end partially obscuring the emaciated bodies of two ex-POWs, answering questions in halting, rasping voices.

How can they even describe it?, thought Sheedy. Poor buggers, how can they ever be normal again?

A group of three Japanese prisoners in dirty, grey prison garb are marched from the hut as Patterson removes the film from his fixed camera. It is pointed towards a strip on a wall, marked in feet and inches. Patterson places the film on a bench, then picks up a couple of chalk boards, marked with the name and rank of the Japanese. He rubs them out quickly, ready for the next batch.

Cooper enters with Corbett, running rapidly through a check list.

'Private Tilson?'

'Repatriated.'

'Private James?'

'Repatriated.'

'Corporal Simpson?'

Patterson turns from fixing photos on the wall to Corbett.

'Played football with him, he had a real boot on him. Says here he's still missing.'

Corbett takes Patterson's sheet and compares it with the one he's checking with Cooper. Corbett sighs and thrusts the sheet back impatiently.

'S-I-double bloody M-S-O-N, Greg.'

Corbett turns back to Cooper.

'Flew out two days ago.'

Cooper has one eye on Sheedy as they approach Roberts' door. He stubs out his cigarette in an overflowing ashtray.

'It's beyond a bloody joke. I can't put a statement in the box and ask it, "is this the bloke who beat the living daylights out of you?".' He stabs an accusing finger at the photo of Ikeuchi.

Corbett veers off to confer with Patterson, as Cooper reaches the door, Sheedy extends his hand.

'Mike Sheedy, *Sydney Herald.*'

Cooper shakes it perfunctorily.

'Heard a press party was due in.'

'You're looking at it, old son.'

Cooper looks sceptically at Sheedy.

'Bob Cooper, Legal Corps.'

'Ah, the Prosecutor. I hope you might be a bit more forthcoming than the Major in there.'

Cooper is tempted to reply but heads straight through the door, leaving Sheedy staring at a pile of documents to which he inexorably gravitates.

Cooper salutes Roberts, who glances up and returns it wearily. Cooper stares at a couple of orderlies stacking files on a makeshift trestle. They get the message and depart promptly. Only the radio operator is left, intent on the whistling static from the set. Cooper produces a pink form from his satchel and slides it across to Roberts.

'Without Mitchell on the witness stand, I might as well pack it in and head home myself. He's my one real shot at Takahashi.'

Roberts studies the form.

'Well, if the medical officer says he's not fit to testify, there's nothing I can do.'

'Frank, he's the only bloke who spoke Japanese. He overheard Takahashi . . .'

Roberts cuts him off abruptly.

'Precisely, Bob. Hearsay evidence is admissible if it's first hand.'

Cooper takes a couple of paces forward, and looks out at the POW compound.

'I thought we were here to give Mitchell and these blokes the one thing they never got from the Japs, a fair go.'

Roberts doesn't like the insinuation. He puts down his pen and stands to face Cooper.

'I know why we're here, and one of our first priorities must be the recovery of these men. As for Takahashi, we haven't got him yet so the point is academic.'

Cooper scoops up a loose photo of the mass grave.

'This . . . is not academic, Major. The only way to crack them is to humiliate their top man in front of them. If this bloody paper war with the Yanks doesn't end soon, we'll never get him.'

Roberts takes the photo with a gesture of resignation.

'You're right. It's not academic. But you've got a flying start with this, Bob. I know the pressure you're feeling but this is a contest of wills.'

The radio operator lifts his headset.

'Think I'm getting them back, sir.'

Roberts steps aside, hands the pink form back to Cooper with a reassuring look.

'The Yanks have promised us Takahashi and we'll get him. Think of the mess they've got to clean up. The entire Pacific and Europe. Meanwhile keep the screws on Ikeuchi, break the number two man.'

Cooper shakes his head grimly.

'These buggers don't crack under pressure.'

He gestures at the photo.

'Even with this, we're up against something we haven't seen before. But give me the witnesses on the stand. Then I'll break 'em into little pieces.'

There it was again, that personal feeling, that potentially fatal trap for a lawyer.

Roberts stiffens and turns back to the operator, who gives him the handset.

'Tokyo, sir.'

Cooper knows that he has pushed too hard. But it was a jigsaw puzzle in which the pieces kept changing shape. He had to keep pushing or be left behind.

'Bob, you're here as a lawyer, not a soldier,' Roberts glares at Cooper, 'don't forget that.'

Cooper salutes sharply and strides out, even more at odds with Roberts than when he walked in.

Roberts takes a deep breath, trying to regain his equilibrium, sinking in thoughts of doubt. What if Cooper was right? What if the system should make monkeys of them all? What then?

He banishes these heavy thoughts and focuses on the clear need for an urgent response from Tokyo. He opens the mike and feels his authoritative voice rising, again with no effort.

'Tokyo, this is Major Roberts, Ambon War Crimes Tribunal.'

Outside, Cooper passes Sheedy, seated, perusing a document, almost lost in a thick cloud of smoke. The proverbial fly-on-the-wall.

Corbett intercepts Cooper as he heads for the door.

'Mr Matsugae's in your office.'

'Can't it wait? We've got to get more from Mitchell.'

'Afraid, not, sir . . . and we've got another cock-up.'

He hands Cooper a new file.

'Four pilots missing, not just Fenton.'

'They came down here?'

'Still checking, sir. But we should get confirmation from Darwin any time. Why haven't we got any flyers in the camp?'

Cooper sighs, hands it back.

'That's a good question, Jack. But keep *on it*!'

In Cooper's office adjoining the large room, a small dapper Japanese man peers closely at the dusty volumes of criminal and military law, perched precariously on a makeshift plank fixed to the wall. He takes in the two samurai swords hanging beneath an Australian flag. Is this a symbol of the justice of the victors? An Australian guard glares at Matsugae, who averts his gaze.

He turns at the sound of footsteps and adjusts his spectacles and his coat. He glances quickly at the photo on the rough hewn desk. A father and two sons, tall, lean and very tanned.

He bows low as Cooper enters. The guard salutes with palpable relief. Matsugae looks up to see Cooper standing rock like inside the door. He can feel his hostile eyes. Perhaps it is his manner or his suit that elicited such contempt. He must approach this Prosecutor with great caution.

'Captain Cooper, forgive my intrusion, but I felt

a great need to talk to you.'

Cooper doesn't move. Matsugae struggles to hide his nervousness, it was most difficult.

'No intrusion, Mr Matsugae.'

Cooper's face was like stone. Would he understand?

'Captain, there is a certain misunderstanding . . .'

'On whose part?'

'On the part of the defendants, Captain.'

'Concerning?'

Cooper still does not move. Should he continue, or admit his shame?

'This presumption of innocence, I have tried to explain to them, but they do not understand why they are on trial in this manner.'

Cooper steps into the office and riffles through files on the desk. Matsugae is puzzled as he watches Cooper, who seems engrossed in some other thoughts. No doubt Cooper enjoyed this predicament facing his clients. He should leave now but is stopped by Cooper's change of tone.

'Mr Matsugae, you'll just have to find the words to explain to them that they are innocent until proven guilty on the evidence.'

So, perhaps they could talk as lawyers. Not just as victor and vanquished.

'Yes, Captain. But I do need witnesses to cross examine in their defence. It would make my task so much easier.'

Cooper hears himself and Roberts. 'Hear, hear,' he mutters *sotto voce*.

Cooper finds the file and looks around at his adversary.

'Well, I don't know what to say, Mr Matsugae, unless they all want to plead guilty and we can all go home. You'll have to take it up with the Judge

Advocate, Major Roberts. Now if you'll excuse me . . .'

Matsugae bows again, as Cooper makes for the door, masking his confused emotions. It was not only the Japanese who could be so enigmatic.

'You should know, Captain, that in Japan, a defence counsel has no contact with his clients before a trial. They are very suspicious of me.'

Cooper is caught off guard. He watches Matsugae with mixed feelings. How can Matsugae explain this to the defendants? They wouldn't trust him.

Cooper lets Matsugae exit before him. Matsugae was the first Jap to show any sign of a 'conscience'. Cooper turns to Corbett, who watches with a flicker of sympathy, as the defence counsel walks away. Cooper is already heading for the entrance, Corbett falls in quickly. Cooper's 'acid level' is high:

'I can't run prosecution and defence.'

This remark overheard by Sheedy as he falls in behind them. They step into harsh sunlight, pausing before a couple of passing trucks. Sheedy looks around, adjusting his US supply sunglasses. Ambonese life has spilled over into the base. Some villagers are plying their trade with a trio of off-duty guards, trading smokes for a couple of dead chickens. Sheedy accelerates to keep up with Cooper.

'How's the shooting party shaping up?'

Cooper ignores him and hands Corbett a file.

'Takahashi's staff? Signals? Adjutants? The Legal Officer?'

'No luck, sir, still at large, all over Japan.'

'I don't care if they're shacked up on Mount-bloody-Fuji, Jack. Get them!'

Sheedy hears the edge of desperation in Cooper's voice. He moves closer to them.

'If you listened to the folks back home, it'd be a lot easier, Captain. They're screaming for blood.'

Cooper stops abruptly, and faces Sheedy.

'Tell them that the punishment'll fit the crime here, Sheedy. Just like any other court of law.'

Sheedy weighs this up and looks over to the POW camp where Japanese prisoners mill around near the wire fence.

'There's one difference, Captain. You'll fix the guilty with a bullet.'

'That's military justice, Sheedy.'

Sheedy nods, breaking into a cynical grin.

'Ah, I see, they'll die as soldiers.'

A plane flies low overhead, banking from an unseen landing strip. Sheedy gestures forcefully to the POW camp, shouting above the whining roar of the engine.

'Our boys didn't get the dignity of a soldier's death in there!'

Cooper tries to suppress his anger, takes a few paces forward, then suddenly swings around.

'I know how our boys died, Sheedy.'

So that's it, thinks Sheedy, a real crusader.

Cooper turns and picks up the pace to Corbett's. Sheedy watches them head for a large Dutch colonial building, the hospital. Near the steps of the building, a few ex-POWs are helped on to trucks by some nurses and Ambonese orderlies.

Sheedy looks back to the prisoners' compound, musing to himself. A hundred 'defendants' all in the dock together. Should be quite a performance.

It starts to rain. Sheedy heads for the shelter of a long barracks verandah.

Keenan steps from the barracks. They watch the Japanese prisoners scurry for cover from the downpour. Sheedy offers Keenan a smoke, who accepts it warily. Sheedy lights it, sizing up Keenan.

'Wonder what's going through their minds, now the boot's on the other foot?', says Sheedy.

Keenan stares at Sheedy then looks back at the compound.

'Is the right boot goin' on the right foot? That's what people want to know. Anyway, who can figure the thinking of savages?'

'Savages? Took a bit of nous to knock out Pearl Harbour and take Singapore, wouldn't you say?'

Keenan now glares at Sheedy.

'Luck!'

Keenan spits out his smoke, stubs it and runs across the grounds to another building. Sheedy shakes his head ruefully.

'Presumption of innocence? Can't see that selling a lot of papers.'

Cooper and Corbett proceed into the large high ceiling room, which has been converted to a ward. The blinds are lowered to defeat the glare. A couple of Australian nurses, sleeves rolled up, sit next to the men, reading letters from home. They move cracked, blistered lips to a smile, but for one man it might have been a letter from another planet, as he stares vacantly at the ceiling.

These were 'men' three years ago. Now, skeletal spectres, stomachs swollen with beri-beri, limbs covered with sores, tropical ulcers, bruises and wounds which look incurable.

Cooper and Corbett walk between the row of beds. Cooper glances at one man. A strong resemblance to Geoff. He averts his sullen gaze and looks at a nurse squeezing water like a baptism over another man, propped up in bed. He has a racking cough.

Next to him, another lost in a cone of moaning and mad ranting.

They reach Mitchell, staring at the ceiling, half singing, half humming to himself 'Ambon Serenade', a sad Indonesian farewell.

Cooper sits on the side of the bed, lights a cigarette, offers it to Mitchell. It isn't taken. Mitchell sings on, oblivious to Cooper's presence. Cooper opens a file.

'Bill . . . you overheard Takahashi discussing executions with Ikeuchi . . .?'

Mitchell continues humming. He shifts his gaze to the patient next to him. He grins painfully.

'Hey, Jim, how we goin' in the cricket?'

But Jim is fast asleep. Cooper places a statement in front of Mitchell.

'Was this before or after the executions were carried out? Could it have been a direct order?'

He looks across to Corbett, who produces a photo of Takahashi and holds it in front of Mitchell.

'Takahashi, was he actually ordering executions?'

No reply. Mitchell continues to hum.

'Bill, was it forty-three, forty-four? Can you remember the month? Wet or dry season? For God's sake, Bill!'

Cooper realises that it is useless, rises reluctantly and takes back the statement. Suddenly, Mitchell speaks, a rasping whisper, a hard madness in his eyes.

'Blow 'em off the face of the earth! Yanks had the right idea! Trials . . .'

He laughs, spasms shaking his body, tears welling.

'*Fuck*ing trials! Fair go for Tojo!'

The spasm sends him into a violent wheezing cough.

'Fair fucking go . . .'

Sister Carol Littell enters with Nurse June Pearson. She strides straight up to Cooper, determined that this will be his last 'interrogation'.

'What in the hell do you think you're doing, Bob?'

Cooper stands his ground.

'My job.'

'Not here.'

Cooper moves to her, shepherds her a few paces away.

'Carol . . .'

Littell sees his determination but this was her territory. He would respect it.

'Bob, I'm not going to stand by and have you wreck all our work just so that you can top a few Japs!'

Cooper gazes around the ward. The noise of the rain builds on the iron roof until it is almost deafening. Cooper leans close to Carol.

'What do we do then, let the Japs walk away? They are responsible for this.'

'And I'm responsible for these men.'

They gaze at each other. On the same side, but with different objectives. Cooper nods apologetically, Littell softens.

'Bob, you're driving yourself too hard. You do have a job to do but you're not made of iron.'

Suddenly, a dreadful scream from across the ward. Littell shouts to Pearson.

'Fenton!'

They hurry across to Jimmy Fenton, a wraithlike figure screaming, tearing uncontrollably at his sheets and bandages.

Cooper steps back to Mitchell, watching Littell soothing Fenton, coaxing him down. She had a real gift. He feels a tug at his hand. He looks down at

Mitchell taking the smoke from his hand, then drawing weakly on it, tears streaming down his face. Cooper lays a consoling hand on Mitchell's shoulder.

'Have a safe trip home, mate.'

He looks up to see Littell observing him. She smiles briefly as she draws a long tassle of hair back under her cap.

Cooper nods to Corbett. They move quickly back down the ward, eavesdropping briefly on a letter being read to one of the men.

'When you're back in Sydney, we'll go fishing again just like we used to . . .'

'They're in for a shock . . .', thinks Cooper.

They exit on to the verandah, watching a truck with ex-POWs pulling away. Cooper shouts above the rain to Corbett.

'Fenton? Didn't you say he's one of the missing pilots?'

'That's Jimmy in there. We're looking for an Eddy Fenton.'

'Any relation?'

'Don't know, sir.'

They make out a figure running towards them. Patterson leaps up the stairs in one bound, shakes himself off then brings out a sodden sheet of paper.

'Sorry, sir, but I thought you should have this right away.'

Cooper hands it to Corbett, grinning.

'It might be wet, Corporal, but that's the best news yet.'

CHAPTER THREE

THE DUEL

Ikeuchi stares straight ahead. Before him, a table. Photos of the graves neatly lined up, crisscrossed by slats of light, falling from the narrow shutters of the hut; a deliberate design by the enemy. Hot, stinking, prison. You do not walk out till you talk.

He looks down at a slender white hand that picks up one of the photos, now curling up at the edges from the heat. It is raised to his eye level by Corbett and held there. A human skull, neatly holed by a bullet between the eyes.

Ikeuchi permits himself a grim smile. This is Cooper's *kabuki* play, the identification of the head— the *kubi jikken* scene. He had seen the great actor, Danjuro the Tenth, perform it in Tokyo. Now he sits in a sweat box on Ambon, an involuntary performer in this bizarre parody.

Ikeuchi stares around as wisps of blue smoke drift into the shafts of light. He feels the craving on his tongue. Tobacco, the most dangerous addiction. A moistening, involuntary, compulsive. Most dangerous. The leveller of enemies. He had seen it in the camp, discipline slackened by the offer of a cigarette.

He looks up as a mask appears in the shaft of light falling from the left. Cold blue eyes, staring, unblinking at him. Cooper. The lawyer. The pursuer. The ignorant.

An angular face, sharp, freckled, thin lips. Does he ever smile? Is he hiding his true genius? Whatever he may say, he is not in the strong position. He could not know. Therefore he would not know.

Cooper steps back towards the wall, then turns around and glares at Ikeuchi, drawing long on his cigarette.

'Killed in battle, were they? Strange, don't you think, soldiers tying themselves together just so they could be shot by you? At point blank range!'

First move. Affirm nothing, deny nothing. Wait for greater desperation, thinks Ikeuchi.

'And then there's the strange fact that most of them were either beheaded or bayoneted to death. And you say that you know nothing of any executions! What was it, mass suicide?'

Why not? So much easier, much less shame.

Cooper walks over to the table, which is groaning under files and statements piled high behind the photos. He selects one at random. He holds it in the light, reads:

One day, Ikeuchi came into the hospital. He was mad, screaming at these blokes 'you get up, you fit to work!' He took a piece of pipe and started beating them, some whose legs were just oozing tropical ulcers. He was like a devil. Anyway this one bloke's leg just came off, right below the knee, and Ikeuchi was still beating him. He died that night.

Lies. Stories to avenge their shame.

Cooper puts it down, grips the table with both arms. He can see it in Ikeuchi's eyes.

'All lies, eh? Well, you and I may disagree on certain "facts". But there is one fact you can't deny. I'll be leaving this island. You won't.'

A man who is convinced of another's destiny is a fool. Time to strike.

'Captain, you seem so convinced by this "evidence" that you have forgotten something.'

Cooper stares at Corbett. What tack will he take now?

As if to underline his point, Ikeuchi goes to push the nearest photos away from him. Corbett grabs his thick, smooth wrist and places it firmly back in his lap. Ikeuchi grins.

'I was never near that grave at that time.'

Cooper picks up another statement quickly.

'You first said "I don't recall being near that grave", now you're changing your story. You were never there? Correct?'

Ikeuchi beams.

'Yes, yes.'

'We have a witness who will swear that you were there, that you directed the execution parties.'

'A native witness, Captain? Come, they only want revenge, and like your men, they could not tell one Japanese officer from another.'

Cooper searches Ikeuchi's face. Was this man really the first pathological liar he had met? If he wasn't so twisted he would be comic. He picks up another sheaf of statements.

'Oh, you're as famous with the natives as with our men. Why is it that everyone hates you?'

Ikeuchi bursts into a cackling, mocking laugh.

'You are putting yourself to so much trouble, Captain. Perhaps you should have let Sergeant Keenan have his way.'

Ikeuchi notices Cooper's hand on the fob watch. Some sentimental attachment? His grin vanishes as he adopts an almost swaggering expression.

'And you are running out of time. If you do not get Vice Admiral Takahashi here . . .'

Cooper shakes his head in cynical amusement. The final ace to fall at the right moment. But it was still a sore point.

'It won't alter the case against you. Under our law, superior orders are no defence to these charges.'

'So Mr Matsugae says. But if we are all presumed innocent, as he says, and only some of us are found guilty, then you have not done your job. Have you, Captain?'

Cooper nods to the guard, Talbot, who steps up behind Ikeuchi, who is so smug, sure that he has scored.

'It doesn't matter what you think, because it was one of your own men who tipped us off about the grave.'

A lightning left hook out of nowhere. But Ikeuchi doesn't flinch.

Talbot grabs Ikeuchi by the shoulder, who doesn't resist as he is drawn to his feet. He gives Cooper a mock salute as Talbot shoves him towards the door. Cooper lights another smoke as Corbett piles statements into an overloaded satchel. He looks up at Cooper, bemused.

'He knows that isn't true.'

'Say it often enough, he'll start to believe it.'

'Divide and conquer?'

'Precisely, Jack.'

Cooper wipes the perspiration from his face with a sodden handkerchief. It had to get easier. There had to be a fissure, a fault slippage that would bring the whole case down on top of them all.

Ikeuchi's words eat at him as they walk from the hut. Suppose the 'guilty' were set free and the 'innocent' . . .?

It was very clear. He could probably link Ikeuchi to the grave. If he could prove he was acting under Takahashi's orders, all the better. Most of the guards involved in the massacre had been posted elsewhere. So that left him with what?—the proof that eluded him, as the massacre had happened just after the surrender and before the POWs were interned.

Now he needed proof that executions were ordered in the camp during the time of Takahashi and Ikeuchi, carried out by men under their command. That would deliver the knockout punch. The capital offence that would cap all the illtreatment.

But Ikeuchi was right again, time was running out and Roberts had sent his sole witness packing. Mitchell was gone. Cooper stops, looks out over the barbed wire fence separating him from the Japanese.

He felt very alone. He was an alien here, confronting people who may as well be from Mars, for all he could know about them.

He yearned for the smell of the wheatfields, his father's bakery, the pungent dough, the heat of the oven. He could see Geoff sliding out the loaves, smiling as he glazed them with fresh honey. Jane's lips on his as they flew along the coast road, reckless, in love. Ambon was the straw that broke that one. She couldn't wait. And there were the attractions of the Yank officer she'd met in Macarthur's office in Melbourne. Would he return then as the famous military lawyer with no one to return to? Maybe Keenan and Sheedy had a point. Just get it over with. 'Military justice'?

Too bloody easy, the voice said. *The world's got to know what they did. And you're goin' to make them tell.* Geoff or his conscience?

He feels Corbett tugging at his sleeve. He follows his arm to two jeeps pulling up at the Legal Corps HQ. Sheedy appears out of nowhere as four Australian officers get out of the jeeps and are greeted with a brisk salute by Roberts on the verandah.

Sheedy tips his hat to Cooper as he walks on.

'Looks like we've got the whole circus now, Captain.'

Corbett looks quizzically at Cooper.

'How the hell does he know?'

Cooper smiles thinly.

'He can't help himself, Jack. It's his nose.'

They walk on, intent on the new arrivals.

Over behind the wire, Ikeuchi walks around groups of prisoners, some cooking rice in a pot, others mending tattered shirts or playing cards in the failing light. Many avert their eyes from his gaze. They knew this measured movement, the presage of a fury to be unleashed on an unsuspecting victim. When the camp had been Ikeuchi's kingdom, it had been the Australian and Dutch prisoners who bore the brunt of it. Now, with the help of his 'lieutenants', he maintained his grip on his new 'prisoners'.

Two burly Japanese walk up behind Ikeuchi as he approaches a makeshift hut. A group of young guards part as the trio approaches. A fresh faced young man looks up from the food cooking before him. Lieutenant Noburo Yamazaki stands expectantly. Ikeuchi halts before the boiling pot.

The pot goes flying, scalding the legs of two prisoners next to it. Noburo goes to pick it up but is grabbed by the two 'heavies', and thrust into the open doorway of the hut.

Other prisoners draw back, a couple going to the aid of the burnt ones, trying to suppress cries that might draw the attention of the Australian guards.

Inside the hut, Noburo is pinned to a post by the sumo wrestlers as Ikeuchi steps up, eyes boring into him.

'Did you squeal, shitface?'

Noburo struggles but is only pinioned harder. He shakes his head vigorously.

'No, honourable Commander. Never. What did I say?'

Ikeuchi slaps him hard.

'Is the Australian lawyer your friend? What did he offer you?'

'I don't know what you're saying, honourable . . .'

Another slap, harder with the base of the palm. Ikeuchi moves in closer.

'You Christians with your devotion to the "truth"! I'll teach you a new truth!'

Noburo tries to flinch from a rain of blows. Suddenly, a voice booms from behind them.

'Stop that now!'

Ikeuchi halts and turns to see the wiry figure of Matsugae standing in the door, shaking with anger. Contempt fills his features.

'Lawyers! This is not your business. Stay out of it!'

Matsugae steps into the room, and stops just short of Ikeuchi's heavy set body.

'I am in charge here. You will release him immediately!'

Ikeuchi stares at him and at the prisoners pressing through the door, looking in on this extraordinary confrontation. Face must be preserved. Who would keep it?

Ikeuchi nods to the heavies. They release their grip. Ikeuchi turns and addresses the prisoners.

'This is just a taste of what can happen to anyone who might think of breaching our unified front. You will say nothing! Or you will pay the price!'

He glares at Matsugae and then grins.

'Yes, take it up with the Vice Admiral. If he ever gets here!'

He pushes past the lawyer and exits with his enforcers, the prisoners drawing back, bowing low. Matsugae steps up to Noburo and examines the gash above his eye. Noburo, ashamed, pushes past him, leaving Matsugae alone staring out at the sun setting over the camp.

Things were not getting better. The chasm was now wider than ever. It had to be crossed, but how?

He steps outside, watching the prisoners dispersing, Ikeuchi striding towards his hut. He looks around at the lush vegetation spilling over the perimeter, the heavy scent of durian and cloves wafting down from the rise behind them filling his senses. Such beauty. A witness to such suffering.

He is distracted by a shout. He looks over to see the Sergeant standing at the fence.

'Hey! Ikeuchi!'

Ikeuchi stops in his tracks, looks over to Keenan who holds up a bullet.

'I've just had this engraved for you! Hope I got the spelling right!'

Keenan convulses with laughter, raucous, vicious, full of hate. Matsugae watches Ikeuchi retreat into his hut. For a moment, he feels an empathy with Keenan's sentiment. But even Ikeuchi must be defended by him to the best of his ability. He was his client.

But now, he needed real authority, something to break Ikeuchi's hold on them. Perhaps the Prosecutor might provide the answer. He had witnessed his first confrontation with the journalist. He sensed a real anger in Cooper. Perhaps it could be turned to advantage. He presented such a cold exterior. But his interior was most likely a white hot furnace fed by the war, tempering his anger to an incredible hardness; combined with a shrewd, acute and logical mind, Cooper made a formidable opponent.

Beyond this lay a shattered world that had to be rebuilt. Would these men be able to adapt? Even if they were freed, how would they respond when they returned to the rubble of their homes? If they had children or relatives in Hiroshima or Nagasaki, how could they cope with a horrible new suffering that could only have been conjured up by the most demonic of imaginations?

His own aunt had been one of the lucky ones. Her home was five miles from the centre of Hiroshima. She had suffered only superficial burns and was still in reasonable health. Whereas others in the same district now lay in teeming hospital wards, their faces pustulating with strange sores, their hair falling out, the victims of the 'black rain'. How capricious it had been in its choice of victims.

It was difficult to acknowledge that those bombs had undoubtedly saved many thousands of Japanese lives, as well as those of Allied soldiers and POWs. But hatred could not be so easily obliterated.

Matsugae felt a sudden surge of anger at his people, at Ikeuchi's narrow, blind obsession. If the result had been different, would his people have been so 'generous'? No, there would have been no 'trials', no 'rule of law'. The sword and the gun would have remained supreme.

A cooling breeze starts to blow up from Ambon Bay. Matsugae looks up, his spirit refreshed, the heaviness lifting. He loved the fishing boats, the outrigger *Perahus* sailed with such skill by the local fishermen. He could have watched them all day, just as he had watched his father launch his fishing boat from the beach near Miyazaki. He could have followed in his footsteps, but for the fateful meeting with the professor on holiday from Meiji University in Tokyo. Sad how this kindly benefactor had been so brutally harassed by the militarists before the war. Yet he, Matsugae Shinji, had managed to avoid 'difficulties' and held on to his post at the same university.

Now he was here, delegated by the Occupation Forces in Tokyo and Imperial Navy HQ to defend their men in the East Indies. If he had known what he was stepping into, he might well have stayed at the university.

Sheedy takes a Bintang beer from a young Ambonese waiter and leans on a cane-topped bar. He peers up at a couple of old photos almost obscured by a couple of potted plants—a large bearded man in a white suit, seated with other white men in suits. Probably the Dutch colonial administrator and his staff. Next to it, a shot of the governor's residence, sepia tinted. The Dutch flag flying proudly. The old world.

It wasn't only the Japs who would have to adapt now. The Dutch were living on borrowed time. Sheedy had been in Batavia and heard the rumours about the new independence movements forming. The Japs had left a real legacy. The white man was not a permanent fixture. He was vulnerable, defeated by an Asian race. The Allied victory was irrelevant. The Japs probably had no idea what they'd unleashed by their example.

But in this officers' mess, only the British and Australian flags were visible. Sheedy studies the faces of the four new men. A couple looked freshly commissioned, the others seasoned campaigners.

He sees Roberts dart him a cold glance, then return to the serious muted conversation. This room had probably been the Jap officers' mess. What discussions would have taken place here? Ikeuchi explaining a better method of water torture as the sake flowed, maybe becoming hysterical, as the Yanks screamed in low for another bombing raid? Very timely for him to muse about the great Allied propaganda theme—the inherently vicious, inhuman nature of the Japs. Maybe, but it could also have been the fact they had been brutalised by their experiences, too long away from home. Roberts had mentioned that most of the detachment sent here were old 'China hands', probably the same gang responsible for Nanking and Shanghai, the infamous Fifth Division. Eight years in battle must do something to any man.

Sheedy's musings are interrupted by the entry of Cooper, satchel under his arm, followed by the ever faithful Corbett—'Don Quixote and Sancho Panza'.

Cooper was definitely the man to watch here. Anyone with that will, that driven, missionary sense of purpose had to be someone worth exploring and getting to know. Sheedy sensed that sooner or later Cooper might have that confessional urge. Things would have to be faced. Sheedy would be there, ready.

The four officers rise as Roberts does the

introductions. The tall sinewy Lieutenant Colonel Johnson, was the President. The others, a Major and two Captains, would form the Bench with him. Cooper shakes their hands in turn then settles down in a thatched chair. Corbett goes for the beer.

Johnson is the epitome of the Duntroon man. Straight bearing, silver hair neatly combed, a relaxed precision even in the ashing of his cigarette. He leans forward in his chair, fixes Cooper with an open, attentive gaze.

'Major Roberts was telling us that things are proceeding smoothly.'

Cooper glances at Roberts. Bloody diplomats.

'Yes, sir. I think we've all been thrown in at the deep end here but we're getting there.'

Johnson considers the answer carefully and looks back to Roberts, who maintains a bland look of agreement. Team solidarity was paramount.

'Of course, Captain. You understand that we can't discuss matters of evidence here. But I'd like to know what you think about the decision to hold this trial en masse.'

Cooper takes a sip of his beer. He looks down into it, choosing his words, then back up at Johnson, waiting expectantly.

'A trial of this size has, I believe, never been mounted before. So, naturally, we're going to have problems. The Japs have not been forthcoming on what happened here. So we'll be relying on statements by the prisoners . . .'

Johnson betrays a certain impatience.

'Captain, I think you may have misunderstood me. I'm interested in what you feel the best strategy might be. We're very much the guinea pigs here. Please continue . . .'

Cooper feels the pressure now.

'I've already discussed this with Major Roberts, sir. I believe we've got to start from the top. The Vice Admiral and Ikeuchi must be the first nuts we crack.'

Roberts leans forward slightly.

'I believe that the Vice Admiral should be on his way here.'

Cooper looks to Roberts for confirmation and receives a tight smile.

'I hope so, sir. He was supposed to have been here last week. The trial's very close now.'

He looks back pointedly at Roberts. He sees Sheedy standing a few paces behind them, no doubt absorbing all this.

Roberts coughs nervously and smiles at the group.

'The Captain can rest assured, the chief defendant will be here in time.'

Cooper sips his beer, stares at Johnson, who moves to sit back. He probably already knew all that he wanted to find out. An awkward silence descends.

Sheedy seizes the moment and steps up to the group.

From his office in the Dai Ichi Building, Major Tom Beckett had a clear view of the moat surrounding the Emperor's palace. SCAP HQ was Tokyo's new nerve centre and Beckett could not help but feel a certain exhilaration at being at the frontier of a new world.

Macarthur had chosen him personally. Respected as a leading member of the American Bar Association, an expert in military law and international law, he worked long hours as Chief of Liaison for the upcoming trials in Tokyo.

It was no easy job, trying to co-ordinate the interests

of all the American and Allied teams who wanted to share the limelight. In fact, the meetings were a nightmare to run. He had helped to establish the International Prosecution Section, which was going meticulously through what was left of the records of Japanese General Defence HQ and the Japanese government. But the bickering between the British, Australians, Chinese and the Soviets, over who would present what evidence, was consuming far more energy than necessary. It would be so much easier if it was an 'All American Show'.

Many records had been burnt in the interregnum between the surrender and the actual occupation. In fact the War Ministry offices on Ichigaya Hill were said to have been a huge bonfire as millions of files went up in smoke, denying the victors the evidence with which they would mete out the 'stern justice' to war criminals, which Macarthur had promised.

But that was the other unexpected nightmare. Working out who in the labyrinthine workings of wartime Japan was responsible for what. The buck almost seemed to stop nowhere but just kept going around and around. The prosecution was not going to have such a dream run here as it would have appeared at first sight.

Beckett was determined that he would be seen as one of the new pragmatists in the SCAP gameplan. The real pain in the ass were the hardliners—those who would have the Emperor and his entire command dragged before a show trial before being despatched to the gallows without delay.

The other pain in the ass were the Russians and the Australians. The former for their insistence on total revenge on the Japanese and their whiteanting of the Americans' reconstruction plans. The latter for their continual baying after the Emperor's blood. Their Foreign Minister, Dr Evatt, never let up.

But now Macarthur had selected Beckett to go on a temporary diplomatic mission. The Supreme Commander was thinking of appointing an Australian as President of the Tokyo Trial to placate the Australian government. He was also interested in the legal skill that they were displaying in mounting such a large trial on Ambon, in the Dutch East Indies. Finally G2/Counter Intelligence head General Willoughby had shown great interest in Vice Admiral Takahashi, the 'Baron', for classified reasons.

As Beckett gazed out over the snow covered ruins of Tokyo, he wondered what kind of reception he could expect from the Australians. They wouldn't like what he had to tell them. But they could not live with false hopes.

He returned his attention to the file before him— *Takahashi/Secret/Eyes only*. But his mind whirls around the almost Machiavellian plotting from which he could not detach himself. His major adversary was Major John Wheeler, the adviser on prosecutions to Macarthur. He wanted to list Prince Konoye, the Emperor's closest adviser, as one of the chief war criminals. Beckett knew that Macarthur was stalling on this one as he believed Konoye would be one of the most useful Japanese in the reconstruction. And he was staunchly anti Soviet. Very important in light of the need to show the Soviets who would remain boss in Japan. Beckett smelt a rat in Wheeler's obsession with the Prince. But SCAP was the new 'Imperial Court' in Japan and he had to weigh his moves carefully. Today's enemy could be tomorrow's ally.

He could only guess at the motives for his being sent off at such a critical juncture. He was being put to some test, he felt. He was being asked to deliver something from this visit to Ambon and Morotai. But whose interests would it serve—Macarthur's, Wheeler's or Willoughby's? Or his own?

Careers would be made or broken here. He had to use all his skill and cunning to ensure his survival and his future. Then he would really graduate to the inner circle.

But he had to really know the players and the rules before he made his move. In the long run, he might be grateful for the breathing space.

Far to the south, in Nagasaki, an unsuspecting player is about to face his greatest test.

CHAPTER FOUR

FLIGHT AND ARRIVAL

Eleven a.m. August 9th, 1945. A moment from which Hideo Tanaka would never escape. He had returned to Nagasaki to marry his fiance, Midori, after getting leave from Naval HQ in Tokyo. His fervent hope was for a new life, to put all the horrors of war behind him. He never thought that his duty would lead him into what he had witnessed on Ambon.

But, that morning, so brilliant and clear, he and Midori had set out from Urakami Cathedral after discussing their marriage ceremony with Father Nishida. They took a track over Mt. Inasa, pausing to look back down on the cathedral nestled at its foot, a carpet of rich green, running back down the hill below. The blazing red of the oleander burst out in pockets, a beautiful contrast to the purple roof tiles and the shimmering blue of Nagasaki Bay beyond.

Hideo wanted to collect the most brilliant of flowers for his love. At a small spring off the track, he had held Midori close to him and pledged to remain with her forever. Then he had cupped his hands under the spring and offered her water to drink. She had just taken a sip when Hideo looked up at a lone American plane overhead, emerging from clouds. A huge black object was disgorged from its belly.

It was the next seconds that were to become Hideo's eternal memory. He saw his hands fly up to Midori, pushing her shoulders back, his knees buckling into hers, launching them together into space. His instinct, honed so well by all the raids on Ambon. Falling, falling, flooded with the most intense light. Most astonishing of all, the moment in which Midori was totally transparent, her skeleton, her spine, her skull all visible as if the air itself was an infinite X-ray machine!

Midori had tried to squirm free, to get up. But Hideo had held her firm. The trees all around them were hit with hurricane force by a wind first screaming then building to a deafening roar.

Hideo held Midori with a vicelike grip. A wave of pressure lifted them and threw them into a ditch below. Hideo looked up momentarily. The pines, the laurels, the chestnuts had launched their boughs like a thousand arrows fired from some giant's bow. Then they too were uprooted and blown away by the giant's breath.

Finally, the roar subsided. An eerie silence descended.

Hideo looked up. Where there had been a thick canopy of foliage, now only the haze of dust and smoke. He carefully brought Midori to her feet with him. They looked around at the forest, stripped, smashed and flattened. They had been lucky. They had landed in a ditch protected by some overhanging boulders. A large clump of trees lay in a crazy heap over the top of them.

Hideo crossed himself rapidly, grateful for their survival. Midori, almost hysterical, buried herself in his arms, weeping, deeply shocked. He comforted her as best he could, wiping blood from lacerations to their arms and faces. And then, the most awesome sight of all.

Over the ridge beyond, a huge angry cloud rising rapidly. A thick column of dust beneath it, swirling at enormous speed. The cloud itself, flashing purple, red and orange, feeding on a boiling fire within it, expanding at a terrifying rate.

'I must be in hell', thought Hideo. 'There is no bomb that could do this.'

Hideo could only stare as the cloud transformed into a writhing mushroom, a black stain on its mile high stem. Midori fainted with fright as she turned to face it. Hideo ran to the spring, cupped his hands again and carefully picked his way back through the fallen trees to Midori, slowly reviving her with the water. How incredible that an act of shared love had become an act of survival in the blinking of an eye.

They stumbled, coughing and half choking on the thick dust, back down to the edge of the track. Then, a sight below so totally numbing that they simply could not take another step.

No green fields, no trees, no flowers, no houses, no sound. No longer the lushness of the mountain, only a red pockmarked ugliness. Desolation stretching as far as they could see. Death had descended on Nagasaki and claimed it as its new kingdom.

Hideo's mind was spinning in such shock that he could only stand paralysed. He could hear the words of some distant sermon, the devastation described as the Apocalypse. But it was all he could do to hold on to Midori, to feel her flesh against his, a tangible contact with a real world he knew, a world of love, of happiness and promise.

Blessed are the meek. For they shall inherit the

earth. This earth? This city?

Then, the shroud of darkness and dust started to shift, sucked towards the swirling stem of the cloud. Hideo peered through the lifting veil.

Urakami Cathedral—a mass of rubble! No roof, no walls, only the facade seemed to have withstood the blast. A roaring fire was consuming its timber skeleton, sending it hurtling into a sulphurous pit beneath. The ancient centre of Japanese Christianity. Gone forever!

Stretching back to the Bay, huge fires raced across the 'city', occasionally joining to form an enormous vortex; sucking all the air, the dust, the wreckage of houses and buildings ever upwards. Offices, schools, the hospital, Hideo's favourite noodle restaurant, the shop where they were to have purchased Midori's wedding ring. All vanished or buried under rubble.

Hideo felt the hot rush of the fires on his face. He wanted to weep. But the tears would not come. And the voice would not scream:

My God, my God! Why have you forsaken me!

Christ's words had struck the city of Jerusalem, shaken it to its foundations. The dead had walked, the wicked were slain. But his holy city of Nagasaki. Burnt, blasted, blown from the face of the earth. Why?

He looked at Midori, her face an ashen mask. He clasped her even tighter as the awful realisation struck. Perhaps they were the only survivors in the whole of the city!

They would have to descend into the inferno. There must be someone alive. Their parents, their brothers and sisters?

They must not lose hope. They must not . . .

Though I walk through the valley of the shadow

It was two days before Hideo stood before the charred ruin of his parents' house with Midori and her parents who had made the luckiest decision of their lives, a day in the valley near Koba visiting relatives.

But Hideo's family were now part of the ashes of the house. Where the kemponashi tree had stood in the garden, tall, proud, a cool protection in summer, now only a pathetic blackened stump. Would it ever grow again in this new wasteland?

Grief almost seemed a forgotten emotion now for Hideo. He desperately wanted to feel it. But this suffering was so great that his heart could not open to it for fear of being swept into a raging torrent in which he would be lost forever.

To face the images of destruction that he had to witness in the following weeks would test his faith in God and His mercy beyond all bounds. But Midori, with her love and her strength, would save him. Their love was a flame that no atomic bomb could extinguish.

He did not know that another great test was approaching as the past reached out for him. Now, the cold winds blew in from the Bay, winter chilling the exhausted, maimed survivors. The land that had been seared by temperatures unknown on earth would soon be covered in snow and sleet.

A large stone head of Christ, scored with heatburns, severed at the neck, faces Hideo. He perches delicately on a charred plank, which was retrieved from the cathedral's ruins with others to build a rough scaffolding.

The Christ head is raised by a primitive pulley. Hideo shouts encouragement to refugees below, who are putting what exhausted strength they have into the task. The head must be returned to the alcove above the temporary altar made from packing cases supporting a rickety bamboo trestle.

The head had been found in rubble a few hundred yards from the remains of the cathedral's facade, lying on its side. The force of the blast had blown it from the body of the statue, the same force that had decapitated thousands at the instant of detonation.

Hideo looks into the dead stone eyes, only feet away. There is no answer to his burning question: Is this your *tenbatsu*—your divine retribution? The cathedral stood only five hundred yards from 'Fat Man's' epicentre. There had to be some answer. But who could answer? Why would God send a plague so great on his own house?

Suddenly, a flash from another time. Hideo feels a momentary dizziness, the shock of a painful memory. He steadies himself. His breath comes in bursts, his palms burning fiercely into the splintered support beside him.

He looks down to Midori, looking up at him, her eyes full of concern. He throws her a reassuring look then returns to the Christ head which is just within reach.

He does not see the plume of dust approaching the cathedral. A US Army jeep threads its way through the ramshackle dwellings, scattering spindled remains along the track to the cathedral. Fires are being lit to warm the hunched, freezing bodies of survivors, many of whose faces are blistered and burnt. Ragged, dirty cowls hiding the more hideous effects of the 'new sickness'.

Dead, lustreless eyes lower themselves from the searching gaze of the two well fed M.P.s, who are scanning both sides of the road—The *gaijin* victors.

They reach an impasse on the road, a pile of charred beams. The roof supports. They alight, step over the rubble and head for the group near the scaffolding, eyes swivelling in every direction.

Midori turns to see them approach an old priest, Father Shirato who is hunched over a large pot from which he carefully ladles soup with a large wooden spoon. A line of refugees moves along slowly, each gratefully slurping the single ration of watery paste, then shuffling on.

She watches inquisitively as they kneel beside him. He puts down the spoon as they produce a crumpled piece of paper. They hand it to him. Midori watches his face darken, a look of sadness and despair as he turns slowly towards the scaffolding. She locks eyes with him. He shakes his head at her, his pain piercing her sharply. He points to the top of the scaffolding. He cannot bear to look as the two M.P.s nod appreciatively to him, rise to their feet and start to head towards Midori.

She sees their eyes fixed upwards on Hideo. Instinctively she screams up to him.

'Hideo! Look! Hideo! Run! Run!'

Her desperate words echo off the fractured facade of the cathedral. Hideo looks down as one of the M.P.s shoves Midori aside roughly. His anger is immediate. But he contains himself, glaring down at them.

The other M.P. merely stands calmly, looking up at him.

'Okay, Tanaka. You can come quietly. Or you can make it hard for yourself. What'll it be?'

For a second, Hideo hesitates. He must defend her from these brutes! Midori screams.

'Run! Now!'

In an instant, Hideo leaps to the next level of the scaffold as the 'persuasive' M.P. starts to climb reluctantly on to it.

Hideo stands against the stark sky, trapped. He sees the M.P. closing, then looks around desperately for an escape route. He looks over at a part of the jagged wall of the cathedral nearest him. It was possible.

He leaps across from the scaffolding on to it, almost losing his footing. Midori cannot bear to look, burying her face in the shoulder of the old priest, who does his best to comfort her. She weeps uncontrollably.

The M.P. hesitates at the edge of the scaffolding. He faces Hideo. He grins savagely.

'You're defying the Emperor's wishes, Tanaka. He wants you to surrender.'

Hideo looks at him then back down to Midori. He shouts: 'Goodbye, Midori . . .'

She looks up but he is gone.

Hideo lands on a ledge some ten feet from the ground, then looks back up to the M.P. on the wall above. The M.P. is about to jump.

Hideo lands on both feet, stumbling slightly, twisting his ankle on a pile of rubble. In great pain, he starts to run, hobbling across the mounds of rubble and charred timber on the floor of the shattered church.

He hears the M.P. land with a thud behind him. His breath shoots out in a vaporous rush as he reaches the opposite wall. He spots a breach, a gaping hole six feet above ground level.

He looks back quickly. The M.P. is only yards away. With all his strength, Hideo pulls himself up through the breach and starts to tumble through the hole as he feels the M.P. grasp one of his ankles.

With a lunging backwards kick, Hideo slips out of his grip and falls out the other side of the wall. He looks down at his bleeding leg, now starting to cramp above the knee.

He hobbles across a crowded section of the camp, survivors making way for his dragging, shuffling escape.

He finds a large pile of rubble, razed sheets of iron and broken charred timber beams. Desperately, he starts pulling the mound apart, then slips under it, burying himself.

A couple of survivors step up, assisting Hideo with the final pulling up of his 'camouflage' over him.

The M.P. runs through the press of survivors. He reaches the mound and looks around carefully.

The one that got away. This time.

As the M.P. returns to the front of the cathedral, he gives a gesture of resignation to his colleague who stands waiting with another young Japanese in handcuffs.

Midori looks up. A smile overtakes her despair.

The M.P. walks up to her, stares at her with his hands on his hips.

'You can tell your boyfriend we'll be back for him.'

Midori lowers her eyes, then watches as they move off to the jeep. She turns to Father Shirato, totally bewildered.

'Father, why do they want Hideo?'

The old priest is equally puzzled. He looks at the jeep disappearing over a rise, dust billowing behind it.

'I do not know, Midori. But they call him a "suspect".'

'Suspect?'

The word was strange. It was difficult to understand. Hideo had been at war. He had followed orders just like the American soldiers. What could he be 'suspected' of?

But Hideo was safe, for now. She must find him and probe him gently with questions. Their marriage had a new urgency.

As the rain drums heavily on the roof of the hospital, Carol Littell carefully rolls her cigarette and lights it. A moment to relax, to ponder. The present: a view from her office down the ward. Men pushed beyond anything she had seen, and 'survived'. It was not like she thought it might be—here she could make up for all the frustration in New Guinea, the orders that kept the nurses away from the Kokoda Front, so she had thought.

The stream of casualties down to the Port Moresby Base Hospital had similar tropical diseases: malaria, dysentery, dengue fever. But here on Ambon, multiple infections were the order of the day. It demanded an exhausting and totally novel approach to recovery. She and June Pearson could not help feeling depressed at their apparent lack of progress.

A glance over the charts told the story. An inch by inch, hour by hour battle with recurrent infections, fevers, slow-healing ulcers. She looks over the chart for Jimmy Fenton. One of the most extreme cases. She had suspected that he had contracted some rare form of tropical meningitis. But the symptoms seemed to come and go. The blindness, the black blood oozing from his mouth, the dementia alternating with stability and long open-eyed staring. Any 'medical scientist' would say that Ambon was a perfect laboratory. The ideal place to study the human immune system under conditions of the greatest stress. So little was known about it. To say nothing of the tropical disease specialists and the endless papers they could publish about it.

But if they had walked in there, she would have given them their marching orders. The future with these men lay not in the hands of those types, but with the loving care and long-term attention they needed.

Long term? Yes, it would demand a commitment from her. She would have to decide soon. A line of Yeats comes to her:

Oh the mind! The mind has mountains, cliffs of fall . . .

That was it. The mind. It held the secrets for the healing of Fenton and the others. If they did not vanish down one of its crevasses, leaving her there holding a slack rope.

She looks up, observes Millie Gaspersz changing one of the plasma bottles. If it wasn't for the Ambonese, the men might not have survived. Their courage, their defiance of Ikeuchi and his goons in sneaking food to the prisoners and hiding escapees, had to be recognised. She only hoped that Cooper was as diligent in prosecuting the ill treatment of the locals as he was with the men. Millie had lost two brothers at the hands of the torturers. Their crime—sneaking some bananas under the wire.

Cooper both unsettled and attracted Carol. She wanted to help him but she could not see any way of guaranteeing it. Cooper's case was critically reliant on the memories of these men. But their recall, in many cases, was gone. And she was the custodian of what was left.

Yet, his drive and momentum could produce brilliant results. If only he didn't lose contact with himself and his sensitivity to others, like herself. He might find feelings he would not admit to. At the moment, he was almost a closed tight ball. But she had seen him with Mitchell. He was not beyond reach.

As quickly as it began, the rain fades away, the clouds parting to let the moon's rays glisten on the soaked vegetation outside the hospital.

She looked through the window to the bay, stretched like a silver sheet below. A thick, dank, smell mixed with the heavy aroma of spice, borne on a slight breeze. So easy just to nod off. A sudden thought—why does Fenton go berserk when it rains? Her head felt heavy. Just surrender, sleep. Then the sight of gaitered boots and khaki in the doorway. She snaps her head back.

'Hello, Bob.'

Cooper steps in, grins at her.

'Didn't mean to wake the dead.'

She stubs out her cigarette, smiles wearily.

'Don't suppose we'd ever catch you napping?'

Cooper produces a rolled cigarette of his own, lights it then studies her.

'We're on the final run, Carol. Thought I'd check with you on what you may have heard lately.'

'Hearsay evidence, Bob?' she grins again.

'Whatever . . .'

He hands her a file.

'It's a list of blokes who went missing in the camp. No one knows what happened to them—except of course, Ikeuchi. And the bastard's not talking.'

'Still?'

Cooper takes a couple of paces, exhales through the screen. He looks down at her.

'Yet.'

She scans the file, puts it down, sighs.

'Carol, Roberts has got a big enough bee in his bonnet about me coming here as it is. I thought you could help this way.'

She looks up at him, sees his openness, his wanting to play it her way.

'Okay, I can help. But you've got to be so careful about what you say to these men, Bob. A word can kill them.'

Cooper seems struck by this, looks at her with what she felt was a professional respect but tinged with, perhaps, another longing?

He leans down, stubs out his smoke in her shell ashtray.

'Thanks.'

He reaches the door, turns back.

'Anything?'

She smiles.

'Anything.'

She studies his back as he leaves. Things were changing.

Cooper strides past the prisoners' compound. He stops at the sight of a lantern flickering in one of the huts. Matsugae and an Australian officer, Reid, engaged in an examination of documents. Reid towering over the Japanese, pointing quickly at various sections on the paper. Cooper cocks an ear as their voices float across, barely audible.

'This plea . . . very risky . . .'

The words fade on a breeze. Cooper moves on. Reid, eh? An old hand at court martial defence back in Australia. He and Cooper had locked horns a number of times. The score was about even. This would be the big one. The largest trial ever. Cooper could not help his amusement. Maybe Reid can explain presumption of innocence to them. Maybe they'll trust him more than their own man.

The next morning, Private Talbot finds himself on duty outside the interrogation hut. Keenan appears with a detail of Japanese prisoners. He halts them a moment, studies Talbot cynically, shouts to him.

'I know you'd rather be at scripture class, Private, but you will be on latrine duty this afternoon.'

A heavy burst of rain and Keenan quick marches the Japanese off. Talbot is drenched but relieved by Keenan's forced exit.

Inside the hut, Ikeuchi is back in the chair. Cooper paces around him as Corbett plays the 'bad cop' today. Corbett slams down a stack of affidavits, an action executed with such ferocity that even Cooper is impressed.

'Ikeuchi beat the living Christ out of me!

'Ikeuchi bashed me with a pipe, broke my kneecaps.

'Ikeuchi was the chief bash artist!'

Corbett picks up another stack of affidavits, slams them down one after the other.

'Ikeuchi! Ikeuchi! Ikeuchi!'

Ikeuchi does not respond, does not move, stares straight ahead.

Corbett moves closer, till he is almost whispering in his ear.

'But you won't be alone at the firing squad . . . there's your men—The Black Bastard, The Regimental Sadist, Creeping Jesus. Remember them? They took their orders from you. They say it themselves.'

How could this fool ever know the loyalty of the *ronin*, his retainers, their devotion to their lord?

Corbett picks up another pile, waves it in front of Ikeuchi. No response. Cooper stands in front of Ikeuchi, his face a mirror of this stone mask.

'Takahashi was in command. But he left the control of the camp to you. But you couldn't order executions by yourself, could you? He had to be consulted. Your records show it. Why are you protecting Takahashi?'

Ikeuchi smiles thinly.

'You know as well as I, Captain. There are no such records.'

He looks up at Cooper, staring at him, again unblinking.

'It would be my word against Baron Takahashi.'

Ikeuchi now grins broadly.

'If you had him.'

A lone plane engine can be heard approaching from across the bay. Cooper takes out his fob watch and checks the time. He gives a grim smile.

'Yeah, if I had him.'

He turns to Corbett, grins broadly.

'Let's see what he's got to say for himself, Jack.'

He catches Ikeuchi darting him an intense, unsettled look. He snaps the fob watch shut.

CHAPTER FIVE

THE TIDE TURNS

Cooper tenses as the US C47 taxies to a halt. His eyes are fixed on the steps being secured to the now stationary plane, oblivious to Corbett and Sheedy beside him. Two guards take up positions beside the stairs. Roberts steps up beside Cooper.

'A big day for us, Bob.'

Cooper doesn't reply. The C47's engines splutter then stop. Roberts wipes his forehead. It was too hot. Maybe he did have the fever, the new bout he feared. But he could not lose control, or authority.

'Bob, I heard you were in hospital last night. I've told you to stay out of it.'

Cooper ignores him. They watch as the rear door is opened. Major Beckett looks out, squinting into the glare. He puts on his sunglasses firmly. Corbett glances to Cooper, just as surprised by the appearance of the tall American as Cooper. Sheedy looks over the top of his glasses, intrigued.

'Who's the Yank?'

Cooper feels that strange sensation on his skin again as Beckett steps aside and Baron Takahashi takes his place in the doorway. Aristocratic, immaculate in a freshly pressed uniform, wearing medals, mostly of British origin. The 'invisible man' was of much shorter stature than Cooper had pictured him.

Cooper sizes up his prey with grim appreciation. But it was his American custodian that had Cooper's mind turning rapidly. Why an officer like him? Why not just M.P.s?

Roberts walks over to the steps as Beckett descends behind Takahashi. The two allies salute each other. Takahashi gazes around with disdain as the guards fall in on either side of him.

'Obviously delighted to be back at the butcher shop,' mumbles Sheedy.

They lead him past Cooper, Takahashi avoiding his searching gaze. Cooper turns to see Roberts standing beside him with Beckett. Cooper salutes.

'Major Beckett, I'd like you to meet Captain Cooper, our Prosecutor.'

Beckett smiles, offers his hand. Cooper takes it, feeling a firm grip, his mind racing.

'Major Beckett is chief of liaison for the Tokyo trials.'

In the long moment that it takes for the two to shake hands, they size each other up. Cooper grins.

'You're a long way from home base, Major.'

Roberts, edgy, starts to shepherd Beckett towards the waiting jeep.

'The Major is here as an observer.'

Beckett makes a magnanimous gesture as he dabs perspiration from his forehead.

'Well, you're putting on quite a show here, Captain, so I just had to come take a look see. Every little bit 'll help the big game back in Tokyo, right Frank?'

Roberts smiles nervously as he and Beckett start to move off. Beckett can feel Cooper's eyes on his back.

'I've been really looking forward to this, Frank. Just look at this place.'

Beckett gestures enthusiastically towards a riot of bougainvillea running back into dense jungle by the strip.

Sheedy moves up beside Cooper, inquisitive over his sunglasses. He mumbles, a smooth American drawl.

'By the way . . . someone tell me where the hell I am?'

He slips his sunglasses on, smiles innocently at Cooper.

Cooper stands outside the interrogation hut with Keenan and Corbett. They watch Takahashi approach, flanked by Matsugae and Reid. Cooper jerks his head towards the door. Keenan disappears inside.

As the defence party reaches Cooper, Keenan appears with Ikeuchi. Cooper studies them both. Takahashi stares right through Ikeuchi.

Finally, Ikeuchi bows from the shoulder reluctantly to his superior. Cooper nods to Keenan, who pushes Ikeuchi forward. Matsugae lowers his eyes, not wishing to give any indication of his feelings.

Cooper salutes Reid and leads them into the hut. Corbett closes the door and stands at ease in front of it. Cooper gestures three chairs before the table. He watches Takahashi seat himself slowly, follows his eyes to the photos of the mass grave laid out like neat plots themselves.

A faint look of shock and surprise crosses Takahashi's oval face. He stares up at Cooper, who sits back studying every facial tic, every nuance.

'Captain, who is responsible for this?' Takahashi says in a clipped, resonant tone, sounding almost plum English. Very convincing.

Precisely, you bastard, thought Cooper.

'I thought you may be able to enlighten me on this matter, Vice Admiral.'

Matsugae leans forward, produces a statement from his satchel, hands it to Cooper.

'My client, Vice Admiral Takahashi, wishes to modify the statement he sent you from Tokyo.'

Cooper takes the statement, suppressing his surprise. He looks over the statement.

'The prosecution never received this statement.'

Matsugae looks at Takahashi then at Reid, baffled. Takahashi calmly takes a cigarette from a silver case brought from inside his pocket and produces an ivory tipped cigarette holder, into which he carefully puts the cigarette. He lights it with a gold encrusted lighter.

Cooper feels Takahashi's utter contempt.

'Your days as a gentleman of leisure are numbered, mate.'

Takahashi smiles condescendingly.

'I'm sorry that you did not receive it, Captain. But, in any case, I wish to amend the statement.'

'Amend? Why?'

Reid signals Takahashi to stop, with a strong cough. He shifts his bulky body forward, wishing to establish his authority before Cooper.

'Captain, I think the previous statement may have given the erroneous impression that the Vice Admiral may have actually given orders for the punishment of prisoners.'

Matsugae anxiously studies Takahashi, then returns his attention to Cooper.

'My client had nothing to do with alleged organised beatings, any alleged forced labour or any alleged execution of prisoners.'

Cooper checks the statement carefully then looks up at Takahashi.

'The men in the photos before you were not prisoners in the camp. They were executed near the airstrip, we believe, just after you took the surrender on Ambon. You recall February, 1942?'

'I can explain . . .'

But Reid cuts him off with a jab to his knee.

'Captain, the defence will modify the statement and discuss it with you later.'

Cooper does not appear to hear.

'If you were the ultimate authority on Ambon, you were responsible for the prisoners?'

Reid nods to Matsugae, who nods to Takahashi.

'That is technically correct . . .'

'I'm glad we can agree on one thing.' Cooper studies Reid. He would have to be on his toes every step.

'But the court martial of prisoners would have been your sole responsibility under Japanese Naval Regulations, correct?'

Takahashi does not flinch, but smiles, not waiting for direction.

'Yes. But no such courts martial took place, Captain.'

Reid glares at Takahashi. He knew Cooper too well. Now the wheels would be really spinning.

'Captain, I think that issue can be explored later.'

Cooper grins at Reid.

'It may well be, Captain Reid.'

Cooper stands suddenly, nods to Corbett who steps over and takes the statement from Cooper.

'The Vice Admiral wishes to modify his statement, Lieutenant. See that it is properly "modified", will you?'

Corbett returns Cooper's stiff salute. Cooper marches from the hut, leaving Reid quietly fuming, Matsugae surprised and Takahashi amused by the relationship revealed between the Australians. Matsugae reluctantly hands him an ashtray in which he carefully ashes his cigarette. Reid rises quickly.

Outside the hut, Cooper reaches for a cigarette from his top pocket. He pauses with the cigarette lighter and studies his shaking hand. Anger.

'Patience.' The voice again. 'You've got him rattled.'

But the arrogance! It was almost as if the war had ended differently for Takahashi. He was the victor. He would decide his fate! The bastard!

Reid taps him on the shoulder. Cooper turns suddenly.

'Bob, the defendants might be more co-operative if you recognised their rank. It might break down some of the barriers.'

Cooper shakes his head and exhales heavily.

'Justice doesn't wear a uniform. Not in my book, Eric.'

Reid observes Cooper's hand, trembling as he takes another puff.

'That's exactly my point, Bob. He might be Japanese but he has a certain rank. He demands certain respect. If you don't show it, the other Japs'll notice. And, he admires British traditions. You saw his medals from the First War.'

Cooper stubs out his smoke savagely.

'Jesus, Eric! Haven't they told you about the Second? We won, the Japs lost! And which tradition led him to execute our blokes? The British or the Japanese?'

'You don't know that for certain.'

'You'll have to have a bloody good explanation for that mass grave!'

Reid is exasperated.

'Pardon the expression, but I'm not going to open that can of worms now. Look, Bob, I wear the Australian uniform just like you. I'm ordered to assist in the defence of men who just yesterday were our sworn enemies. But I'm going to do the best job I can and bugger my personal feelings!'

Cooper stares at him fixedly. Reid shakes his head wearily. Who in the world would have their jobs?

'There's an easy way to do this job. And a hard way. I don't want to see it run into a bloody great obstacle course. We could be stuck here for years. Ambon's a stepping stone in our careers, Bob, not a dead end. Tokyo's going to be the place where we can leave our mark. Think about it. Takahashi could be very useful to both of us.'

Cooper is not convinced but gives Reid an encouraging nod. Reid, satisfied for the moment, turns back to the hut. Cooper looks across the grounds to Roberts' office. The sound of laughter, a distant tinkle. Who really is Beckett? What is his relationship with Roberts? Is he the one who said who could be admitted to the 'big game' in Tokyo and who could not? Is Ambon really a 'dry run' for that one? Or is there some other agenda?

Cooper observes the Japanese prisoners as he crosses the compound. How would they know whether justice had been done? How would anyone know? Reid's taunt about 'personal feelings' meant that there had to be some standard by which to assess the outcome. What was it? A 100 percent conviction rate, or significant sentences for the major culprits? To appease the chorus of blood and revenge back home, or to satisfy a real standard of proof and guilt? How would he be judged?

One thing was certain. All the effort put into getting Takahashi back must not go to waste. He had to link him and Ikeuchi through executions. Orders that only Takahashi could give because he was required to. That proof still had to be found. The trial started in the morning.

Cooper walks through the evidence room, glances at another batch of three Japanese being photographed by Patterson. He turns back, pulls Patterson aside.

'Takahashi's staff?'

'No luck yet, Captain.'

Cooper strides on to Roberts' door, knocks and enters. The air is thick with smoke. Beckett, just by his presence has made Roberts' office his domain. Roberts is clearly nonplussed by Cooper's arrival. Beckett picks up a bottle of bourbon, offers Cooper a glass.

'I won't refuse.'

Beckett keeps his eye on Cooper as he pours a shot.

'Yep, I'd say you wouldn't see this standard of alcohol around here too often.'

He hands Cooper the glass. Roberts refuses another, finishing what he held. Beckett smiles, raises his for a toast.

'Ambon and Tokyo. Sister cities of justice.'

Cooper raises his glass, clinks it with the others. He drinks a small amount, puts down his glass.

'I won't stay long. Just wanted to thank the Major for delivering the chief defendant.' Cooper smiles thinly at Roberts who remains pokerfaced.

Beckett continues his expansiveness.

'No trouble, all part of the job, rounding up the

Emperor's old guard around the Pacific. We fought a war together, gotta clean up the peace the same way. Right, Frank?'

Roberts stares at Cooper discouragingly.

'My word.'

Cooper delays a little longer with his drink.

'The Emperor's "old guard", Major? Come to think of it, that's not a bad description. Hopefully, Takahashi's conviction'll bring us one step closer to the throne.'

Beckett glances at Roberts, then fixes Cooper with his best 'trust me' expression.

'I guess you haven't heard, Captain. It was just decided before I left. Emperor Hirohito's been granted immunity from prosecution.'

Cooper can feel his lips moving but his mind is paralysed by one word—'How?'

'What great genius dreamed that one up, Major?'

Beckett sees that Australian obsession with Hirohito rising on Cooper's face. Mr 'Diplomacy' will answer.

'General Macarthur. And I believe the President and Congress were also involved in the decision. Cooper, we're dealing with a defeated and demoralised nation. Rubbing their noses in it isn't going to win us any Brownie points.'

Cooper cannot suppress a caustic laugh.

'Oh, I see. So, if Hitler was still alive, then you blokes would just rap him across the knuckles and tell him to go stand in the corner?'

Roberts' anger is barely contained.

'I think that's enough, Captain!'

Beckett gives Roberts a placatory gesture.

'It's okay, Frank. The Captain's feelings are perfectly understandable. Many of our people feel just like you, Cooper. But your comparison with Hitler is way off the mark. The Emperor's a sacred institution in Japan. If we were to put him on trial, we would have the entire nation against us. It would be our backs that'd be against the wall. Then there's the simple lesson of history. Use the conquered leader effectively and everything else will fall into place. Look at the way the British ran the Raj in India.'

Cooper digests this information a few moments, looking down into his drink. He could not take another sip. So this is what the 'big game' in Tokyo was really about? He just could not see the point of any trials unless the Supreme Commander was held responsible. God, if this was in reverse, the Japs'd have the President and Congress up against the wall! No trials, no 'due process', no questions asked. Cooper shakes his head.

'So, Japan is the American Raj?'

Beckett grins broadly, appreciating the parallel.

'That's good. That's precisely the kind of thinking we need in Tokyo, Captain.'

'You're not dealing with a Western culture, here, Major. That should be bloody obvious by now!'

Beckett looks out over the base grounds.

'We've got to find a political solution now, Captain. Not a military one.'

Cooper salutes both of them and turns to leave. Beckett steps around the desk to open the door for him. Cooper faces Beckett squarely.

'I'll keep all that in mind, Major, when I'm prosecuting some fanatic who swore on oath to the Emperor to wipe us all off the face of the earth.'

Cooper's final jab catches Beckett short for a moment. He covers with a chuckle.

'I'm sure you will, Captain.'

Roberts shares his polite laughter. Beckett closes the door on Cooper and shrugs to Roberts, masking his real unease. It was such moments that made Beckett pine for the old comforts of the Boston bar, the clients who were wealthy and respectful.

But the stakes were higher here. And so were the potential rewards.

For Matsugae also, the stakes could not be higher. Outside the long assembly hut, he moves slowly with Takahashi at his side past the massed Japanese defendants. A heavy silence weighs down on them as he reads their faces, many lowering their eyes from the intensity of his searching gaze. The only sound is that of laughter and conversation floating across from the Australian mess.

Matsugae stops before Ikeuchi, standing at rigid attention in front of the defendants. They stare at each other a long moment. The contest of wills would now be resolved.

Matsugae steps back on to a raised platform with Takahashi. He had never been a devoted follower of the military, particularly after what they had done in disgracing his benefactor, Professor Yoshida, forcing him from his post.

But now he felt a peculiar satisfaction in standing before these men. For it was into his hands that they would now entrust their fate. Perhaps he felt just a twinge of revenge. But a sobering thought immediately comes. He glances at Takahashi. If he was not successful in Takahashi's defence, he might suffer the same fate as Yoshida.

Takahashi's voice is stern and deep, almost barking at his men.

'I have returned to stand with my men in this hour

of our country's need. Our actions are to be examined in great detail by the Australian court. We will uphold the great tradition of the Imperial Japanese Navy. Our conduct will be impeccable, even though we face the greatest test in our divine history. His Majesty the Emperor wishes that all his subjects co-operate with our former enemies, however galling that may be for many of you.'

What an extraordinary change from the silken tones used on the Prosecutor, thinks Matsugae.

'For this purpose, Imperial Navy HQ has sent Mr Shinji Matsugae, one of our country's most respected and experienced legal experts to represent you. You will listen carefully to him and follow his every instruction. He has my full backing and authority to represent us, with our best interests uppermost in his mind.'

Takahashi nods to Matsugae who steps forward nervously. Ikeuchi stares fixedly at Takahashi, silently demanding his attention, but not receiving it.

'I wish to thank the Vice Admiral for his kind remarks. It is true that our people's eyes are upon you, as well as those of our former enemies. Even though you may burn with the shame of your imprisonment, you will conduct yourselves with the honour you displayed in battle, as the Vice Admiral said.'

Matsugae looks across the rows of faces, finally stopping at Ikeuchi, whose eyes are still fixed on Takahashi.

Defiance incarnate, thinks Matsugae.

'But some of you may be tempted to take the honourable way out. This would be a terrible mistake for all of us, for it would expose us to even greater danger! You will not do this thing!'

Matsugae pulls himself up, feeling himself slipping into the haranguing tone of Takahashi.

'If I am to conduct your defence to the utmost, then your feelings must not stand between you and the truth, whatever your rank. This must be your new *giri*—your new duty. Truly, *giri* is the hardest to bear!'

He pauses. Was he really getting through to them? One final statement of authority was imperative.

'You are soldiers of the Emperor! I am his emissary!'

Matsugae bows to them, an action only perfunctorily mirrored by Ikeuchi and his 'lieutenants'. Takahashi raises his arms in the traditional salute.

'*Tenno heika . . .*'

A hundred pairs of arms fly up as a hundred voices yell: '*BANZAI!*'

Across on the mess verandah, Cooper stands with Corbett and Littell, each with a beer. The thunderous chant continues.

'*TENNO HEIKA BANZAI!*'

Sheedy appears beside Cooper, beer in hand.

'*TENNO HEIKA BANZAI!*'

Cooper downs his beer, looks straight at Sheedy.

'Long live the bloody Emperor!' A harsh, bitter tone noted by Littell.

Sheedy raises his glass, grinning sombrely.

'Yeah, to his continued good health!'

Cooper exits with Corbett, watched with concern by Littell. Sheedy drinks, muses to himself.

'How long does it last?'

Littell turns to him.

'What?'

'The hate, Sister Littell, the hate.'

Littell turns away. There was no 'medical' training that could answer that. If time heals all wounds, that would be the hardest.

Cooper walks hurriedly into his office. Files and papers scattered along a long table, illuminated by paraffin lamps overhead. Corbett adjusts the lamps, turning them up full. The dull sheen of the samurai swords becomes a blazing silver reflection.

Cooper ponders them a moment. They had been captured just after the surrender was taken. Maybe they were the actual weapons used by those elusive 'executioners'. He sits at the desk, feeling overwhelmed by what faced him. He looks up at Corbett, standing ready with a file.

'What's that?'

Corbett sighs.

'It took a while, but it's the confirmation on those missing flyers.'

He hands it to Cooper who reads slowly.

'Says that their last position was somewhere off the island. Someone's lost the flight tape in Darwin. They're trying to find it, get the exact position. Not much joy with this one, Jack.'

'No sir, but I'll keep on it if you want.'

Cooper returns to the pile of affidavits before him. He hands each of them for Corbett to file under each defendant's name. Cooper looks up at Corbett who seems puzzled.

'What's up?'

'It's just all a bit strange. I mean, sir, Takahashi arrives here the day before but his statement never arrives. Doesn't leave us with much time, does it?'

'Or the defence. Yeah, but now he's here, let's look at it. Our best shot is with the mass grave. We know

70

Takahashi was here to take the Australian surrender. Next best is Mitchell although it doesn't nail him down tight. But it's bloody good circumstantial evidence that he and Ikeuchi met and discussed executions. Only a couple of occasions but it might be enough. Next the prisoners' statements on the bashings and food supplies. We can use the international law angle and their own regulations on that one. It might square away both of the buggers. Did you see Sister Littell?'

'Yeah, she has what you might call "hearsay" evidence. Rantings and ravings, particularly from that bloke Fenton. But nothing coherent.'

It was vital to keep the link to Carol open. He would arrange for her to 'run into' Corbett and the information could be exchanged. But they were still lacking that vital piece—what had happened to the eleven blokes who had disappeared from the camp. Possible grave sites were still being excavated without any new bodies found yet.

Cooper leans back in his chair. It might be more difficult but it might just work.

'Jack, get over to Roberts' office. We want a requisition, no, we want to subpoena any documents from the Japanese Naval Command that are kept in Tokyo. Find out what clearance we need to get them.'

Corbett leaps to his feet.

'I just hope it doesn't take as long as Takahashi, sir.'

Cooper grins, pleased with this brainstorm.

'If it's not so hard then who knows what we'll turn up?'

Corbett exits, leaving Cooper to ponder his opening address. This was going to be the most unique and challenging address he had ever done. To tell the story of what happened on this island over the last three and a half years. A real feat of narrative and legal organisation. Was he up to it?

He looks across at the photo of Geoff and his father. If only they could be there to witness it.

Behind the wire, Takahashi stands, smoking, as he observes the night sky, the rhythmic pulsations of brilliant galaxies of stars. He finds himself navigating his way across the Indian Ocean, a time long gone. Who would remember now how the Japanese Navy escorted British and Australian ships across those treacherous waters, crawling with U-boats? No one.

He hears a rustling behind and turns around. Ikeuchi, standing a respectful distance from him. Head slightly bowed.

'We must talk, Honourable Vice Admiral.'

Takahashi turns his face away, and looks back to the heavens.

'We have nothing to discuss.'

Ikeuchi stands his ground but conceals his fury. Takahashi walks away, no hint of anxiety. Ikeuchi looks across to the building where last minute construction is being supervised by Keenan. The old Dutch schoolhouse being converted to a courtroom.

His performance would be impeccable. No one would escape his wrath in that pit, on his stage—on his own *hanamichi*, in his *kabuki* play. The Australians would find themselves as the pupils, not the teachers.

CHAPTER SIX

THE TRIAL THE PANIC

Cooper feels a jolting sensation. He was being lifted from dark, watery depths, writhing in a battle with a swirling vortex trying to suck him back down. He opens his eyes, a pool of water caught in a sunbeam. Has he escaped? He tries to focus, looks up. Geoff's face!

The faces comes into focus. Corbett, with a puzzled, concerned expression.

'Sir, it's time.'

Cooper lifts his head, sees that he has slumped over the desk. His head is a balloon of heat, radiating waves of blinding pain, stabbing his temples and slicing his skull with thin long blades.

He looks down at the pool of water. His sweat, seeping across the pages of his opening address. Carefully chosen words now smudged and deformed. Would it matter? Couldn't he speak from the heart? Have them all in his hand, regardless?

Suddenly, the dream comes back. The pool is at the bottom of the mass grave. Ikeuchi raises a sodden corpse, its face covered in mud. A thunderous downpour starts. Ikeuchi drops the corpse nonchalantly, stares back up at Cooper, grinning widely. The rain washes away the mud on the corpse's face, revealing its features. The pale, angular face of Geoff.

Cooper's grief comes in a raging torrent. He leaps into the grave, hurls Ikeuchi back, and falls to his knees, his body shaking in violent convulsions. He prises Geoff free with his shaking hands, and stares into his face, bloodied, scarred and slashed. He falls back against the grave's muddy wall, clasping his brother close, weeping, wanting to burst from his body.

He looks up through rain and tears. Takahashi stands above the grave, staring into the distance, completely detached from it all. Waves of grief transform into a sharp, hot filament of rage. Cooper feels his skin charged with a burning as he feels the tightness in his stomach directing this searing filament, now a taut piano wire with which he tears the throats out of Takahashi and Ikeuchi.

'Sir?'

Cooper observes his shaking hands on the desk, then looks up at Corbett, now at the open door, satchel heavy with papers. Slowly, Cooper takes out the fob watch and checks the time. He continues to stare at Geoff's image in the cover, then nods wearily.

Suddenly, an explosion of angry shouts from the compound. Jeering, yelling, deep throated and high pitched voices. Men and women in a chorus of hatred.

Cooper finds his feet quickly, and pushes papers and files into his satchel. He grabs his cap and steps through the door into blinding light.

Outside the compound, dozens of Ambonese swarm around the two lines of Japanese being marched from the camp. Keenan yells at the guards who form a chain to the courthouse, pushing back the locals, many of whom bear the scars of torture and ill treatment by their former masters.

Talbot looks around nervously, as he uses his rifle

to block two old women screaming insults at Ikeuchi and the others. Takahashi leads the way through the 'parade of honour', immaculate in a freshly pressed uniform.

Cooper is jostled as he approaches the rear, open end of the courthouse. He and Corbett spot a gap in the crowd and are slipped through the line of guards by Keenan who whispers harshly to him, jerking his head at the locals.

'Well, someone's got the right attitude!'

Cooper looks up at the sky. Dark thunderheads gathering over the bay, spiralling up into a bright sky, charging the air below. Some Frenchman had the words for this moment—*apres moi, le deluge.* So it would be today.

He proceeds into the long hut that is filling up with the defendants. Any confusion by them is quickly resolved by a firm shove by M.P.s standing at each of the five long benches that form the 'dock'. It is separated from the prosecution and defence tables by a wooden barrier. The witness chair stands next to the interpreters and court orderlies, who sit at adjacent desks nearby, ancient typewriters ready and waiting. The Judge Advocate's desk is seated at an angle from the Bench, a long table covered in dark cloth, raised above the others on a trestle platform.

Sheedy catches Cooper's eye as he gazes around. He gives him a two fingered salute and stubs out his cigarette as he produces a notebook from his 'campaign jacket'. He stands waiting in front of an observer's bench. Both he and Cooper study Beckett closely as he enters, escorted by an M.P. to his seat next to Sheedy. Beckett looks across, a tight smile and a nod to Cooper.

The Bench led by Johnson and Roberts file in.

They stand before crossed Australian and British flags, centred on a portrait of the King. Cooper looks across at Matsugae and Reid at the defence table, files neatly laid out in rows before them. Corbett continues to remove a mass of documents and lay them out hurriedly. Cooper takes his time sliding documents from his satchel. A quick smile at Reid who remains expressionless. The perfect card player.

Cooper gazes back at Takahashi and Ikeuchi who are standing, staring ahead, aloof. That facade would melt when exposed to the heat of Cooper's questions. It could not survive. Cooper feels a tightness in his chest, a moment of doubt.

He looks across to the Ambonese, continuing to shout and jeer around the open sides of the courthouse. No doubt there. The verdict was in long ago. Cooper stiffens at the sound of Johnson banging the gavel loudly.

'Silence! Silence! Silence! This court will come to order!'

Some of the Japanese defendants on the edge of the court have to lean away from the grasping arms of the locals reaching through the ranks of very nervous M.P.s and guards ringing the courtroom.

'Sergeant Keenan, you will remove the observers from the perimeter of this court!'

Keenan jumps to it, gesturing to the Australian guards rapidly. Talbot and the others put their backs into it, pushing hard against the groups of locals who are gradually driven back. Any sympathies with them are momentarily suspended. Order descends as the concerted chorus fades to the occasional shout or jeer. The guards return to their positions.

Keenan snaps his fingers. A number of thatched panels are slid into position around the court, blocking the view and reducing the glare. Cooper observes the shadows falling over the participants. It was a pity that the clear view of the POW camp had to be blocked out.

Keenan looks around, satisfied that order is in place. A grim satisfaction tinged with the same regret as Cooper. The camp was no longer visible. Keenan steps forward, snaps to attention, and salutes the Bench. He moves back to his position before the mass of defendants.

Johnson nods to Roberts who stands ramrod straight behind his desk. All eyes are on him except for Sheedy, head slightly bowed as if in danger of nodding off. The rapid shorthand in his notebook distracts Beckett momentarily who then returns his attention to Roberts.

Roberts clears his throat.

'I hereby convene the Australian War Crimes Tribunal Ambon, in accordance with the Australian War Crimes Act 1945.'

Roberts and the Bench take their seats, followed by the entire court.

A young court orderly steps up with one of the Japanese interpreters to face the seated defendants. He produces a clip folder from which he reads.

'The accused are charged under section three and section nine, subsection two of the Australian War Crimes Act 1945, with the deliberate and concerted ill treatment of prisoners of war. How do you plead?'

Cooper turns sideways in his seat, intent on Takahashi who rises as the interpreter barks the charge in Japanese.

'*Musi*. Not guilty.'

An audible ripple of dissent from the Australian guards.

Takahashi resumes his seat, impervious to Cooper and the 'unofficial vote'.

Ikeuchi rises, hesitates for effect, then lingers on each word as he looks straight at Cooper.

'Not guilty!'

He congratulates himself on a flawless delivery. But the audience think otherwise. The ripple becomes a loud murmur. Roberts bangs the gavel loudly.

'Order!'

Ikeuchi enjoys his moment of adulation, then sits, grinning at Cooper. He takes no notice of Matsugae's reproving expression.

Ikeuchi is followed by each of the Japanese rising to pronounce themselves 'not guilty'. Cooper keeps his head down, studying his address. He glances up to the Bench and Roberts, sitting impassively as the word *musi* runs on like a cracked record.

As the last defendant sits, Cooper reaches for the fob watch and opens it. He checks the time, then closes it gently, whispering *musi* to himself. Corbett turns to him, his eyes full of expectation. The months of work, the sweat soaked days and late nights, the concentration, the frustration, the confrontation— all for this moment. Cooper is all that he aspired to be. Tough, inspirational, a quick wit and a mind like a steel trap. He could not fail.

Cooper rises slowly to his feet, looking around the court, feeling the total concentration of all the faces before him. He looks down at his address, then steps away from his table, as if lost in a reverie.

He turns back to face Takahashi and Ikeuchi seated just behind him. He studies them like they were some sort of exotic specimens. Exotic but deadly. He looks over the faces of the other defendants, some of whom lower their eyes from his penetrating gaze, others who stare right through him, uncomprehendingly. They had no idea what they were caught up in.

Cooper turns to face the Bench, waiting.

'Vice Admiral "Baron" Takahashi, Captain Wadami Ikeuchi and the other ninety defendants listed in the indictment now sit in this court, next to the prisoner of war camp that they ran for over three and a half years.

'We must first pay a perverse compliment to the defendants. In that time, they managed to turn this island from paradise into a pocket of hell. No easy feat. But their concerted and dedicated approach to this task will be proven beyond all doubt.

'With the surrender of the Australian Second Twenty First Battalion, "Gull Force", and the Dutch garrison, on February 3rd, 1942 to the vastly superior forces of the Japanese Navy, the reign of terror began.

'Shortly after the surrender, three hundred men of the Gull Force Battalion "disappeared" near the Laha airstrip, not far from this court. Their fate was to remain a mystery, even to prisoners in the camp, for the entire war.'

Cooper moves over to a table on which are placed gruesome exhibits, axe handles stained with blood, bayonets, swords, lengths of wire whip.

'We now know their fate. They were executed en masse.'

He lets this fact sink in as he looks down at the instruments of suffering.

'Six hundred men were then interned in this camp. With the Japanese surrender three years later, one hundred and twenty were left, barely alive.'

He looks around at the faces of the Bench, Roberts, Corbett, Matsugae and Reid intent on every word.

'What was the nature of the ill treatment with

which the defendants are charged? Mass beatings, torture, executions. The forced labour of men barely able to stand.'

Cooper starts to pace, as if his feet are a drum-beat for his words.

'Death marches. The deliberate denial of food, of medicine, of any care or any consideration. The prosecution will prove that the chief causes of the prisoners' deaths were starvation and disease, a death rate which was only worsened by the other ill treatment, as the strategic position of the Japanese deteriorated in 1944 and '45.'

He looks again at Takahashi, who sits imperiously, as if the court did not exist.

'We can only speculate as to what happened in the final weeks before the surrender. When all records on this island . . . "vanished". The prosecution will also contend that the Japanese administration of Ambon violated international law and had a deliberate policy to ensure the concerted and continuous ill treatment of both prisoners and the local population.'

He steps to the prosecution table, takes a sip of water from a glass and is handed a sheaf of statements from Corbett. He walks over and stands beside Takahashi.

'And who were the chief architects of this policy? Vice Admiral Takahashi, who was responsible for the island as part of his Navy's fleet headquarters, and Captain Ikeuchi, who controlled the POW camp on the island, under his command. The other defendants, officers, NCOs and guards were responsible for the implementation of this policy.'

Cooper holds up the sheaf of statements.

'Their actions will live forever in the memories

of those "fortunate" enough to have survived the living hell of Ambon. The prosecution will submit the statements of those survivors. Their words bear close examination.'

He drops the statements on the table with an audible thud.

'The story they tell is truly overwhelming. Their words will prove to be the final weapon for which the accused have no answer.'

Cooper gazes around the faces before him. Roberts, scowling at those final words, Beckett impassive, Sheedy with one eyebrow cocked in thought, the Bench mildly impressed, the President, Lieutenant Colonel Johnson, making a couple of notations with a fountain pen.

Finally, Cooper sits, head down to the evidence. Corbett slides across a piece of paper.

'Great.'

Roberts nods to the Bench and looks back to Cooper.

'The case of the Commonwealth and Vice Admiral Takahashi will proceed first. The prosecution may call the defendant as its first witness, unless it wishes to call others.'

Cooper exchanges a look of surprised relief with Corbett, then rises.

'Thank you, Your Honour. The prosecution calls Vice Admiral Takahashi to the stand.'

Takahashi rises, indomitable, and is escorted by Keenan across to the witness chair. He bows to Roberts and the Bench, then adjusts his jacket as the orderly steps up to him.

Takahashi instinctively raises his right hand as the Orderly states the oath.

'Do you swear that the evidence you are about to

give this court will be the whole truth and nothing but the truth?'

'I solemnly swear.' That resonant, silken tone again.

Takahashi seats himself with precision. Sheedy glances at Beckett, whispers out of the side of his mouth.

'This bloke knows his onions.'

Beckett moves his shoulder, half turning, distancing himself from Sheedy who gets the message, quietly amused.

Cooper steps up beside Takahashi who sits calmly facing the Bench. Matsugae leans forward, listening closely.

'Vice Admiral Takahashi, you were responsible for the Imperial Japanese Navy's Fourth South Seas Fleet base on Ambon?'

'That is correct.'

Cooper walks away, addressing the court.

'Which was a position of great honour, wasn't it? Ambon was to be the main forward naval base for the invasion of Australia?'

Takahashi considers it carefully.

'That would be correct.'

'Yes, it would be but for the fact that the invasion was cancelled.'

Cooper turns back, a grim smile.

'And you were left with the supervision of the prisoner of war camp on this island?'

Takahashi maintains his calm composure.

'Yes . . . but the 20th Garrison Unit responsible for the camp was left entirely in the hands of Captain Ikeuchi.'

'Not entirely. Didn't Captain Ikeuchi have a duty to report prisoners' violations of camp regulations to you?'

Takahashi chooses his words very carefully, glances at Matsugae then back to Cooper.

'It is impossible to know whether every violation was reported.'

Cooper moves in closer.

'Answer the question, Vice Admiral. Did Captain Ikeuchi report violations to you?'

'On rare occasions.'

'Did you investigate these violations?'

'Certainly. Every violation that was reported by him was investigated.'

A tremendous clap of thunder overhead. Takahashi looks up. An unfortunate omen? Rain, heavy drops on the tin roof, then a thunderous downpour.

Cooper waits, staring at Takahashi. The rain eases slightly but Cooper raises his voice to be heard.

'How did you respond to these violations?'

Takahashi's voice booms out.

'I left that in the hands of Captain Ikeuchi.'

Cooper looks back to the Bench sceptically.

'Captain Ikeuchi . . . but your office had a clear view down to the camp, didn't it?'

The rain eases further. A gentle drumming on the roof. Takahashi smiles.

'Except when it rained. It rained often.'

Cooper retrieves a file from Corbett, turns back to Takahashi slowly.

'Did you investigate an incident in August, 1943 when thirty prisoners were beaten from dawn to dusk? A beating . . .'

Reid whispers to Matsugae who rises instantly.

'Objection, Your Honours.'

Cooper nods to Roberts, looks back at Takahashi, sighs.

'Correction. An "alleged" beating in which four men . . .'

He glances at Matsugae pointedly.

'Allegedly died.'

'I do not recall the incident.'

'If such incidents were reported to you and you say you investigated them, how is it possible that you don't recall it?'

Takahashi thinks carefully.

'I was in Batavia in August 1943, at a meeting of senior naval officers.'

'Are there records of your attendance at that meeting?'

'If they still exist, they would be in Tokyo.'

Cooper glances at Beckett.

'If they still exist . . . Vice Admiral, can you tell this court what happened to the records of your command on this island?'

Takahashi manages to sound almost regretful.

'They were destroyed by Allied bombing raids.'

Cooper looks across at Reid incredulously.

'Every file? Every scrap of paper? What did you do? Put a sign on the roof—"please bomb here"?'

A wave of sniggering sweeps through the guards. Roberts bangs the gavel.

'Captain Cooper. Humour has its place but not at this time.'

Corbett suppresses a smirk as Cooper turns to Roberts.

'Your Honour.'

He turns back to Takahashi. Time for the jugular.

'From early 1944 to the surrender, over three hundred prisoners in this camp died. We "allege" that prisoners' rations were reduced to below starvation level! We "allege" that there were no medical supplies! We "allege" that one rotting bandage had to last the whole camp for a month. We "allege" that men on their last legs were forced to carry sacks of cement until they dropped or were "allegedly" beaten to death!'

The savagery of Cooper's tone starts to rattle Takahashi.

'Captain Ikeuchi was . . .'

'Do you deny this happened under your command?'

'You don't understand . . .'

'Do you deny you had a duty to prevent it?'

Takahashi leans forward earnestly.

'You don't understand. We were subjected to daily air raids! Ten raids in a day! Supply lines cut! By your blockade. Everyone suffered!'

'Some more than others!'

Cooper refers to a folder he picks up from Corbett.

'Are you aware of the Imperial Japanese Navy regulation concerning prisoners who—escape, resist or disobey orders from guards, escorts or those responsible for supervising prisoners?'

'Yes.'

'What was the penalty for such offenders?'

Takahashi is sombre, apologetic.

'Death.'

'Who would make such a decision?'

Takahashi treads very carefully, feeling a trap closing.

'The commander of the garrison.'

'Yourself?'

'Theoretically, yes.'

'Theoretically?'

Cooper selects a statement from the folder.

'Well, let me refresh your memory, Vice Admiral. I read from a sworn statement from Private William

Mitchell. You remember Private Mitchell?'

'No.'

'Let me refresh your memory again. Private Mitchell was a prisoner you used personally as a gardener around your headquarters. He spoke Japanese unbeknown to you or any of your staff.'

A glance to Ikeuchi. A stone statue.

'I quote: "Takahashi often held meetings at Fleet HQ to discuss the execution of prisoners with Ikeuchi".'

Takahashi is alarmed but feigns indignation.

'He is a liar!'

Reid nods to Matsugae who rises.

'Objection, Your Honour. Private Mitchell is not in court. How well did he speak Japanese?'

Cooper looks away, his momentum spoilt.

'I don't know.'

'Objection sustained.'

Cooper turns back to the table and accepts a new handful of statements.

'In the three years of your command, in spite of admitted escape attempts by prisoners, and I submit statements verifying these attempts . . .'

He hands them to the orderly.

'In spite of all those violations, in those three years you never witnessed any brutality?'

'No!'

'You never ordered the punishment of any prisoner?'

'I did not.'

'And you never had to make a decision on the life or death of a single prisoner?'

'Never.'

Cooper steps away, taking the pressure off, studying the Bench. No real reaction. Takahashi takes a folded handerchief from his pocket and wipes the perspiration from his hands and dabs at his face. He folds the handkerchief neatly and places it back squarely in his pocket.

Sheedy makes a note in his pad—'Bullshit'.

Cooper hands the statements back to Corbett and is about to turn back to Takahashi when he sees the file on the missing flyers in amongst the ones below him. He turns slowly back to Takahashi.

'The frequent air raids over Ambon. Can you tell this court what would have happened to pilots captured during these raids?'

Takahashi seems genuinely bemused.

'I do not recall any pilots having been taken prisoner.'

'That wasn't the question. What was the regulation governing captured pilots?'

Takahashi smiles condescendingly.

'There were no pilots taken prisoner.'

Cooper smiles thinly in return.

'So it is a hypothetical regulation, Vice Admiral?'

'I do not understand the word.'

Cooper refers to the file before him.

'I think you understand perfectly. Didn't you graduate with honours in law? From Oxford?'

Takahashi glances to the Bench, smiles ingratiatingly.

'Under international law, a captured pilot would have been treated like any other prisoner of war.'

'And if a pilot had violated international law?'

Reid whispers to Matsugae who stands, not quite sure of himself.

'Objection, Your Honour. This seems irrelevant.'

Roberts looks at the Bench then at Cooper, puzzled.

'What is the prosecution's intention?'

'I am attempting to define the extent of the Vice Admiral's duties, your Honour. Since, he is so reluctant to do so himself.'

Reid rises instantly.

'Objection!'

'Objection overruled. Proceed, Captain!'

Cooper turns back to Takahashi but keeps one eye on Reid.

'Under Imperial Japanese Navy law, who would have decided whether a violation had been committed or not?'

Takahashi is about to remove his handkerchief again, but thinks better of it.

'The President of the court martial.'

'Who held that position on this island?'

Takahashi pauses before answering softly.

'I did.'

Beckett leans forward slightly, tensing. Sheedy watches him.

'Please repeat that for the court.'

'I was the President.'

'Of the court martial.'

'Yes but I repeat! There were no pilots taken prisoner.'

Takahashi smiles again. But a tremor in his eyes. Cooper registers it and steps away, looks at Reid, who knows Cooper may have the ace. Cooper turns back.

'There were no pilots taken prisoner during your command on this island. Tell me, Vice Admiral, how was a court martial constituted?'

Roberts sees Reid rising to his feet.

'Captain, unless you have a very good reason, I see little to be gained by this line of questioning. I am sure the court has a clear picture of the Vice

Admiral's responsibilities.'

'Yes, Your Honour.'

He turns back to Takahashi.

'One further question, Vice Admiral. How do you explain the mass grave near the Laha airstrip?'

'Mass grave?'

'Yes. You took the surrender here and three hundred men were executed soon afterwards, near the Laha airstrip?'

'I did take the surrender but then I was called to Manila for an urgent meeting. I was not aware of this until I arrived here two days ago.'

Cooper looks at Takahashi, the Bench and Beckett.

'And I suppose the records of that meeting are in Tokyo?'

'I would not know.'

'Vice Admiral, I put it to you that you were in command here, regardless of where you happened to be. It is hard to believe that such a major "event", such as the execution of three hundred men, could not have come to your attention. The choice is very simple, Vice Admiral. Either you ordered Ikeuchi to go ahead with the executions or you failed to order him not to? What's it to be?'

Takahashi looks to the Bench, to Matsugae, then to Ikeuchi. He shakes his head.

'I can only repeat what I said. I knew nothing about this incident.'

Cooper stares at him for a few moments. Pathological liar number two. He turns to the Bench. No visible response. Surely they could see through this.

'Your Honour, I request an adjournment.'

Roberts is surprised. The schedule didn't permit many adjournments.

'On what grounds, Captain?'

'Your Honour, the Vice Admiral's case is a complex one. It requires more time for crucial evidence to be processed if the case is to be properly presented.'

Roberts confers with the Bench. Johnson makes a couple of notes then looks up at Cooper, noticeably irritated by the request. His tone is curt.

'Request granted. You have twenty-four hours, Captain.'

Cooper feels the protest opening his lips but holds himself in check. Roberts can see it and brings down the gavel quickly.

'This court is adjourned.'

Keenan springs into action with the guards, shuffling the confused Japanese from their seats as the court rises. Cooper and Corbett pack their satchels quickly, Cooper pausing to observe Takahashi being escorted out. He turns to Corbett.

'Get Darwin back on the line. We need that tape priority urgent.'

Cooper ignores Reid's glaring expression and strides out the side. Every second counted.

Sheedy walks from the court with Beckett, pausing with him to observe the compound into which the Japanese are being marched by the guards.

'Off the beaten track, aren't we, Major?'

Beckett looks at Sheedy closely.

'Have we met before?'

'Mike Sheedy, the *Sydney Herald*. We might have run into each other at the surrender on the *Missouri*.'

Beckett hides his jealousy. A lousy newspaperman had been preferred over him at such an occasion?

'I don't recall. Anyway I'm just paying a friendly visit.'

Sheedy grins lopsidedly.

'Keeping the natives honest?'

Beckett smiles thinly.

'They're doing just fine, Mr Sheedy. Nice talking to you.'

Beckett walks off to join Roberts, who is walking from the court. Sheedy lights a half smoked cigarette, watching, now very intrigued.

In the Legal Corps evidence room, Cooper, Patterson and two Australian staffers stack up all the statements of the prosecution and defence and commence to comb through them.

Corbett enters hurriedly, files tucked under his arm. He walks rapidly down the long room. He taps Cooper on the shoulder, hands him the files. Cooper takes a last puff on his cigarette, looks over the files which have the Japanese 'mug shots' attached to the flaps.

'No luck with Darwin, sir. Or Tokyo.'

'Tell 'em they can burn the midnight oil just like us. It's vital, Jack.'

Cooper drops the files, disappointed.

'More guards. Jesus, I need Takahashi's staff. Where's the Legal Officer?'

'Shimada?'

'That's the bloke. Shimada can verify Takahashi's orders.'

'Still searching.'

'And the Signals Officer?'

'Tanaka?'

'Yeah. He could explain the so called "missing records".'

'Still looking for him, too.'

Cooper shakes his head wearily. Corbett exits quickly. Cooper looks at the others, poring over the documents. Patterson races through the documents, then grins at Cooper.

'I took a speed reading course in Melbourne.'

'Now you tell me.'

Cooper looks up as Carol Littell enters apprehensively.

'Sorry to disturb you, Captain.'

She walks up to Cooper and hands him a piece of paper from which he reads aloud.

'Bastards, leave Eddy alone?'

'It's like a recurring nightmare for Jimmy Fenton the last couple of days. Maybe it means nothing but I thought you should know.'

'Thanks, Carol.'

He picks up the file on the missing flyers as she stands staring at the large map of Ambon, dotted with flags and markets.

'Eddy? Eddy Fenton!'

He hands her the file. She looks at the photo closely.

'Yes, there is a resemblance, isn't there?'

Cooper's face takes on a new determination. He turns to the others.

'I'm tempted to say "Bingo!", boys, but keep reading!'

Cooper shepherds her towards the window.

'Anything else?'

'Not really. They just don't want to talk, Bob. Unless they start ranting like Jimmy.'

'And I'm not allowed to talk to him.'

She looks up at him encouragingly.

'There are ways!'

They are interrupted by Corbett bursting through the door.

'Got it, sir!'

He runs to Cooper, almost out of breath, hands him a rumpled piece of paper. Cooper makes a beeline for the map as everyone swings around to watch.

He notices Sheedy amble into the room as he crosses over to the map.

'You're out of bounds, Sheedy.'

'Roberts assured me I wouldn't be in the way.'

'Nice of him.'

Cooper reaches the map and refers to the co-ordinates on the paper.

'Do you know where this would be, Jack?'

Corbett places a marker on the map just off the coast.

'Here. South of the peninsula.'

Cooper steps back to find Sheedy standing behind him.

'Say one word about this and you're history.'

Sheedy places his hand over his heart in his best 'trust me' expression.

Cooper reads aloud.

'Radioed they'd been hit . . then nothing.'

Corbett ponders and turns to Cooper who has been joined by Littell, totally involved in the investigation.

'So, if Darwin picked up their signal . . .'

Littell nods slowly.

'Then . . .'

Cooper looks back at the map and traces an invisible line from the red flag to the camp. He looks back to them, his arm hovering over the point.

'Exactly, Carol. Right here.'

Corbett isn't so sure.

'It's deadly 'round that whole area, sir. Reefs, sharks.'

Sheedy looks pointedly at Cooper.

'Not only in the water, old son.'

Cooper hesitates a few moments, weighing it up, then strides across to the desk, picks up the file, slides them into his satchel and tugs his cap on. He grins at Corbett who is mystified by Cooper's move.

'No time like the present, Jack.'

He heads for the door, the others are irresistibly drawn into his wake.

Ikeuchi wakes to the sound of feet running past his hut. He looks out to see his fellow prisoners hurried along by guards. Suddenly, he sees the bulky form of a guard enter the hut.

Keenan grasps Ikeuchi by the collar and yanks him to his feet in one swift move. He finds his feet leave the earth as he is propelled across the room and out the door. Keenan drops him into the line of defendants moving up an open area between the huts.

Keenan strides up to the head of the line where a Japanese interpreter stands beside Cooper and Corbett, who holds a torch over the photos of the four flyers. The interpreter repeats the question.

'Do you recognise these men?'

As each defendant steps up, he is forced to follow Keenan's finger across the photos. Cooper studies each of them, searching for a glimmer of recognition. Each gives a shake of the head in response.

Ikeuchi reaches the head of the line. He stares past the photos at Cooper. Keenan leans over to him.

'Don't play silly buggers, Tojo. Do you recognise these men, Ikeuchi?'

Cooper gazes intently at Ikeuchi studying the pictures. Finally, Ikeuchi gives an insolent shake of the head and he steps away. Keenan pulls him back.

'Answer the question!'

'No.'

Keenan holds him there. Finally, Cooper shakes his head and Keenan lets Ikeuchi move on. Ikeuchi's other nemesis, Lieutenant Noburo Yamazaki is next in line.

He steps up, starts to scan the photos. A flicker of recognition. But Cooper is distracted by a shout from Matsugae.

'Captain! I must protest!'

Noburo lowers his eyes, trapped, not knowing which way to look. Cooper stares at Roberts, who follows closely behind Matsugae. They halt beside Cooper. Roberts fumes.

'What do you think you're doing, Captain.'

'Mass trial. Mass interrogation, Major!'

Takahashi is escorted up to them by Talbot and another soldier. He appears elegantly unruffled in his white kimono. Matsugae stares angrily at Cooper.

'The defendants have legal rights, Captain.'

Keenan moves Noburo on. Takahashi is deposited before Cooper who sees the antagonism building in Roberts' eyes. But he could not back down. Not now. He turns to Takahashi.

'Do you recognise any of these men?'

Matsugae is almost imploring.

'You do not have to answer, Vice Admiral.'

Takahashi waves him aside with a generous gesture, but takes his time bringing a pair of glasses from inside his jacket pocket and putting them on. He leans forward, studying each of the photos closely. Finally, he straightens, removes his glasses, returns them to his jacket and faces Cooper.

'I cannot be of any assistance.'

Roberts steps forward.

'You're closed down, Captain. My office. Now! You too, Mr Matsugae!'

He turns abruptly and walks off. Cooper and Matsugae square off in a long silence until Cooper finally returns the photos to his satchel, aware that Takahashi has not taken his eyes from him. Keenan escorts Ikeuchi back up beside Takahashi. Cooper snaps the satchel shut.

'Those flyers went down here. I'm going to find out what happened to them. Sleep on that!'

Keenan leans over to Cooper, an audible whisper.

'Give them to me. There won't be a mark on them.'

Cooper feels that hot fire in his chest. But he is a lawyer.

'Put 'em to bed, Sergeant.'

Cooper follows Matsugae from the compound, past Sheedy who draws on a cigarette, a witness to everything. Further on he notices Beckett holding back in the shadow of a hut, also a witness to the line up.

Beckett turns as Cooper walks past, unaware that he is observed by Sheedy, whose mind is going ten to the dozen.

In his office, Roberts sits at his desk, with Beckett who produces a pack of Camels. Matsugae and Cooper wait before them. Reid enters, looking very put out by it all. Roberts glares at Cooper.

'If you've got the evidence, then what is it? If you haven't, you'll stop wasting our time!'

Cooper glances to Beckett, who snaps the lighter closed. Beckett shrugs.

'I'm not here.'

Cooper places his satchel on the desk.

'Takahashi was in charge of the court martial here. Captured pilots had to be tried by court martial and executed. Their law.'

Reid sighs wearily.

'And where are the bodies, Bob?'

'I haven't found them yet. But they came down here and they're not listed as having died in the camp, and we didn't send them home.'

Roberts cannot hide his bewilderment.

'For God's sake, why are you chasing four phantoms when you have the hard evidence of the mass grave?'

'That's the work of Ikeuchi and his men. Takahashi could have ordered it or he might not have. But he had to order those pilots . . .'

'You're making the one mistake a lawyer cannot afford. You're making this a personal crusade.'

'Personal? For God's sake, this could well be the key to breaking Takahashi once and for all!'

Matsugae turns to Cooper.

'Is that your "presumption of innocence", Captain?'

Beckett steps past Cooper to the ashtray on the desk, mumbling a low comment to Roberts.

'Amen.'

Roberts nods in agreement then looks up at Cooper.

'You can't waltz into court with "maybes" and "perhaps". And I won't have you harassing the defendants in the pursuit of some fanciful notion. Facts, hard facts! Do I make myself clear?'

Cooper stares pointedly at Beckett.

'Nothing's clear about Takahashi's case . . .'

'And an apology to Mr Matsugae is in order.'

Cooper considers the order in strained silence then finally turns to Matsugae.

'You have my apology, Mr Matsugae.'

Matsugae bows curtly.

'Thank you, Captain.'

Cooper salutes Roberts, ignores Beckett and exits. He closes the door, relieved, to find Sheedy leafing through a statement, taking notes.

'Don't you ever sleep, Sheedy?'

Sheedy looks up, grins.

'And miss all the good bits?'

Patterson walks up slowly to Cooper. He hands him a statement, absorbed in thought.

'This might be something, sir . . .'

Cooper examines it. Sheedy steps up reading quickly over his shoulder.

'Christ, this has been sitting right under our noses?'

Patterson looks sheepish.

'It's a real jigsaw puzzle, sir . . .'

Cooper glares at Roberts' door.

'Nothing a dozen more staff and a bit more co-operation couldn't fix.'

He opens his satchel quickly, inserts the statement and closes it, heading for the door. Sheedy shadowing him.

Outside, the compound is quiet, crisscrossed by floodlights manned by guards in the bamboo towers. Sheedy quickens his pace to keep up with Cooper.

'Two brothers. Different services. Same camp. Long odds wouldn't you say, Captain?'

Cooper turns back to Sheedy, not concealing his blood scent.

'War's riddled with long shots. If I can pin just one execution on Takahashi, I've shortened the odds.'

Sheedy is beside him but Cooper accelerates again leaving his next question on the edge of his tongue.

'Goodnight, Sheedy.'

CHAPTER SEVEN

THE DESPERATE GAMBLE

Talbot was glad to be able to put the day's events behind him. He did not feel comfortable pushing old women around, Ambonese or whoever they might be. It went against the grain, all those years of lectures by his father, the Anglican minister for West Perth.

A Christian gentleman treats women with the highest respect. They are God's vessels for bringing life into this world.

But, he had to obey orders. He had hoped to see some action, but as he'd volunteered late in '45, he had to take whatever came up. Now, he was becoming increasingly intrigued with Ambon and its long Christian history. Even the famous Catholic missionary, Saint Francis Xavier, had passed through. Maybe he could make contact with some of the local missionaries or priests. Perhaps his posting here was all part of some divine plan.

But such thoughts could not last as he tinkled away on a battered old piano. He looks up. Three soldiers, faces flushed, are weaving over from the mess bar. A rangy fellow with clumsy fingers spills his beer as he reaches down for the keyboards, completely upsetting Talbot's melody.

'Hey, Talbot, you know "The Road to Gundagai"?'

Talbot hums to himself a moment, the tune comes back. The trio join together as Talbot hits the keyboards with feigned gusto.

There's a track winding back, la . . la . . . la . . ., on the road to Gundagai . . .

Keenan is at the bar, holding up his hand to the barman and two corporals, who are fascinated by the small black mark in the middle of his palm. The other hand steadies his body, swaying towards the floor. He is very drunk.

'Told the bastards, I wasn't Jesus bloody Christ, for all the good that did me!'

Keenan wobbles around, throws a drunken mock salute to Littell at a nearby table and stumbles over to Talbot's group. Talbot looks up apprehensively at Keenan, who is rousing along with the chorus.

Suddenly, Keenan stops. A malicious leering grin.

'Hey, sonny Jim, how 'bout one of your "mazin" graces . . .'

Talbot tries to ignore him by concentrating on the keys.

'Soldier, I'm giving you an order!'

The other three are pushed back as Keenan steps behind Talbot, grips him firmly by the wrists and thumps his hands on the keys. He bellows the words in a harsh tuneless voice.

What a friend we have in Jesus . . .
All our . . . daa . . . da das to share . . .

He turns to the soldiers, throwing his head back, delirious.

'Come on! Don't want Talbot here to think we're a bunch of heathens!'

Louder now. And very threatening.

What a friend we have in Jesus!

The buzz of conversation in the room stops. Talbot

fights against the vice of Keenan's hands, singing angrily above him.

Amazing grace, how sweet the sound
That saved a wretch like me . . .

Keenan pulls back in disgust. Talbot stops, the last note an abrasive echo in the still room. He stands, faces the simmering Keenan. A couple of the soldiers stumble back. A 'blue' was imminent.

Cooper stands in the doorway. Keenan gazes unsteadily across to him. He straightens himself, chuckles, then slaps a hand on Talbot's shoulder, trying to make light of it. He turns to the room, meeting a wall of stony faces including Littell. He holds up his crucified hand, his mind in alcoholic turmoil.

'Tried to tell 'em . . . tried . . . not Jesus bloody . . .'

The silence has a sobering effect. He wipes the back of his hand across suddenly dried lips, and backs to the door, almost colliding with Cooper.

Cooper glances at Talbot, then returns his attention to Littell as he approaches her. She sees the question etched on his face before he opens his mouth.

As they approach the hospital steps, Carol glances about nervously.

'Bob, it's one thing to pass on a scrap of information but Major Roberts has to authorise this.'

They reach the door. Cooper takes a quick look around then opens it for her.

'The rules, Carol! Turn the other way for five minutes.'

'I know your five minutes.'

Cooper stops her in the corridor. He hands her the photos of the flyers.

'Have him look at these.'

She looks at them for a few moments, then bites the bullet. She hands them back.

'You're not winning many friends after that stunt you pulled tonight. If Major Roberts finds out you've been here, I know nothing about it.'

She leads him into the ward, looks around, then turns to him.

'Kid gloves, all right?'

'Scouts honour.'

She stands back watching as Cooper approaches her most fragile patient. Cooper stops short of Fenton's bed. He lies, eyes open, staring into an abyss, lips trembling in an indiscernible whisper. Locked in a waking nightmare.

The chorus of screams rising and falling, the cracking of bones, the blood exploding from ulcerous legs.

Cooper sits on the side of the bed gently.

'Hello, Jimmy.'

Fenton's eyes don't move from the ceiling. Cooper brings up the photo into his eyeline.

'Is this your brother, Eddy? Was he here on the island?'

Fenton stares right through it.

Cooper leans closer, a loud whisper.

'Was Eddy here? You told Dave Cartwell, remember? What happened to Eddy?'

No response.

'Jimmy, what happened to Eddy?'

Littell's hand on his shoulder. He looks up at her realising it is useless. Very slowly, Fenton's skeletal hand moves towards the photo. His fingers trembling as they touch it. A low moan.

Cooper feels the photo being tugged from his grasp.

He stands, and leans over Fenton with a new urgency.

'Jimmy, what happened to Eddy?'

Fenton starts to shake, tears streaming down his face, the photo clasped to his breast.

'Jimmy!'

Littell pulls on Cooper's sleeve.

'Bob, he's on the edge. Don't tip him over!'

Cooper looks back to her, a harsh whisper.

'He knows. Don't you see? He knows!'

Littell pulls him away.

'Out!'

Cooper pulls back, riveted by the sight of Fenton, sobbing, the photo pressed onto his protruding ribs. He grabs the other photos and his satchel and starts away. Littell stops him gently.

'Bob, you must always remember what he's been through.'

She sees Cooper's own grief and regrets her words. But it had to be said. With a heavy reluctant sigh he exits. She turns back to Fenton and fetches a damp sponge from a wash basin. She applies it to his feverish face. Softly, soothing.

'It's all right, Jimmy. It's all right. You and Eddy. You were close, weren't you, Jimmy?'

Night is falling over Nagasaki. Midori pulls her shawl tighter against the cold blasts from the valley below. She can just make out a rough track ahead, winding through clumps of dead trees, a light snow starts to fall. She quickens her pace, a shivering, seemingly frightened figure in a barren world.

She moves with a strong determination, her bare feet swollen with the cold, crunching into the twigs and leaves as she continues her climb.

She reaches a high ridge, lined with a ghostly

spectre of blackened disfigured trees. She remembers how it was, how she would climb up here with Hideo, the days when the world was a wide green carpet, when the cherry blossoms were in bloom, when they had just fallen in love.

She stops. Sudden movement nearby. She looks around carefully, whispering.

'Hideo? Hideo?'

Hideo appears, ragged, half crouching as he approaches. He gathers her to his side, leading her higher on the ridge. They huddle together, the snow swirling around them in a thickening shroud.

Hideo reaches a camouflaged space, a natural tunnel, covered with dead blackened tree limbs. Midori edges under the boughs, the snow now a blinding cover around them. She wraps her shawl around them, their hands and arms clasped tightly together, sharing the warmth of their thin bodies.

She takes a couple of rice cakes from a cloth under her shawl, hands one to Hideo. He eats ravenously. Midori takes a small bite, looks at him with great apprehension.

'They have come back looking for you.'

Hideo feels the growling of his stomach subside as the delicious rice cake is devoured. He looks out into the snowstorm.

'I have to get away . . . far away where they can't find me!'

'And our marriage? Father Shirato wishes to know . . .'

Hideo shakes his head in despair.

'What can we do, Midori?'

Midori feels the urgency of knowing. The past. She must know!

'This thing you've done?'

Hideo turns to her, both afraid and angry.

'Please do not ask me.'

She withdraws momentarily, handing him the rest of her food which vanishes rapidly. She must know.

'You were a soldier, following orders. They must understand that.'

Hideo flares.

'They don't want to understand us! They have made up their minds! I am guilty! Look at our city, our beautiful Nagasaki, Midori. Why? Because we are all guilty! You, me, my family!'

Hideo's grief bursts forth at last in a great rush. He buries himself in her breast, sobbing uncontrollably. Midori runs her fingers through his matted, tangled hair, rocking him back and forth, whispering her love for him.

'I cannot run away, Hideo, but I must be with you.'

Hideo wipes away the tears across his grimy face and looks into her eyes.

'Perhaps, I can send for you when it is safe?'

Midori considers. There had to be a new way, new hope.

'If we all run like animals, when will it ever be safe? How can anything ever be different? How can we ever be anything other than a defeated people? No hope, no chance of facing the world again . . .?'

She looks at him. Love, concern, yearning and fear whirling in her breast.

'I don't want to live if that is all there is to live for . . .'

She pulls Hideo even closer to her. His arm reaches around her, embracing her gratefully. The snow shroud has lifted. In the distance they see the campfires around the cathedral.

The lights of hope?

Ikeuchi sits, waiting. The stage, the *hanamichi*, was his domain now. This would be the *oshimodoshi* scene, in which the demon Cooper approaches and he will be forced to retreat. He would be rendered impotent.

He looks over from the witness chair to Takahashi. Would his superior 'stand with his men' as he said he would? They would soon know.

Cooper steps up beside Ikeuchi. But he looks directly at Takahashi.

'Captain Ikeuchi, did Vice Admiral Takahashi ever issue instructions for the punishment of prisoners?'

What would it be? Revenge or blind loyalty?

'I believe he did. But he never issued written orders.'

Cooper thinks that at last he may be penetrating his armour.

'Did he order verbally or otherwise the execution of any prisoners?'

Fool! Such an honour was not bestowed lightly.

'I know nothing of any executions.'

Cooper steps back to the prosecution table, taking a thick folder from Corbett, and turns back.

'Then, how do you explain this? I submit the results of autopsies just completed on the remains of the men you dug up from the mass grave.'

He hands the document to the orderly who passes it to Roberts.

'The results show conclusively that these Australian prisoners were shot at point blank range, decapitated or bayoneted to death. I'll ask you the question once more, Captain. Did Vice Admiral Takahashi ever order the execution of prisoners?'

Ikeuchi stares at Takahashi then at Noburo, who lowers his eyes from his gaze.

106

'I know nothing of any executions.'

Cooper turns back to the table again, then swings around and walks up to the chair. He holds the photos of the four flyers in front of Ikeuchi.

Roberts leans forward, ready to pounce.

'Do you recognise these men?'

Study them slowly. Then sweet revenge. On both.

'Yes.'

Cooper, unprepared for the answer, catches a glimmer of terror in Takahashi's eyes, who manages to catch himself. Matsugae looks at Reid, greatly alarmed.

'You say you do recognise them?'

Ikeuchi grins defiantly.

'Yes. I was dragged out of bed last night and forced . . .'

'That's not what I meant! These men were here!'

The court is in uproar, Matsugae and Reid both jump to their feet!

'Objection! Objection!'

Cooper cannot stop.

'Here in this camp! What did you do with them?'

Roberts bangs the gavel ferociously.

'Objection!'

'Captain Cooper!'

'Why is it that not a single Australian airman survived in this region. Not just these four! Any airman!'

'Captain Cooper!'

Cooper then makes the gesture that gives Ikeuchi the greatest satisfaction. Retreat! Retreat! The demon was defeated!

'I withdraw the question!'

Roberts almost snarls.

'Unless the prosecution conducts itself properly,

this court will be forced to review its commission!'

Cooper glares back at him.

'Yes, Your Honour.'

Matsugae glances at Takahashi, very relieved but still very much on edge. Ikeuchi was incorrigible.

Cooper dumps the photos insolently on his table, then carefully picks up another statement. He turns the pages carefully.

'Captain, I have here a sworn statement from Corporal David Cartwell, a prisoner in the camp from 1942. He states:

'Jimmy Fenton reckoned the Japs executed his brother Eddy and three other Air Force blokes.'

Reid pushes Matsugae to his feet.

'I beg the court's indulgence but the defence has not read this statement. May we look at it, if the court pleases?'

Roberts nods to Cooper who hands it over reluctantly.

Matsugae and Reid scan it carefully. Reid points at a part, using sign lanuage to explain something about a crazy man. Cooper observes Ikeuchi, highly amused by the theatrical gestures of Reid. Matsugae looks up, adjusts his horn-rimmed glasses.

'I ask the prosecution to read the last part of that paragraph.'

Cooper takes the affidavit, pursing his lips in distaste.

'Jimmy always was a bit of a nutter. Lived in a dream world. We never saw his brother or those other blokes.'

Mastsugae nods to Cooper.

'Thank you, Captain.'

He sits, leaving Cooper stranded. Roberts taps his pen idly.

'Have you any further questions, Captain?'

Cooper is about to sit.

'No . . .'

But straightens again.

'Your Honour, I call Major Beckett to the stand.'

Beckett, Roberts and the Bench are equally startled.

'For what purpose, Captain?'

Sheedy puts a tick in his notebook next to Cooper 'Strikes'. There is already another tick.

'To draw upon his unique knowledge of vital Japanese records.'

He grins slightly.

'After all, we're all on the same side.'

Sheedy simply taps his pencil on his notebook, glances at Beckett, almost tempted to make a comment.

Reid rises abruptly.

'Objection!'

Beckett stands suddenly, rising to the challenge.

'I have no objection to answering the Captain's questions.'

Roberts nods to the Bench, then turns back to Cooper.

'This is a highly unorthodox move, Captain. You will confine yourself solely to the matter of records.'

'Yes, Your Honour.'

Beckett takes the stand, recites the oath, not taking his eyes from Cooper. Taunting him with a suppressed smile.

'Major Beckett, you are chief of liaison for the Tokyo trials under the Supreme Allied Command for General Macarthur?'

'I am.'

'Your job would entail, I assume, a knowledge of the evidence to be presented in those trials.'

'It does, yes.'

'Your Tokyo prosecutors have in their possession all records left by Japanese High Command at the surrender?'

'What's left of them. Like the Nazis, Japanese High Command ordered all command sections to destroy their records before they fell into our hands.'

'Are there records relating to this region amongst those you recovered?'

'Possibly, but they're going to take months, maybe a year to catalogue fully. Our people are fully stretched just sifting through the evidence for the major trials in Tokyo.'

Cooper nods in apparent appreciation.

' "The big game". However, Major, what we are searching for could well be near the top of the heap?'

'Or the bottom, if they exist at all.'

'Thank you, Major. You have been most helpful.'

Roberts looks relieved and nods to Beckett.

'You may stand down. Thank you, Major.'

Beckett leaves the stand, straightening his jacket. As he passes Cooper, he grins and mumbles out of the corner of his mouth.

'That's good!'

Cooper turns to the Bench.

'Your Honour, I request an adjournment while a search is made through the Tokyo records.

Johnson looks at Roberts. No precedent for this one.

'A search for what, Captain?'

'Records of courts martial held in this region between 1942 and the surrender, and any other orders from Tokyo on the treatment of prisoners.'

Roberts isn't satisfied.

'Courts martial of whom, Captain?'

'Captured pilots, Your Honour.'

Matsugae needs no encouragement from Reid.

'Objection, Your Honour!'

Roberts hesitates, looks at Johnson ambiguously, then back to Matsugae, intent on his ruling.

'Objection overruled.'

Relieved, Cooper picks up documents and hands them to the orderly.

'I have warrants out for key members of Vice Admiral Takahashi's fleet headquarters staff. I need time for their delivery into custody.'

Matsugae glances anxiously at Takahashi, but receives no response. Takahashi projects an air of tranquil confidence.

Roberts peruses the documents and passes them via the orderly to Johnson. He inspects them carefully, then looks down to Cooper, admiring his thoroughness, but annoyed by the delay in the trial.

'Request granted. Court is adjourned for twenty-four hours while an approach is made to Supreme Command in Tokyo for these records.'

Roberts bangs the gavel instantly. Keenan and the guards quickly start to move the defendants from the courtroom.

Cooper places the photos and files back in his satchel, looks up, sees Sheedy give him an encouraging smile, then leans over to Corbett.

'How long for Takahashi's staff, Jack?'

Corbett is embarrassed.

'We're going like the clappers, sir.'

Later in the afternoon, Ikeuchi finds himself seated again. The ritual was becoming somewhat tiresome. Cooper circling the hut, smoking, thinking he has the upper hand. How would they ever understand?

'I've seen some dumb pricks in my time but you

take the cake. Anyone with half a brain can see what Takahashi's up to. "It wasn't me! Ikeuchi ran the camp! If there were beatings" . . .'

Cooper's eyes are almost bulging.

' "Executions, then Ikeuchi was responsible. I saw nothing! Heard nothing!" And your only defence is that there were no executions! You've dug up three hundred bodies! They were executed! And you're going to cop the lot!'

Ikeuchi watches Cooper turn his back to him. He glances at a pack of cigarettes lying on the table before him. He picks it up, removes one and lights it with a box of matches slid from his jacket.

Cooper turns at the sound to see him drawing on the smoke. Almost as if they were taking a break in the mess! Ikeuchi chuckles but his voice is of quiet steel.

'You and your British justice. Your books of law. You don't understand the Japanese way.'

Cooper stops dead, waiting.

'Before the war, to you we were just little yellow monkeys. We could not make a plane that flew or a ship to sail. Could not even make war. Now, to you, we are savages. Your only way is to crush our spirit, destroy our honour . . .'

He shakes his head, amused.

'If we do the things you accuse, if we could take an axe handle and a man, and by bringing the two together . . .'

He grips his hands in a contemptuous motion.

'We then destroy his very essence, his living soul. If we could do this thing with no remorse, no . . . "conscience"? nothing! . . '

He sees Cooper struggling for control. His hands suddenly fly apart!

112

'Then how can you expect to break us?'

Cooper steps forward abruptly, containing his fury. Ikeuchi observes him calmly, as Cooper takes the cigarette from his lips, drops it to the floor and stubs it out, like he was exterminating a dangerous spider.

'Remorse, conscience? Well, Takahashi doesn't have any "remorse" or "conscience" about your ancient beliefs. As far as he's concerned, you're the past—and he's the future. He's going to bury you!'

They are separated by inches. But it may as well be the diameter of the Milky Way. Cooper yells to the door.

'Sergeant!'

Keenan appears in the open door.

'Escort the Captain and his "conscience" back to the camp, will you?'

Keenan crosses the hut, pulls Ikeuchi up roughly and shoves him out the door.

Cooper stands for a few moments. It was the sheer persistence in the teeth of facts, of believing that nothing had happened. Perhaps they fabricate a fantasy world, they can't face the outside world. They were isolated for centuries. Now, when confronted with this, they cannot cope but rely on all the ancient beliefs, the Emperor and all that warrior *bushido* crap.

You're getting closer, says the voice again.

Cooper stands in the doorway, whirling in these thoughts. He looks down to find Sheedy squatting outside the window, smoking.

'I've seen some dumb pricks in my life but he takes the prize, Sheedy.'

Sheedy considers a moment.

'I don't think he sees it quite that way.'

Cooper shakes his head, half amused by this strange

echo of his own thoughts just moments ago.

Cooper heads for his office but is intercepted by Corbett running from the Legal Corps offices.

'We've got through, sir. They're referring the request to someone in the International Prosecution Section.'

Cooper nods knowingly.

'More red tape.'

'And Fenton's had a relapse, sir.'

Things were not going well. They both turn at the sound of an empty truck entering the camp. Cooper points at it almost despairingly.

'If Shimada or Tanaka was on that, we might have a different story.'

Corbett shrugs helplessly. Cooper lays an encouraging hand on his shoulder.

'Don't know what I'd do without you, Jack.'

Corbett looks away embarrassed, as if distracted, then pulls a folded paper from his top pocket.

'And there's this, sir. From the President.'

Cooper reads it. A grimace of 'duty'.

'I'll have to, I suppose. Might be interesting. For a while. But don't let up on Tokyo. We've just got to find that bloody Legal Officer if we can't get those records.'

'Maybe they'll give us an extension of time.'

Cooper shakes his head. He wishes he could believe it.

Rain has driven the Ambonese dancers inside the mess where the dinner party seats itself at a long table. Chaos reigns as the lanterns are the only flickering light. The generator had failed again.

The dancers resume their welcoming ritual to the assembled guests. Roberts, Johnson and the Bench all in full dress uniform on one side of the table, laden with fruit and flowers in bowls, wine glasses and the best dinner service. Opposite the brass, Sheedy, his tie done up, hair neatly combed, sitting next to Beckett, who has his attention on Littell's graceful neck only a touch away, silhouetted against the soft lantern light.

Beckett takes a cigarette from the pack beside him. Sheedy reaches over, lights it, as the dancers build to a mesmerising, whirling climax. Littell drums her fingers on the table in time with the rhythm, delighted by the swirl of rich yellow and green silken costumes. The dance suddenly stops, the dancers frozen in position. Then, with consummate ease, they link hands and bow to the loud applause of the Australians.

Sheedy leans over to Beckett who claps politely.

'Partial to a two step, myself.'

Beckett, smiling at Littell, could just as easily ignore the intrusion. He turns to Sheedy, humouring him.

'You don't strike me as the dancing type, Mr Sheedy.'

Sheedy lights his own cigarette, studies Beckett.

'Now that's what makes life interesting. When things aren't what they seem.'

He looks up, pleased at the arrival of the wine. Talbot and two other guards acting as waiters.

'Take this island, for instance. Flying in here, first thing I see is . . . nothing. Until I realise the "nothing" is mist. A shroud, if you like, for . . . all this.'

Beckett's patience is thinning.

'All what, Mr Sheedy?'

Sheedy gestures expansively as he takes a sip.

'Life. You realise, these people have been

performing these dances for generations. Long before the American Revolution or the pilgrims on the *Mayflower*. This piece of ground of theirs has a special history, all of its own. Here we are, holding trials on their piece of ground. We'll shoot the convicted on their piece of ground. When it's all over, we'll pack up and leave.'

He pauses now that he has the attention of everyone.

'What I'm wondering, Major, is how can this piece of ground ever be the same again?'

Beckett gives a polite shrug, smiles noncommittally. What was Sheedy trying to say? He was never direct. Obliqueness was his forte and Beckett was not about to be tripped up. A very delicate web would have to be spun here. Any provincial snide remarks would be jokingly tolerated but it was the real challenge that Beckett would have to expect.

He turns to see the most likely challenge enter and take his seat beside Roberts. Beckett could almost feel Sheedy's anticipation as he stares at Cooper, very spruce in his full uniform, with Littell also joining the silent chorus of approval.

With the wine glasses filled, Johnson raises his glass and his other hand for silence.

'This occasion is in honour of Major Beckett's visit to our humble proceedings. Welcome, Major. And our compliments on these wonderful steaks that you arranged for us.'

All raise their glasses, with Sheedy watching Beckett's expression closely. Someone would have to get through that benign mask.

'Anything I can do to make life more comfortable here, just name it. So, thank you for the honour. Enjoy.'

Cooper looks at Littell with a knowing expression, raises his glass to her. She returns the gesture, noted by Beckett.

Talbot and the others serve thick steaks from silver platters. Sheedy tucks into his with gusto, watched with some distaste by Roberts. Beckett watches Cooper, ignoring his steak, reaching for some papaya instead.

'Something wrong with your steak, Captain?'

Cooper shakes his head wearily.

'No appetite, Major . . .'

Sheedy nods.

'The heat . . . or the Ambon amoebas, Captain?'

Cooper glares at Sheedy, who returns his attention to his steak. He looks across to Littell who has a puzzled look on her face. Was Bob hiding a case of dysentery? Cooper grins at her.

Beckett slices his steak with easy grace.

'Heat never really bothered me, which is strange considering I'm from Boston. I've got one of those temperaments, I guess, adapts to any environment.'

A barely audible, 'Hear, hear.'

Roberts picks up on it, gives Sheedy a stern gaze as their eyes meet. Sheedy acts the innocent, pouring a glass of wine for Littell. She tilts the glass, enough, and looks back to Cooper, sipping from his glass. Beckett looks at Cooper inquisitively.

'Where are you from, Captain?'

Cooper swirls the wine in the glass, the amber colour enriched by the lambent glow of the lanterns. A shiver of memory. How similar was the glow of the lantern in the living room of the old stone house as dusk came down and the cicadas started their rasping buzz near the creek.

'The wheatfields in the west of New South Wales.

A small town called Parkes.'

'Maybe like the mid-west of the States, then?'

'I've never been there but it could be like the photos I've seen. Wide plains, fields of grain, old farmhouses.'

'Must take a look, one day. Bring my father. He's from South Dakota.'

Johnson coughs politely, putting down his cutlery gently.

'Perhaps, Major Beckett might like to tell us all about the organisation of the trials in Tokyo?'

Beckett is glad to have the floor, but watches Cooper carefully.

'Well, I wish I could say, Colonel, that it was as well organised as the show you're putting on here . . .'

Roberts and the Bench are basking in it.

'But we're still drawing up the charges against nearly thirty major war criminal suspects. "Class A" we call them. The top men. From Tojo on down.'

Beckett smiles at Littell. She had to be impressed with this.

Cooper nods, a defiant look.

'With one or two exceptions, Major.'

Roberts glares at Cooper who waits for Beckett. A considered reply but uncompromising.

'Necessary exceptions, Captain.'

Sheedy looks at Cooper, reading his fine edge of decision. He wanted to do it but 'protocol' was the barrier. Sheedy see Roberts' direct glare at him but he takes the plunge.

'Does that mean, Major, that the Emperor will not be standing trial?'

Beckett stares at Cooper. Was this a set up?

'That's correct, Mr Sheedy.'

118

'But he will be called as a witness?'

Beckett's stony expression replies. Sheedy grins.

'I look forward to covering this one. When Tojo and the gang attempt to pass the buck to the little Emperor.'

A tense silence. Cooper looks into his glass, grateful for Sheedy's bullseye. Johnson looks at Beckett, a thinly veiled mask of fury. He looks back at Roberts, adopting a concerned smile.

'And who will be represented at the trials, Major?'

Beckett is again his magnanimous self.

'Just about everyone. Us, you, the British, the Philippines . . .'

Sheedy leans forward, ignoring Roberts' warning look.

'What about the Chinese and our local friends the Dutch?'

Beckett sips from his glass, dabs at the corner of his mouth.

'Yes, them too. I'm sure they'll have a lot to say . . .'

Sheedy grins.

'Especially the Chinese, after Nanking and so on.'

'Absolutely.'

A pause. Beckett smiles at Roberts and Cooper.

'Yes, it should be the forum for great careers to be made. The whole world will be watching.'

Roberts glances to Cooper.

'Yes, you'll never know who'll be watching, right, Major?'

'Correct. And I'd have to say, Major, that the Captain and yourselves would feel right at home up there.'

Cooper is not convinced. Beckett offers Littell a cigarette from a gold case. She accepts, watching the veiled seduction with the same detachment with which she parries Beckett's interest in her. Cooper strokes his glass thoughtfully.

'I guess that there will be careers made up there.'

Beckett pours wine for Littell, smiles at her and Cooper.

'Is that such a bad thing, Captain? Reward for effort?'

'As long as justice is served? No.'

Roberts is quick to intervene.

'That goes without saying.'

Beckett studies Sheedy with an ingratiating smile then looks back to Cooper.

'Absolutely. It's what we're all in this for.'

Cooper downs his glass. This deserved some further exploration.

'It seems to me, Major, that in a trial like Tokyo, the committee could end up in total disagreement. Surely someone'll have the casting vote?'

Beckett sighs almost contentedly, grins widely at Cooper and the Bench.

'Well, you may not know it but you guys'll have the jump on us there. General Macarthur has decided to appoint an Australian as President on the main International Tribunal.'

Cooper is caught for words but watches the sceptical expression growing on Sheedy's face.

Johnson, beaming, raises his glass in a toast.

'A wise decision on General Macarthur's part.'

Roberts and the other members of the Bench raise their glasses in response.

'Hear, hear. General Macarthur.'

Beckett raises his almost fervently.

'General Macarthur.'

Cooper is the last to raise his glass, looks directly at the mute Sheedy.

'To his continued good health, Major Beckett.'

Beckett is not quite sure how to take this, but drinks the toast in silence, pondering the hidden irony or barb in Cooper's remark. He raises his glass again to Cooper.

'Tokyo.'

Cooper raises his slowly. There is only Beckett and himself now.

'Justice.'

Cooper reaches across and touches his glass firmly against Beckett's glass. Beckett feels his glass pushed back by the impact of Cooper's. Littell watches.

It was almost as if two knights were jousting for the honour of Lady Justice. But who was the 'dark knight'?

Outside, the air is thick and dank with the smell of rotting durian. Cooper and Littell walk slowly, lost in their own thoughts. She turns to him, a shy smile.

'Thanks for giving me an exit out of there.'

'Anything to protect our women from marauding Yanks.'

'He's not that bad.'

'They're all the same, those blokes. They think we're just like any dumb natives. Fly in with the cargo and we'll fall at their feet, calling them "Oh great one!" '

Littell is amused by the analogy.

'I think he's got a difficult job, just like you.'

'Yeah, they're experts at making it easy on themselves and hard for everyone else.'

They walk on studying the clouds scudding low across the bay. A pale half moon on the rise.

Cooper stops, pulls a smoke from his jacket, studies the hospital, lamps burning low inside. Its perimeter swept by the rhythmic probe of the arc lights.

'I heard about Jimmy Fenton's relapse.'

Littell is weary but defensive.

'All I can see are doors closing with Jimmy at the moment.'

Cooper sees her sensitivity but presses on.

'There must be some way you can stop it, Carol.'

'For God's sake, Bob, he's dying!'

Cooper swings on her, venting his frustration.

'You want him to die for nothing? Is that what brought you here? A mission of mercy? Finish them off with a kind word and a soothing brow?'

'That's outrageous! And what makes you the expert?'

'It's the last thing Jimmy needs!'

'What makes you think you know his needs?'

She sees another barrage coming but grabs his arm forcefully.

'I'm trained for this but I question myself every day. Am I doing the right thing? Was that a wrong move? Bob, this is uncharted territory, we've never had to face this . . .'

He sees her face running with tears, and moves his arm around her waist, drawing her closer. Her voice comes in racking sobs.

'Of course I want to make . . . it . . . right . . . for Jimmy. Show him . . . he went through it . . . all . . . for something.'

Cooper gently wipes tears from her face. She gathers herself and looks up at him, breathing deeply to calm herself.

'He does deserve that. But all the learning in the world can't prepare you for this.'

Cooper brings the cigarette up to her lips. She draws on it gratefully. Cooper moves them into the shade of a tree as he sees Beckett and the Bench stroll on to the verandah of the mess. An urgent whisper to her.

'You're here because you know what you're doing, Carol. You're here because people can rely on you.'

She draws on the cigarette and smiles weakly at him.

'You know, I've got this crazy idea, Bob, that one day, someone's going to ring a bell and say "Righto, everything's back to normal". Trouble is, we won't know what "normal" is any more.'

Cooper searches her face, open, fragile, caring and vulnerable. Slowly, he bends forward and places a light kiss on her lips. She smiles up at him.

'I suppose that would still be normal. Good night, Bob.'

She squeezes his arm and walks back towards the hospital. From the shade of the tree, he watches her walk. She had released something in him. He did not know what. But he could feel a part of himself suddenly alive.

He turns around to see Beckett, Roberts and the Bench being served nightcaps by the soldiers. Was the enemy behind the wire or within?

CHAPTER EIGHT

SURRENDER

The President clears his throat officiously.

'Captain Cooper.'

Cooper stands expectantly.

'It seems that Supreme Allied Command in Tokyo is unable to guarantee production of the records you require within a reasonable period of time. It also appears that the prosecution has not located any of Vice Admiral Takahashi's staff at this time.'

Johnson glances along the Bench, confirming a unanimous decision.

'On both these grounds, we are unable to grant your request for an extended adjournment.'

Johnson looks to Roberts who addresses Cooper curtly.

'Does the prosecution wish to call any further witnesses in this case?'

'No, Your Honour. We rest our case.'

Corbett studies Cooper as he sits. Had the fire and thrust deserted him? He hoped not. But there was a sense of shrunken hope, a bitterness almost palpable. Perhaps it was the heat, enervating enough for the strongest of men?

Roberts turns to the defence.

'Mr Matsugae?'

Matsugae rises, adjusts his glasses. He takes his

time as he steps from the defence table to stand alone, facing the Bench. His test had come. Very aware of Takahashi's eyes upon him. Judgment for both of them.

'Your Honours, the prosecution charges are false. There are no records to indicate standing orders for the ill treatment of prisoners on Ambon. On the contrary, the Vice Admiral and his men were guided by the Imperial Precepts of His Majesty the Emperor. These are contained in the *Field Service Code* carried by all these officers and men. I quote from this book.'

He selects a page carefully.

'If you pretend bravery and act with violence, the world will in the end look upon you as wild beasts.'

He puts the book down thoughtfully.

'Is this the policy of "deliberate and concerted ill treatment" that the prosecution alleges my clients to have authorised here?

'Surely not.'

He takes a sip of water and glances to Cooper, head down, ignoring him.

'The defence will prove beyond a shadow of doubt that the actions of the accused were not systematic atrocities. If the prisoners did receive beatings or were "victims" of other so called "illegal actions", then we will prove that they had violated regulations vital for maintaining camp discipline.

'It should be known that this was the very same treatment that Japanese soldiers could expect from their own officers if they breach Naval regulations.

'In summary, the defence will prove that the chief reason for the unfortunate deaths of prisoners was their long confinement in tropical conditions to which they were not suited . . .'

He steps back to the table and takes a sheet of

paper from Reid who looks across at Cooper, expectant.

Matsugae hands it to the orderly.

'Your Honours, I would like to submit a plea of dismissal of all charges against Vice Admiral Takahashi and twenty-nine other defendants.'

Cooper is stunned. He looks at Corbett then sees Reid's studied avoidance of his gaze. He looks back to the impassive Takahashi. But Ikeuchi cannot hide his own surprise. Or was it anger?

Cooper rises at once.

'Your Honour, this plea must first be referred to the Judge Advocate General back in Australia.'

Roberts is dismissive.

'Thank you, Captain, we're familiar with the *Manual of Military Law*.'

Cooper is on a knife edge. Reid was exploiting a bloody loophole. But it could just work.

'Your Honour . . .'

'That'll be enough, thank you, Captain.'

Cooper takes his time, finally sits. He glares at Reid who sits smugly waiting. Cooper glances to Beckett straightening the crease in his trousers. If they were any sharper, they'd cut.

Cooper looks back as the President clears his throat nervously.

'The court rejects the plea of dismissal for Vice Admiral Takahashi in the first instance. It reserves its decision on the other defendants until the Vice Admiral's case is heard.'

Reid gives a shrug to Matsugae who bows to the Bench courteously. Cooper, relieved, grimaces at Corbett, deep in thought. Cooper feels a new surge of concentration as he watches Matsugae turn to Roberts.

'Your Honour, I call Vice Admiral Takahashi to the stand.'

Takahashi is escorted again by Keenan to the stand. Sheedy draws up three columns in his notebook: 'Convicted', 'Acquitted', 'Sentence'.

After taking the oath, Matsugae steps up to Takahashi respectfully. Beckett attuned to every word.

'Vice Admiral, what was your first action when you took over the command of Ambon?'

Takahashi gazes around imperiously.

'I held a meeting of all my officers and men. I told them: "Japan is not a signatory to the Geneva Convention for the treatment of prisoners. But I insist that you behave as if we are".'

'Your orders then were that your men must adhere to international law?'

'Yes.'

Cooper rises.

'Objection. This island was governed by Japanese Imperial Navy regulations.'

Matsugae looks back to Reid. A discouraging shake of the head.

'I withdraw the question, Your Honour.'

Cooper sits. Matsugae turns to Takahashi.

'Vice Admiral, you spent some time in England?'

'Four years. I obtained my degree in law . . . at Oxford.'

A couple of the Bench exchange impressed looks, notations made. Sheedy notices, whispers with a mocking chipper, British accent—'I say, old bean!'

Beckett glances darkly at him. Sheedy presents him with a blank look, then puts his first tick in his 'Acquitted' column.

Matsugae studies the Bench then turns back to Takahashi.

'You joined the service upon returning to Japan in 1914?'

'Yes, although I spent much of the time with my European friends.'

'And you went on to serve as the Captain of a destroyer, the *Yamamoto*, used mainly for escorting British and Australian ships? Yes?'

'Yes. We used Perth as a base for our escort duties across the Indian Ocean.'

Talbot, on guard beside the Bench, is astounded to hear this.

Matsugae holds up some medals, glinting in shafts of glare shooting from behind the court's side partitions.

'Vice Admiral, could you tell the court what these medals are?'

Matsugae hands them to the orderly, who hands them to Takahashi. He looks at the two medals, almost lovingly.

'Yes, they are decorations awarded to me in the First War. One is British, the Distinguished Service Cross. The other is Australian, a Navy award for bravery in action. I would wear them at ceremonial occasions on Ambon and Ceram, even though I knew that many of my junior officers did not approve.'

Takahashi hands them back reverently to the orderly who then passes them to the President.

Matsugae glances back to the Bench. Even the President's usually sober expression shows a sign of approval.

'Vice Admiral, in Tokyo before the war, you were the only Japanese member of the European golf club?'

Cooper rises abruptly.

'Objection! This is irrelevant! The Vice Admiral was not here to improve his golf handicap!'

Laughter from the guards and Sheedy. Roberts bangs the gavel.

'Silence! Mr Matsugae?'

'This evidence is essential to gain an understanding of Vice Admiral Takahashi's attitude towards Australian prisoners.'

'Objection overruled. Please continue.'

Matsugae nods to Takahashi.

'Yes, I was the only Japanese member. But I was accepted by all the members as their friend.'

Matsugae glances to Reid. Strange how his fellow counsel, a recent enemy, seemed to gain satisfaction from the way the case was proceeding.

'And so, Vice Admiral, what was your reaction when war was declared in 1941?'

'I would have to fight against people I respected. Many more than my own countrymen.'

A glance at Ikeuchi.

Matsugae steps up beside Takahashi, as if ready to hear the confession of the day.

'Vice Admiral, I want you to consider very carefully the following question.'

Cooper edges forward. This would be it.

'How do you explain, as the Supreme Commander of this island, the bodies of the prisoners uncovered in the mass graves?'

Ikeuchi gives no hint of the anxiety he is feeling.

Takahashi is confident but suitably contrite.

'As I explained to Captain Cooper, I was not on Ambon immediately after the surrender in 1942. But Captain Ikeuchi was here. He never informed me that such mass graves existed. You would have to ask him the details of what happened to those men. But I do know that, during my command, we buried prisoners who had died of tropical diseases or who had been killed during Allied bombing raids along with my own men.'

A solemn look straight at Ikeuchi.

'I am very distressed by what I now know.'

He looks back to Matsugae humbly.

'This appears to bring no credit to my command, but I cannot be held responsible for actions which took place when I was not here.'

Cooper is intent on the Bench. The wheels were turning adversely, it seemed. Was Takahashi wrapping them around his little finger? Reid had been bloody clever. Don't address the real issues but play the nostalgic Anglophile strings for all they were worth! Then dump all the blame for the mass grave on Ikeuchi.

Matsugae bows to Takahashi and then the Bench.

'Thank you, Vice Admiral. No further questions, Your Honour.'

Roberts raises his hand to Matsugae.

'Does the defence wish to call any further witnesses?'

Reid shakes his head. Matsugae bows.

'No, Your Honour. The defence rests.'

Roberts turns to Takahashi, almost respectful.

'You may step down, Vice Admiral.'

As Takahashi is escorted back to the dock by Keenan, Sheedy puts another tick in his 'Acquitted' column and looks across to Cooper sympathetically. If ever there was a time for a rabbit from the hat, this was it.

Littell slips in beside one of the guards, takes her seat beside Sheedy. Cooper notices her. She smiles at him. He returns it gratefully. The cheer squad was most welcome.

Roberts makes some notes then looks up. The

courtroom is a blur. His head feels like it is filled with thick jelly. Barbed wire tightening around the inside edge of the skull. Matsugae and Reid are waiting, puzzled. Their faces swim in a sea of spinning images. Roberts nods to them.

'Counsel will proceed with summing up.'

Roberts wipes his glasses carefully. Gradually, clear vision returns as he watches Matsugae step from his table. All eyes are upon him, except for Takahashi who sits as if the result is a foregone conclusion.

Matsugae studies the Bench carefully, very aware of the abyss awaiting him if he should fail.

'Vice Admiral Takahashi is an officer of special qualities. Educated at the finest university in England. Awarded some of the highest decorations by the British and Australian Imperial navies. An admirer of British justice and the rule of law! A man of honour who did everything in his power to alleviate the sufferings of the prisoners and his own men when Ambon was under total siege!'

He looks around to Takahashi respectfully.

'One man can do so much. Was this the man who would authorise such a barbaric act as the mass execution of three hundred prisoners? Was this the man who would authorise a policy of "concerted and continuous ill treatment" as the prosecution alleges. I humbly submit that the Court consider these questions very carefully in judging the Vice Admiral's case. The defence believes that these charges are false and without any foundation in fact. The prosecution has not produced one witness or one statement that could prove the Vice Admiral's guilt beyond reasonable doubt. Not one shred of evidence that could satisfy this burden of proof.'

Masugae looks to Cooper, whose eyes are fixed on

a point behind the Bench. Preparing his last onslaught.

'I humbly request that this court consider Vice Admiral Takahashi worthy of acquittal on all charges.'

Matsugae bows low to the Bench and returns to his seat. A small, reassuring smile from Reid. Matsugae adjusts his collar and wipes some drops of perspiration from his forehead. He looks at them with some surprise. His anxiety must have been intense. This was the first time his skin had so reacted.

He notes the back of Cooper's shirt, darkened by a large sweat stain. His anxiety must be as great as the expectations of his people.

Cooper steps a couple of paces towards the Bench, gazes out through a sizeable crack in the side partitions to the camp beyond. Then back to Takahashi.

'Vice Admiral Takahashi. The golf playing, "British gentleman"? The Oxford educated lawyer, endowed with every privilege of the elite of Japanese society? No, the man who commanded the POW camp with the highest death rate in the Japanese Empire.

'As the Vice Admiral was in command here for nearly three years, it is not open to him to deny that he had a duty to carry out his command function. It was part of his duty to ensure that the prisoners were given adequate rations, adequate medical care and proper treatment by the men under his command.'

Cooper gazes around at the defendants.

'But, as the overwhelming weight of evidence shows, the prisoners' conditions deteriorated into a hell on earth, particularly in the period from 1944 to the surrender. If the war had not ended when it did, the "policy" of starvation, disease and brutality would have been totally "successful".'

He steps back, stands in front of Takahashi, looks down at him.

'This evidence is now given even further weight by the discovery of the mass grave near Laha.

'The issue is one of responsibility. The defence that Takahashi did not order such acts carried out by Ikeuchi and his men, fails to address the clear and simple fact. Takahashi did have responsibility for such actions. It is not necessary to establish that he personally ordered such horrendous crimes.'

Takahashi gazes straight ahead. Cooper looks back to the Bench, sombre.

'But it is quite clear that only he had the power to prevent them.'

Cooper steps back to the defence table, gazes down at Reid and Matsugae.

'It is, therefore, strange that the defence should raise the Vice Admiral's education at Oxford and his admiration for all things British as evidence of his total sympathy for the prisoners. The Vice Admiral is clever, privileged. And that is the point. He cannot use it to exonerate himself.'

He looks straight at Ikeuchi.

'The fact that this truth is not obvious to the defendants does not mean that it should not be transparently obvious to this court.'

He faces the Bench defiantly and then paces deliberately back to block Takahashi's view of the Bench.

'Such a clever man would be totally familiar with international law. As he was, on his own admission. But there is not a shred of evidence to show that the Vice Admiral employed his "privileged" knowledge for the welfare of the prisoners he "respected" so much.

'Such a clever man could not be blind to what was going on around him! He would be fully conscious, fully aware of his repsonsibility. Such a clever man would have known about the mass executions of Laha. He would have known from his subordinates the number of Australians captured at the surrender and then the number actually interned in this camp. Simple arithmetic would have told the Vice Admiral that if there were six hundred men in this camp, then three hundred other prisoners were mysteriously "unaccounted for"! Such a clever man could not have failed to notice this!'

Cooper raises his voice to a thundering shout!

'How could such a clever man have not known! How?'

He glares at Roberts and the Bench, who seem almost pushed back in their seats by the sheer power of Cooper's delivery.

Cooper lowers his voice menacingly.

'He would not have known, either because he chose not to or because he himself was responsible. Whichever way you view it, ignorance of the facts in this case is simply not credible.'

Cooper gazes around the edges of the court, sees that he has the rapt attention of Sheedy and Littell, the concern of Beckett and the grudging respect of Keenan. He looks around again, as if trying to see beyond the partitions blocking the view.

'The screams of men beaten, men tortured and men dying still echo through this camp. And Vice Admiral Takahashi does not hear them.'

He turns and faces the Bench directly.

'Will we?'

There is a long muted silence in the court, no one wanting to be the first to speak or move. Cooper surveys the faces of the Bench, Beckett, Takahashi, Ikeuchi, Keenan and Talbot, standing almost as if in a trance from what he has just heard.

Sheedy gazes down at his notebook, no longer certain as to the outcome.

Cooper sits slowly beside Corbett and exhales deeply. He suddenly felt very tired. When was it like this before?

He is back on that dirt track, the 1935 mile championship. Arms flailing, his lungs screaming and legs buckling as he lunged at the tape. A photo finish. But inches in front, a young Aboriginal from a Moree school whose stick legs had swallowed the ground in that last lap. He had collapsed on top of him, the dust covering him as he fell into a roaring inferno of voices, the earth rushing towards him. Then darkness.

He had gone beyond a boundary of pain and exhaustion. But this was a new race and this pain, this memory, could not be so easily shrugged off.

Cooper looks up to see Roberts' lips moving but the words sound strange although familiar.

'. . . and to remind this court that a fundamental presumption of innocence applies in these proceedings, just as it does in an ordinary criminal or civil court. I ask the court to keep this always in mind when considering the verdict on Vice Admiral Takahashi.'

The President bangs his gavel.

'Court is adjourned until further notice.'

Cooper and Corbett stand, watching as Takahashi and the other Japanese are escorted out. Corbett sees

Cooper's exhaustion and leans over as he packs his satchel.

'That was really something, sir. I think you really had them eating out of your hand.'

Cooper appears not to hear but turns to see Beckett and Roberts making their way together across the grounds. Nothing could be guaranteed.

He looks back at Corbett who sees the question in his face. If only he could deliver what Cooper wanted. He shakes his head.

'No news from Tokyo, sir.'

Cooper is about to exit, when he sees Littell standing, waiting patiently.

He stops as she approaches, nods to Corbett, and faces him. Her face full of simple admiration.

'I think you'd better talk to Jimmy, Bob.'

Lanterns, flickering across burnt and disfigured faces, making their way slowly past a huge bell mounted on a tripod of timber beams. Three sturdy Japanese men keep pushing the bell in a rhythmic motion, producing a slow, doleful clanging that rings out across the dark ruins of the cathedral.

The survivors gather before the shattered facade, facing the makeshift altar, ghostly spectres against the jagged walls and the wasteland beyond.

Candles glow softly on the altar. Midori stands, nervous, staring up at the head of Christ, lit from below. The eyes stare out across the destroyed city. Midori ponders the story of Christ's agony in the garden that night before the crucifixion. How he had sweated blood before his betrayal by Judas. Was Nagasaki a modern re-enactment of his crucifixion? Would it 'rise again on the third day'?

She looks back at the group of refugees gathering.

ABOVE Sergeant Keenan (Nicholas Eadie) orders Captain Wadami Ikeuchi (Tetsu Watanabe) to dig! (The Film 1989-90)

BELOW The remains of Australian soldiers unearthed from the mass graves. (The Film 1989-90)

ABOVE   A moment of high tension at the excavation of the mass grave. (far left) Sergeant Keenan, (centre) Captain Wadami Ikeuchi, (background) Captain Cooper (Bryan Brown). (The Film 1989-90)

BELOW   (right to left) Japanese defence counsel Mr Matsugae (Sokyu Fujita) addresses 100 Japanese defendants, while Vice Admiral Baron Takahashi (George Takei) and Captain Wadami Ikeuchi observe. (The Film 1989-90)

ABOVE *Ambon Island, 1946. Ninety-one Japanese charged together with war crimes concerning the mistreatment of Australian and Dutch POWs.* (Australian War Memorial negative no. P427/14/11)

BELOW *One hundred Japanese defendants, faced by Mr Matsugae and Baron Takahashi, raise their arms in unison to swear allegiance to Emperor Hirohito and shout: 'Tenno heiko Banzai!' ('Long live the Emperor!').* (The Film 1989-90)

ABOVE Sister Carol Littell (Deborah Unger), Captain Robert Cooper and Lieutenant Jack Corbett (Russell Corbett), attempting to locate where four 'missing' Australian pilots may have crash-landed. (The Film 1989–90)

BELOW (left to right) Major Beckett, US Chief Liaison Officer (Terry O'Quinn), Vice Admiral Baron Takahashi and Captain Robert Cooper. (The Film 1989–90)

ABOVE *Vice Admiral Baron Takahashi cross-examined by the Prosecutor, Captain Robert Cooper.* (The Film 1989-90)

BELOW *Vice Admiral Baron Takahashi undergoing intense questioning by Captain Robert Cooper. (far right) Major Beckett observes from behind.* (The Film 1989-90)

ABOVE   *Prosecutor Captain Robert Cooper, Captain Wadami Ikeuchi and other Japanese POWs in the background.* (The Film 1989–90)

BELOW   *(left) Major Tom Beckett informs Major Frank Roberts (John Bach) and Captain Robert Cooper that Emperor Hirohito will not be brought to trial in Tokyo.* (The Film 1989–90)

ABOVE *Ambon, 1946. Officials from the court which tried 91 Japanese officers and men for war crimes related to the mistreatment of Australian and Dutch POWs. The Prosecutor John Williams is in the front row, far left.* (Australian War Memorial negative no. P427/14/13)

BELOW *The four officers forming the Bench for the War Crimes Trials in Ambon. The President of the Bench (Ray Barrett) is second from the right.* (The Film 1989-90)

ABOVE   *Ambon, 1946. War Crimes Trials. Members of the court trying Japanese officers and men for war crimes.* (Australian War Memorial negative no. P427/14/09)

BELOW   *Ambon Island, 1946. War Crimes Trials. Japanese officers and men undergoing prosecution.* (Australian War Memorial negative no. P427/14/08)

ABOVE *Ambon Island, 1946. War Crimes Trials. Some of the Japanese defendants.* (Australian War Memorial negative no. P427/14/10)

BELOW *Captain Wadami Ikeuchi, POW camp commander, rises to pronounce himself: 'Musi!' ('Not Guilty!').* (The Film 1989-90)

ABOVE   Captain Robert Cooper asking Sister Carol Littell
about Private Jimmy Fenton. (The Film 1989–90)

BELOW   Private Jimmy Fenton (John Polson) restrained by
Captain Cooper, Private Talbot and Sister Littell, as he gives
evidence in court. (The Film 1989–90)

ABOVE   *Four Australian pilots.* (The Film 1989-90)

BELOW   *Major Frank Roberts advises Captain Robert
Cooper to play by the rules.* (The Film 1989-90)

Private Talbot (Jason Donovan) stands with Captain Robert Cooper outside the interrogation hut. (The Film 1989–90)

The courtroom. Captain Wadami Ikeuchi is asked to indentify the 'missing' Australian pilots by Captain Robert Cooper. (The Film 1989–90)

ABOVE *Private Talbot takes particulars from Lieutenant Hideo Tanaka (Toshi Shioya) after his arrival back in Ambon, having surrendered himself to US M.P.s in Nagasaki.* (The Film 1989-90)

BELOW *Lieutenant Hideo Tanaka and his defence counsel Mr Matsugae in the interrogation hut.* (The Film 1989-90)

Lieutenant Hideo Tanaka waits in the prisoners' compound prior to his final courtroom appearance. (The Film 1989-90)

ABOVE   Sergeant Keenan criticises Private Talbot for talking to the prisoner, Lieutenant Hideo Tanaka. (The Film 1989–90)

BELOW   After the trial, Captain Robert Cooper, journalist Mike Sheedy (John Clarke) and Mr Matsugae share a common concern over the outcome. (The Film 1989–90)

Would Hideo appear? She felt her fingers knitting into a tense ball. She smiles uncertainly as Father Shirato appears and takes his place before the altar, bowing to the Christ head, and turning to face Midori and the congregation.

He looks around carefully, then steps forward and takes Midori's hands in a reassuring grip then gently strokes her face. Midori adjusts her frayed, white veil, feeling very conspicuous without Hideo. Surely he would not shame her by not appearing?

Father Shirato blesses the congregation and then steps back on to a large box to gain a better view. A murmur amongst the refugees is stilled as he holds up his hands for silence. Young Japanese children, holding rough stick crosses, stand in a line on either side of him.

'We are gathered here tonight to bear witness to the marriage of Hideo and Midori. But before the ceremony commences, I would humbly request that the leader of our parishioners, Dr Nagai, say a few words to you. As you know, he has been here long before I, who arrived after the calamity that befell Nagasaki and your beloved church.'

He turns, extending an arm of welcome to a shuffling, older man who steps on to the box vacated by Father Shirato. Midori looks up at him, full of admiration although still anxious. Dr Nagai had had a miraculous escape from death at the Nagasaki Hospital and even though he had suffered burns and radiation sickness himself, he had worked ceaselessly to organise medical aid for the thousands of victims of the bomb. He was the epitome of Christian self-sacrifice and would be recognised as one of the heroes of Nagasaki, later confirmed as one of the national heroes of Japan by the Emperor himself.

'I have now heard that the atom bomb was destined for another city.'

His voice comes in a wheezing burst. But his eyes radiate an intensity as he surveys the congregation, gauging its mood.

'Heavy clouds rendered the target impossible and the American crew headed for their second choice. Nagasaki. A mechanical problem then arose and the bomb was dropped further north than planned. It burst almost above our cathedral, this tiny enclave of faith. And, in an instant, eight thousand Christians were called to God.'

Midori looks around for any sign of Hideo. Why was he late?

'I believe that it was not the American crew who chose this place. It was God's providence.'

A murmur of dissent wavers through the congregation.

Dr Nagai raises his voice to meet it.

'Was not Nagasaki the chosen victim? The lamb without blemish, slain as a whole burnt offering on the altar of sacrifice?'

Men shout denials, women wail.

'How can you say this? How can you justify the indiscriminate slaughter of innocent women and children?'

Midori looks around fearfully. Suddenly, she notices movement at the rear of the line of children. Hideo appears. She looks to Father Shirato as the tumult in the congregation grows into a swelling roar of denial.

Dr Nagai and Father Shirato both hold up their arms for silence. Gradually, the shouting subsides. Hideo walks across the line of children and heads straight for Midori. Somehow, he had managed to find a clean shirt and pair of trousers. He takes his place beside her, squeezes her hand, searching her face, stained with tears of relief.

Dr Nagai smiles down at them then continues sombrely.

'At midnight of that day, in the Imperial Palace, His Majesty the Emperor made known his sacred decision to end the war. On August 15th, the Imperial Rescript which put an end to the fighting was formally promulgated and the whole world saw the light of peace. August 15th, the feast of the Assumption of the Virgin Mary. This cathedral is dedicated to her. Is it not significant, the convergence of these events, the end of the war and the celebration of her feast day?'

The congregation is still. Dr Nagai a wraithlike figure in the flickering light. But Hideo is leaning forward, intent on every word.

'Yes, only this *hansai*, this burnt offering, was sufficient.'

He gestures to the cathedral ruins.

'Here was the one pure lamb that had to be sacrificed as *hansai* on His altar, so that many millions of lives might be saved.

'Happy those who weep, they shall be comforted. We must walk the way of reparation, ridiculed, whipped and punished for our crimes, sweaty and bloody. But we can turn our minds' eyes to Jesus carrying his cross up the hill of Calvary. The Lord has given and the Lord has taken away. Blessed be the name of the Lord.'

He bows deeply to the congregation. The air is still, a cloud of vapour rising into the cold night air from the human beings below. Midori stares at Hideo who appears shocked by what he has just heard. He tries to smile at her but cannot feel the emotion. If the Lord did move in mysterious ways, then this was his most mysterious plan.

Father Shirato resumes his position on the box. He holds up his hands again.

'Dr Nagai's words are not words of despair, but hope. Let us look forward to the future in hope. It is from the union of the faithful like Hideo and Midori that our future will be assured.'

Hideo looks up at the Christ head in deep reverence. He too would have to accept his fate. There was deep wisdom in Dr Nagai's words that was just out of reach for him.

As Father Shirato commences the ceremony, two M.P.s appear and make their way to the front of the group. Father Shirato sees them but continues with the exchange of marriage vows.

Hideo produces a ring, hand made, a burnt, scratched copper. He places it on her finger lovingly and gazes into Midori's eyes, full of delight at his courage and initiative. Into his line of sight steps one of the M.P.s. He looks up at him unafraid.

Midori turns, sees them but checks her fear and looks up as Father Shirato blesses them both. Hideo and Midori embrace gently. Hideo holds her to him and whispers in her ear.

'I always love you, Midori. I will come back to you.'

Midori's tears come in a rush. She feels a sudden anger at herself. She had used such persuasive words to make Hideo face this moment. Now, it had come when she had least expected it. She grips Hideo tightly, grief overcoming her anger.

'I love you, Hideo. I will pray. You will be in my thoughts and in my heart.'

Midori lets slip her arms from him as he turns to face the two M.P.s. He separates himself and steps towards them.

Father Shirato takes Midori's arm, comforting her as the congregation starts a murmuring, then growing into a quavering emotional hymn, led by Dr Nagai.

'The Lord is my shepherd . . .

'No evil will I fear . . .'

Midori stands with Father Shirato, sobbing softly, but finally joining the chorus of voices sending Hideo off into the night, to face what he must.

Hideo looks back at the cathedral and the people, Midori now a tiny figure before the altar. But the voices, the voices, pure and clear, ascending to the stars.

CHAPTER NINE

THE BOMBSHELL

Sheedy types away at a battleworn typewriter next to an open window of his hut. He looks up occasionally, mopping his forehead with a sodden handkerchief. The thumping clang of the keys echoes across the grounds. He pauses to take a swig from a half empty bottle of whisky, stubs out his smoke into an overloaded ashtray and continues.

Keenan appears at the window.

'Awful bloody racket you're making. Enough to wake the dead.'

Sheedy grins and pulls the sheet from the typewriter.

'Deadlines. Bane of the wordsmith.'

Keenan eyes the whisky bottle, an empty glass next to it. Sheedy puts a new sheet into the carriage, gesturing the bottle.

'Help yourself.'

Keenan pours a large shot and angles his head around to read from the first sheet.

' "Ambon, island of mist . . ." Pretty bloody poetic.'

Sheedy checks some notes, looks at Keenan indulgently.

'Colour.'

Keenan is bemused.

'It's called colour. Dress it up a bit for the reader. Give 'em a sense of place.'

Keenan drinks, nods and cocks his head, conjuring an 'image'.

'Ambon . . . an island that the devil'd be proud to call home . . .'

He smiles thinly at Sheedy.

'Put that in your story. Give 'em a sense of real bloody place.'

He pauses, gazing into his drink then lifts his glass in a toast.

'Where the politicians and lawyers put us soldiers out of a job . . .'

He downs the last of it and slams down the glass.

'Tell 'em that back home.'

He walks off. Sheedy looks down at the glass. It has left a wet ring on the page, smudging the words.

Across the grounds, Cooper and Littell sit in an all night vigil at Fenton's bedside. Cooper holds Fenton's hand, whispers to him gently.

'Jimmy, you can help us. You know what happened to Eddy. You can tell us what happened to Eddy.'

Cooper leans forward as Fenton starts gurgling, low guttural noises. Nothing comprehensible. He looks up at Littell who reads a letter beneath the lowering lamplight.

'He says that':

the real fear came when I reached the dock.
Who'd be there waiting? My wife? My kids?
Would they all be strangers, how would they look
at me, a walking skeleton, who used to be her
husband and their father.
Well, sis, I'm glad to say that they were there
and they are really looking after me real well. But

143

I couldn't 've made it without you, honest to God. If you're ever in Brisbane, please drop in and have tea with us.

Cooper shakes his head in sympathy. Littell puts the letter down and looks at Jimmy.

'Will it ever end for these men, Bob? They'll live with it every day of their lives . . .'

'And you? Are you going back to help 'em?'

Littell hesitates.

'I still don't know. I think I've got something to give but a lot to learn yet.'

'Any family that's waiting?'

'Well, I don't know about my husband Jim. Last thing I heard he's run off with, of all people, a nurse from the United States . . .'

She feels embarrassed at the revelation, lapses into silence. Cooper nods, a grim smile of empathy.

'Yeah, I know about that one. My fiance, Jane, she ran off with, of all people, a Yank officer stationed in Melbourne.' He pauses. She waits. But he only shakes his head in semi-amusement. Perhaps it was a long time ago.

'I really wonder sometimes whether the Yanks saved us or invaded us.'

They stare at each other. A shared pain felt less burdensome. She smiles and shakes her head. Cooper wouldn't be the sort to take that one lying down. She tries to imagine what kind of argument they might have had. If it had been like his courtroom performance, the girl would have collapsed in a total, screaming heap.

Cooper looks down at Jimmy, twitching, sweat soaked. Was even sleep not a relief from his suffering? He takes Jimmy's hand again.

'Jimmy, you can help me, you know what

144

happened to Eddy, don't you? Eddy was here, wasn't he?'

She takes Jimmy's other hand, stroking it rhythmically as she takes over this gentle 'interrogation'.

'Jimmy, I know you can hear me. You remember Eddy?'

Cooper watches her as she continues her soothing probe. Her face showed the signs of strain of the months of caring. Deep lines on the forehead and the natural curve of her 'laugh line' very noticeable. But that warmth, that radiance of concern and healing kindness. It only increased his desire to explore, to follow that feeling from that night.

Cooper rises and takes a smoke from his pocket. He nods to her.

'Just stepping out for a quick one.'

She looks up at him as he walks down the ward. They had to face it. Their feelings had crossed the almost indefinable barrier from 'professional' to 'personal'. They had become allies in an apparently lost cause—Jimmy Fenton. Where would they be after that?

Out on the verandah, Cooper surveys the camp, still, peaceful. But there were boiling currents under that placid exterior. What were the Bench discussing at that very moment? Probably a split decision with the pressure on the wavering member to make it unanimous?

Another fact was now clear. Sheedy could be a very useful ally. He could ferret out information and approach the whole game from another angle. It was time to act on that one. Beckett and Takahashi? There was a hidden agenda. There had to be. Both he and Sheedy could discover pieces of it. And then compare them?

As for Carol and himself, it was all in the realm of the possible. But they might not be able to follow through. The thought of Tokyo had not lost all attraction, particularly with an Australian judge as President. There could be some fireworks there with Tojo and the others and it would be a shame to miss it. The issue of the Emperor would have to arise as Sheedy had said in puncturing Beckett's balloon so neatly at the dinner.

But it was all a moot point until the trials were over on Ambon and Morotai.

He gazes across at the compound. Takahashi and Ikeuchi, both Japanese but like chalk and cheese. Ikeuchi was for the bullet, there was no doubt, and he would keep Takahashi out of reach because of their code of loyalty. A strange thought: Maybe it was similar to 'standing up for your mates'. But, how could Ikeuchi regard himself as a 'mate' of Takahashi? No, the Japanese must have a much more rigid society based on obligations that you could not even see. Perhaps the trial would bring them out for the first time.

If only he'd got his hands on Takahashi's staff. Life was now full of 'if onlys'. If only Fenton could remember.

If only, if only. The voice, closer now. *You remember what the old man said: there are no mistakes in life. That's one way of lookin' at things. You have to run your own race.*

Rain starts, droplets then the rapid downpour. Cooper throws his cigarette into a gully of water and heads back inside.

Suddenly, the most dreadful scream erupts from the ward. Cooper runs down the corridor into the ward to find Carol struggling to hold Fenton down.

He is delirious, wild eyed, thrashing at the sheets. Cooper studies them for a long while. This is the key! As the rain subsides, Carol manages to soothe Jimmy back to a less frantic state. Still shivering, mumbling, almost catatonic but controllable.

Copper walks up slowly beside the bed as she wipes his feverish face with a wet sponge. Fenton settles down, on the edge of sleep again.

Cooper leans over to her and whispers.

'It's the rain, isn't it Carol? We've got to ask him.'

She looks at him, fearful.

'Try it, but I'll have to stop you if . . .'

He nods agreement, leans over to Jimmy and whispers.

'Jimmy, did something happen to Eddy in the rain? Was it during the rain, Jimmy?'

No response. Cooper repeats himself. Fenton opens his eyes slowly, looks over the ceiling. Suddenly, they are filled with tears. Cooper squats beside the bed and looks up at her. She shakes her head.

'Don't say a word. Just let it come.'

Cooper stares at Fenton. He and Carol were like untrained surgeons probing into Jimmy's mind. They were peeling back layers of trauma to reach their goal. But would it vanish before they got there? That was the risk, the unknown. Carol was right. It was a whole uncharted territory.

Fenton closes his eyes, exhausted. Cooper leans over and repeats it, staring at Carol who now holds Jimmy's hand.

'The rain, Jimmy. Tell us about the rain.'

Cross legged before a single fluttering candle, Takahashi sits alone in his hut. Beside the candle, a small rounded green stone sitting on a perfect circle of dirt. Takahashi contemplates it with equanimity.

At the time of greatest test, he could immerse himself in the memory of those pilgrimages. The stone gardens in Kobe and Kyoto. How his father had taken him by the hand around them. Then made him sit for hours contemplating the harmony between the rocks, the gardens, the rock pools and the pebble paths. Sketching them, observing the concentric balance, so unique to Japanese culture.

As for the trial, he would be prepared for whatever was decided. The Australian judges would know the exigencies of command and would have to appreciate his unique background. He looks down at a copy of T.S. Eliot's poems. He loved their seriousness of purpose, inventive language, and the memories they contained of many long nights at Oxford, rapt in the discussions of those themes that Eliot explored so profoundly. If it were not for the intervention of a certain duke and his wife, he might now be married into British royalty. Such love should not have been hostage to racial prejudice but he also knew the perils waiting for him back home by entering into such a marriage. Still, as Oscar Wilde had noted, Oxford was the home of grand passions and lost causes.

But if Japan needed a new international outlook then, it needed it now more than ever. He must be part of this new destiny. It was almost as if his life had been a training for the greatest challenge facing the Japanese nation. Recovering national pride and esteem was important. But of the greatest importance was the reconstruction of a modern nation, adopting the best of the West's science and technology and fusing it with the craft skill and aesthetic genius of the Japanese.

Suddenly, it comes back to him. 'The Hollow Men',

Eliot's great meditation on the puny modern man. Might the title have come from Shakespeare's *Julius Caesar?*

But hollow men, like horses hot at hand,
Make gallant show and promise of their mettle
But when they should endure the bloody spur,
They fall their crests, and like deceitful jades,
Sink in the trial.

Would he be judged a 'hollow man' who had 'sunk in the trial'? Would he be led whimpering to the slaughtering post? No. His life had been of value. He would not deny it in death. He would be fearless and face it like his ancestors. A true warrior to the last.

The mode of thought, the insight in Eliot's poems could emerge from the still points in the 'gardens of stone'. This would be the way for Japan. He contemplates the parchment scroll and the calligraphic pen to the other side of him. He would write on these themes, if he had to compose last words to his family. Further contemplation was needed.

Ikeuchi lies awake, watching the strange glowing half moon of light creeping slowly across the thatched roof. The Australians could throw light into the darkest corners of this place. But the darkness in their minds would be permanent.

He had almost triggered the great *Shibaraku* scene in the court! Wait a moment! He had seen the fear in Takahashi's eyes. And the retreat of Cooper. All at once. A triumph of double play!

Cooper's clumsy attempts to undermine him had become ludicrous to observe. But Takahashi had not 'stood with his men'. They would need a new hero.

They would need to be reminded of the true 'Imperial Way'. Not the lies told by the smart lawyer from Tokyo.

The time was approaching for such a demonstration.

On his bed in Sugamo Prison, far to the north, Hideo reflected on the letter he would write to Midori. This day had been special. He had actually passed General Tojo when he was despatched on a work detail to clean the latrines. Sugamo was a hive of activity with Japanese and American military lawyers passing frequently on their rounds of their clients—the men who held ultimate power over Hideo. The chiefs of the army and the navy and the civilians in Tojo's Cabinet.

Hideo would tell her that he took some comfort that the mightiest men in the land were also facing trial. Not only humble officers like himself. He couldn't quite understand it, because he had not yet been accused of anything, but was wanted as a witness. But, still it felt that he was like an accused.

Perhaps, it was Providence that he was here. One of his cell mates was also a Christian, General Miyamoto, who had served in China. He was a character with a great sense of humour and an endless gift for telling stories. He also had a very interesting view on the trials and postwar Japan. He said that—'Japan had seen the hell of war and now it must face the purgatory of peace'.

But, he was very optimistic that Japan would emerge all the stronger from the trials and that the real evil doers would not go unpunished. This was a great comfort to hear and it would be very interesting to see how it applied back on Ambon with Vice Admiral Takahashi and Captain Ikeuchi.

He had also heard about the exclusion of the Emperor from the trials. If the Americans could show such wisdom then they might redeem some of their reputation. However, no one would stand trial for the destruction of Nagasaki and Hiroshima!

Hideo stands quietly to look out across Tokyo Bay. The cold icy winds would soon give way to the heat and humidity of Ambon. He would brace himself. But, after the recent months, he probably could face any adversity. The shock, the despair, were not so distant and would still descend on him. He must pray and think of Midori and the love to which he would return.

Cooper opens his eyes, shaken gently by Carol. Before him, a steaming mug of tea. He rubs his bleary eyes, and looks around. He had fallen asleep in the chair beside Jimmy's bed.

He takes the mug, smiles weakly at her.

'Two sugars?'

'One. Sorry, we're on rations, Bob.'

He takes a sip. Strong brew, straight to the brain, a quick starter.

'Thanks. I fell asleep. Anything from him?'

She shakes her head. Cooper nods, wearily, resigned. It was worth a shot but it was too late. He looks up to see Corbett standing at the end of the ward.

He gets up, downs the last of the mug gratefully and picks up his cap and satchel. He shares a last look with Carol. She smiles but her eyes don't conceal her feelings of sadness.

Cooper steps into the harsh sunlight and walks quickly with Corbett. They pass a few sullen

Ambonese, watching as Keenan and the guards march the Japanese double file into the courtroom.

'Major Roberts was looking for you, sir.'

'What did you tell him?'

'Said that you were down in the town, interviewing some possible witnesses.'

Cooper grins in appreciation.

'Good man.'

'I just can't get any response from Tokyo, sir.'

Cooper sees Sheedy approaching the courtroom, chatting with Patterson who has his camera and tripod slung over his shoulder. Photos for posterity. Would it be an anticlimax?

'There might be another way.'

Corbett is puzzled, shakes his head. Sheedy tips his hat to Cooper.

'Morning, Captain.'

'Mr Sheedy.'

Sheedy steps away. Cooper looks back to see Roberts and Beckett striding towards the back of the courtroom. Yes, careers would be made in Tokyo but Major Beckett will be conducting interviews on Ambon today. Late applications will not be considered.

Cooper and Corbett enter and stand at their table. Cooper glances at Takahashi. No hint of any feeling at all. The heat is already stifling, radiating down from the tin roof.

The Bench files in, stands at their table looking down on the packed courtroom. The orderly steps forward.

'The Australian War Crimes Tribunal Ambon is now in session.'

The Bench sits followed by the court. Matsugae glances nervously at Reid who radiates confidence.

Matsugae looks at Cooper, ignoring him, and then back to the Bench. His hour had come. The droplets of perspiration starting to run down the back of his collar.

The President of the Bench looks up at Keenan.

'Sergeant, escort the defendant Takahashi to the Bench, please.'

Keenan taps Takahashi on the shoulder. He rises, and walks the final steps of his destiny, stopping just short of the Bench table. Keenan snaps to attention, salutes the Bench and returns to his position.

Cooper glances at Beckett, apparently impassive but totally alert. Sheedy sits next to him, pen poised over his notebook. He crosses his fingers as he sees Cooper's look.

The President takes his glasses from a leather case, unfolds them and puts them on. He picks up a document, his voice clear and resonant.

'The case of Vice Admiral Takahashi is almost without precedent.'

Cooper feels his pulse racing, a sudden craving for a smoke.

'Vice Admiral Takahashi appears not to have exercised any effective authority in the course of his duties.'

Takahashi stares right through the Bench, keeping a rigid mask of detachment towards them. But his own heart joined the others now beating faster and faster with each word of the decision.

'We are also faced with a man who, although Japanese, appears to have been strongly influenced by British values.'

Matsugae nods, noticed by Reid. The point had been made.

'However, although the Vice Admiral has been scrupulous in providing proof of his personal background, he has not been so scrupulous in furnishing the court with the records of his command. This could be deliberate, this could be incompetence or it could be, as he claims, the result of the chaos and destruction which preceded the Japanese surrender on Ambon.'

Sheedy makes a notation in his notebook. 'Could be bullshit'.

Cooper studies the President's face, the lines of perspiration creeping down his lean cheeks.

'The court has no way of telling which alternative is correct.'

He looks up, straight at Cooper.

'The prosecution has failed to convince this court that Vice Admiral Takahashi authorised a policy of brutality against prisoners here or that he ordered the execution of any prisoners.'

Cooper glances at Beckett, very comfortable with the direction of the decision.

'This is not to say that turning a blind eye might not have had the same effect. Nevertheless, what is required is proof beyond reasonable doubt. The attempt by the defendant Ikeuchi to implicate the Vice Admiral in what was undoubtedly a reign of terror and violence has failed to persuade this court conclusively of the defendant's guilt.'

Corbett looks to Cooper, shaking his head in disbelief. He sees the firm setting of Cooper's jaw, the anger growing. He glances to Keenan, bewildered, filling with suppressed rage.

The President removes his glasses, glances along the Bench to present a unanimous face.

'Therefore it is with a great deal of regret that this

court must acquit the defendant on all counts.'

Sheedy puts a heavy tick in the 'Acquitted' column, as a growing murmur of dissent is silenced by the bang of the gavel.

Cooper stands immediately.

'Your Honour, I request that Vice Admiral Takahashi be retained as a material witness in the case against Captain Ikeuchi and the other defendants!'

Beckett tenses, observed by Sheedy. The President looks to Roberts who doesn't hesitate.

'Your request is out of order, Captain. The defendant is free to leave this court.'

Cooper stands defiantly, urged on by the silent chorus of support throughout the room. Matsugae is alarmed.

'Then I request that the Vice Admiral be retained while the Judge Advocate General in Australia reviews his case.'

Roberts is almost apoplectic.

'His case will be reviewed, Captain! But there is no necessity to detain him further.'

'Is that the opinion of this court, Your Honour?'

'It is!'

'Is it?'

Cooper scoops up his battered Manual, flicks open the page, steadies his quivering hand, and reads with one eye on Roberts.

' "The court shall take the proper steps to procure all witnesses whom the prosecutor or the accused desires to call." I repeat my request!'

'Request denied! The defendant is free to leave this court!'

The President bangs his gavel.

'This court is adjourned till further notice!'

The Bench rises followed by the whole court. Cooper watches as Takahashi is escorted out the rear of the court by Keenan, then turns to see Reid clap his hand on Matsugae's shoulder in congratulations. Matsugae glances at Cooper almost sympathetically, then turns back to Reid.

Sheedy steps up to Cooper, studies his face and shrugs.

'Can't beat the old school tie, Captain. I was half expecting them to give Takahashi the V.C. for good measure.'

Cooper keeps his eye on Roberts as he walks across the grounds.

'It's not over yet, Sheedy.'

Corbett is startled by this statement. Sheedy weighs it up, shrugs again. Cooper leans over to Sheedy as he packs his satchel.

'If you want to make yourself really useful round here, you could make certain inquiries from your contacts in Tokyo.'

Sheedy sees the request on Cooper's face, nods slowly. Cooper turns to Corbett.

'Introduce Mr Sheedy to that radio operator down in the town, will you, Jack?'

Corbett, puzzled, looks at Sheedy who stands waiting, somewhat amused by this proposed assignation.

'Now, sir?'

'Yes, Jack, now.'

Corbett picks up his satchel and exits with Sheedy, who is buoyed up by this new move.

'Ever been in the intelligence gathering side, Lieutenant?'

'No, Mr Sheedy, I haven't.'

'Then, welcome to it.'

Cooper stares at the near empty courtroom and the portrait of the King at the juncture of the two flags. The 'King's men' had just acquitted 'the Baron'. But the rights of the 'commoners' were not yet exhausted.

In his office, Roberts pours a large shot of whisky for himself and Beckett. They barely have time to take a sip when there is a knock at the door. Cooper enters.

Beckett can see the impending explosion and downs his glass.

'I think I should leave you two for a while.'

Cooper steps in, placing himself beside the door.

'That's good, Major.'

Beckett does not like the sarcastic echo of himself, but smiles at Roberts and exits past Cooper, ignoring his angry gaze. Cooper shuts it slowly, turns back dismissively.

'Beckett's the joker in the pack, isn't he, Frank?'

Roberts sits calmly. But the room is starting to melt. Those hot needles again.

'What do you mean?'

Cooper steps forward and places his satchel on the desk in front of Roberts.

'Takahashi's guilty. You know it and so do the Bench!'

'Do I? Well I do know that you didn't deliver the goods, Bob.'

'Was I the one who sent Mitchell home? The only witness?'

Roberts studies Cooper closely, the slight blur of his face coming into focus again.

'Takahashi's case is closed.'

Cooper leans forward on his satchel, his sinewy forearms like taut cables supporting his poised body.

'No, it's not. And there's still the High Court.'
'Try it and you're dead!'

Roberts rises to face him but Cooper is undeterred.

'Everywhere I turn, it's the system. I tried to sign on for this war. There was the system. Too good for cannon fodder. Into the Legal Corps for you.'

Roberts is affronted, wishing that it was a straight line. He'd have had Cooper court martialled instantly.

'Very few men have the privilege of what we've been given, Bob. And the system, as you call it, works! A presumption of innocence! Remember that phrase?'

'The system is too smart by half.'

Cooper glances at his satchel and stands back, sombre.

'Yes, maybe Keenan was right. We should've lined the lot of them up and just pulled the trigger.'

Roberts' anger is still contained but growing.

'Do you realise the implications of what you've just said?'

'Do you realise the implications of Takahashi's acquittal?'

Roberts shakes his head, almost derisive.

'Why all this, when you've got the real bastard?'

Cooper sees this tack, mirrors his amused expression. 'Ikeuchi?'

'Yes! He's named in every single statement! He's the bloody monster! Bob, I know you too well. When you've got a fire under you, you'll go for broke and bugger the consequences! Don't throw away all those years by trying to make a hero of yourself. The rules are all we have.'

Cooper studies him as he sits again. Neither of them was backing away.

'Is that what justice is to you. Rules?'

Roberts detonates.

'Why don't you open your bloody eyes for once? Without these trials it'd be the law of the lynch mob! That'd make us the savages! Can't you see, without the rules we're lost?'

Cooper shakes his head in astonishment.

'You buy that, you really do buy that, don't you?'

Roberts sees that they are not advancing.

'I know you're disappointed about Takahashi but life goes on after Ambon, Bob.'

Cooper picks up his satchel, removes a form and drops it on Roberts' desk abruptly.

'The "rules" still allow an appeal. Sir!'

He salutes and exits quickly. Roberts sighs heavily, relieved for the moment. But this would colour the rest of the trial without doubt. And then there would be the explanation to the Army Minister. It was going to be tough.

He looks up at the portrait of the King. It is noticeably askew, as if Cooper's very presence had tilted it over. He rises and adjusts it thoughtfully. What if Cooper did find the evidence that could have convicted Takahashi? What then? He returns to his desk, a new burden added to the already considerable load.

Beckett falls in with Cooper as he strides back to his office.

'I'd like a word in private, Cooper. Maybe away from here?'

Cooper waves Patterson aside as he approaches with a load of files.

'I'm very busy, Major. So, whatever you've got to say do it fast, as you say.'

They step out into the shade beside the Legal Corps

building. Cooper lights a cigarette. Beckett hesitates. Cooper was worth another shot.

'You did one hell of a job here. I'd rate you as a star performer.'

'I didn't realise that I was auditioning.'

Cooper cannot bring himself to face Beckett who moves to catch his eye.

'I mean that. It'll be prominent in my report.'

Cooper faces him.

'When you write that report, Beckett, you tell Macarthur and the President and Congress, they can breathe easy. Hirohito and his "old guard" will be there to dance every time you call the tune.'

Beckett lights a Camel, shakes his head.

'Cooper, you're a smart guy. This is an island in the middle of nowhere. What happened here will be forgotten in no time . . .'

Cooper leans closer to Beckett.

'That's all it's ever been to you lot, hasn't it? We mop up the dirty work while you take all the glory? Half you blokes don't even realise we fought a war with you! A lot of good men died here!'

Beckett's voice is pure steel with an edge of sympathy.

'I lost my brothers in the war. I had Hirohito in my sights! How do you think I felt when Macarthur told me of his decision?'

Cooper turns at the sound of an approaching jeep. In the back seat, erect, indomitable, Takahashi and a guard. Beckett offers Cooper his hand.

'I'm leaving now, Cooper. But I hope to see you with the team in Tokyo.'

Cooper studies the outstretched hand and then gazes at Takahashi.

'Yeah. When I come for him.'

He steps back into the building, deserting Beckett, his face perplexed and angry. Roberts emerges as Beckett approaches the jeep and climbs aboard.

Cooper watches from his office as they exchange a few words, shake hands and salute. The jeep lurches forward and drives off, dust billowing behind it. Cooper watches Roberts stand, watching the departure. Further along, near the wire, Keenan and a platoon of Japanese stand watching the jeep drive through the gates. Keenan's anger all in the sharp turn of his head and a swift audible rebuke to some of the Japanese, who bow instinctively towards the passing jeep.

'If you bastards think you'll be joining him, you bloody won't. Because he's left you high and dry.'

Cooper stubs out the cigarette in his old coconut ashtray. He looks down at the photo of Geoff.

'Just when you think it's all over, it's only begun.'

CHAPTER TEN

OUT FROM THE NIGHTMARE

Hideo surveys the road through the main streets of the town, Amboina. The impressive, turquoise domes of the many mosques that had barely escaped air raids. The spires of the white churches against the early morning sky. The Ambonese strolling beside the road, carrying fruit and other goods on their heads.

As the truck turns up towards the track to the camp, the vivid appearance of chains-of-love-flowers, rich peach coloured and filling the air with a heady sweetness. Then, from below, the sound of a choir of Christian Ambonese, swelling to an ethereal harmony, floating in the still morning air. Hideo felt a sudden pang. How strange that he had been 'farewelled' by the ragged choir of Midori and his friends. And now 'welcomed' by this. The choirs that evoked the memories of fleeting joys and deep sufferings in both places.

Talbot, seated opposite Hideo, notices the crucifix swinging from the chain around his neck. He attempts to maintain a look of indifference but notices Hideo's glance at him. Their eyes meet for a long moment. Hideo's calm is almost unnerving, a real contrast to the furtive glances he had observed of the other Japanese in the courtroom. And it is

162

very different to Ikeuchi's arrogant, knowing expression.

The truck rolls into the base grounds. Hideo looks around, taking in the bombed out remains of his former office and the shattered remnants of the former HQ. The truck halts suddenly. He jumps down from the truck, grabs his pack and is steered by Talbot towards the front of the Legal Corps building. As he walks, he looks over to the barbed wire fence.

Ikeuchi faces him, drawing thoughtfully on a cigarette. He cannot conceal his concern at this new arrival and turns away suddenly. Hideo looks back, puzzled as he is taken inside the evidence room. Ikeuchi has vanished.

Talbot positions Hideo in front of the height measurement as Patterson loads the camera. He stands back, intrigued by Hideo. His attention is distracted by another staffer who searches Hideo's bag. He prods Talbot with a photo of a beautiful Japanese girl. Midori.

Corbett walks in behind Talbot and stands watching. It takes a few moments for Hideo's slate identification board to register. 'Tanaka Hideo Lt. Signals Officer.'

Corbett wheels around and heads straight for Cooper's office, bursting through the door.

'Captain, we've got him. The Signals Officer!'

Cooper looks through the open door to Hideo, now being photographed in profile.

'Good. If he can verify anything on Takahashi, we'll have his plane turned around in mid flight! Take him to the hut.'

'Sir'.

'Oh, Jack, anything from Sheedy?'

'Not yet, sir.'

'Get Matsugae over as well.'

'Sir.'

Corbett exits hurriedly. Cooper studies Hideo for a few moments then looks back down at the file on the four pilots. Would this Signals Officer remember?

Talbot escorts Hideo into the hut and takes up his position beside the door. Matsugae enters, followed by Cooper and Corbett. Corbett seats himself at the table opposite Hideo and his counsel. Hideo glances nervously up at Cooper then looks to Matsugae, who smiles reassuringly.

'I am here to assist you, Lieutenant Tanaka, as your legal counsel. My name is Shinji Matsugae.'

Hideo nods, hands him a written statement in Japanese, but keeps his eyes directed at Corbett who opens a file.

'Lieutenant Tanaka, you were in charge of the Signals Section on Ambon, in the headquarters of Vice Admiral Takahashi?'

Hideo glances to Matsugae who nods slightly.

'Please answer the question, Lietenant.'

'Yes.'

'Did you ever send or receive any orders relating to the courts martial of prisoners on the island?'

'No.'

Cooper leans on the table, studying Hideo who seems slightly dazed by the alien proceedings.

'Did you ever receive orders for the destruction of camp records?'

Hideo glances at Cooper, shakes his head, puzzled.

'No.'

Corbett leans forward anxiously.

'Did you ever intercept transmissions from Allied planes?'

'Yes. We were under continuous attack.'

'Do you recall one particular flight, July 24th, 1944?'

Hideo strains to remember, increasingly bewildered by the line of questioning.

'There was always great confusion . . . much radio traffic . . . in code.'

Cooper leans forward, gazes at Hideo, willing him to remember.

'July 1944. The island wasn't under heavy air attack. One particular flight. Reconnaissance.'

Matsugae leans over to Cooper almost pleading.

'Captain, please be reasonable. The Lieutenant has just told you that he can only recall great confusion.'

Cooper ignores him.

'Answer the question, Lieutenant.'

Hideo stares up at Cooper.

'Much has happened since I left Ambon. I was on leave in Nagasaki . . .'

He looks down. Matsugae scans Hideo's statement then shakes his head at Cooper.

'The Lieutenant lost both his parents and his brothers in the atomic bomb, Captain.'

Cooper leans back, the wind taken completely from his sails. He catches Talbot's shocked expression, then turns back to face Matsugae, who stands and bows to him.

'Captain, do you intend to lay charges against Lieutenant Tanaka?'

Cooper looks at Corbett disconsolately.

'Not at this time.'

'Then, in view of the fact that Lieutenant Tanaka surrendered voluntarily, unlike the other defendants, I formally request that he be allowed to return home.'

Cooper looks through the window to the courthouse. If Tanaka knew so little, what was the point? But then again. He turns back to Matsugae.

'We'll retain Lieutenant Tanaka. He may be called

as a witness in the case against Captain Ikeuchi. That will be all, Mr Matsugae.'

Matsugae gestures to Hideo to rise. They both bow curtly and exit as Talbot opens the door for them. Cooper lights a cigarette, subdued. Corbett shrugs.

'Bit of a strange one, sir.'

'Yeah.'

He looks out at Talbot escorting them back to the compound.

'Nagasaki, home? Jesus . . .'

As the dusk descends, Cooper and Sheedy share a drink on the verandah, away from the buzz of conversation of the Bench and the NCOs.

Sheedy listens to the shouts and clapping resounding across from the prisoners' compound. Two large sumo wrestlers are visible, locked in combat before the assembled Japanese in front of the main assembly hut.

'Must be one of their national days.'

Cooper is preoccupied.

'What's the word from Tokyo?'

Sheedy glances around and moves a step closer.

'I can't get any precise details but it seems that Takahashi's got quite a name for himself in certain circles.'

'Such as?'

'Well, put it this way, Captain. You know the Yanks are sweet on Hirohito. Well, the little Emperor's got his network of cronies. Without which he's rooted. Which means that Uncle Sam is also rooted.'

Cooper looks over to the President and other members of the Bench in quiet discussion.

'You're saying that Takahashi's part of that mob?'

Sheedy shakes his head and grins wryly.

'Now, that's where it's difficult to get a precise fix. Macarthur's under a lot of pressure up there to bag the Emperor's mates. So who knows who's really in whose pocket, if you know what I mean.'

'What about Beckett?'

'Well, he's not the sort of bloke who would usually mix with us colonials. I'd say he was part of some softening up process for us in Tokyo. But, I did find out that he's part of the push in Macarthur's HQ to go easy on some of the "cronies". Reform not revenge is their motto.'

Cooper sips his beer. It was clearer but it was even more elusive. Sheedy lights a kretek, blows a fragrant cloud into the still air.

'It doesn't alter the fact that for a bloke who ran a butcher shop here, Takahashi was treated like someone up on a driving charge. So, what's next, Captain?'

'We'll proceed with the case against Ikeuchi and the rest of them. Unless some miraculous evidence drops out of the sky . . .'

'I wouldn't hold your breath.'

Cooper downs his beer and places his glass on the verandah rail. He turns to Sheedy.

'Thanks. Just keep your ear to the ground.'

'I'll do my best. Oh, by the way, you know we gave the Poms a hiding in the first test?'

Cooper grins.

'Time to bring in the spin bowlers?'

Sheedy picks up Cooper's analogy.

'Well, when you've tried out the real speedsters and they're not getting the wickets, the pitch should be ready for some top spin.'

They stare at each other, attuned to the same idea.

Cooper walks off. Takahashi might seem to have

hit them for six but this did not mean that the right bowler couldn't get his scalp. He could not shake his hunch. That ball was only a matter of time.

Sheedy returns his attention to the sumo wrestlers locked in combat in front of the assembled Japanese.

Squatting in the dirt with the other Japanese, Hideo and Noburo watch the huge wrestlers, Ikeuchi's 'lieutenants', almost naked except for loin cloths. Ikeuchi makes his way from the back of the group and slides down beside Hideo, who attempts to ignore him. Ikeuchi smiles thinly.

'The Christian.'

Hideo rises but Ikeuchi grabs his arm and forces him back down.

'It is the duty of an officer to stand by his superiors.'

He moves closer to Hideo, his foul breath covering Hideo. He grabs the crucifix around Hideo's neck, pulling hard on the chain.

'Even if it means sacrifice of himself.'

He snaps the chain and throws the cross into the dirt.

'Whatever I am asked, I will tell the truth.'

Ikeuchi shakes his head, a savage grin.

'You think they are interested in the truth? They have already acquitted Baron Takahashi and you say they are interested in the truth!'

Hideo contains himself as Ikeuchi rises and pushes his way back through the other defendants. Noburo picks up the crucifix, hands it back to Hideo with a look of alarm.

'Captain Ikeuchi is right.'

Their faces are splashed with heavy drops of rain. As the downpour descends, they run with others to the shelter of the huts. Noburo stands next to Hideo under the overhang of a hut, glancing at him anxiously.

'Hideo, why did you come back?'

Hideo threads the cross back on the chain carefully.

'We were soldiers following orders. They have to understand this.'

Noburo is perplexed.

'But you were free. You could have run. They would never have found you. Don't you see? They don't want our understanding. They have made their minds up. We are guilty! All of us!'

Hideo faces him.

'Noburo, if we all run like animals, when will it ever be different? How can we ever be anything than a defeated people? No hope . . . no chance of facing the world again?'

He searches Noburo's face but all he can see is bewilderment and fear. The downpour is now a thunderous torrent, cascading rivers of water down the roofs of the huts.

In the hospital, Jimmy Fenton is wide awake, his eyes burning, his breath coming in urgent gasps. He reaches for the photo of Eddy Fenton.

Carol gazes out over the grounds, awash in a muddy quagmire. On her desk, illuminated by the lamp, her last report. She lights a cigarette, watching the activity in the Legal Corps offices. Bob would be preparing the cases for the rest of them. How they ever expected him to convict the lot was beyond her.

Suddenly, the lights dim and fade out.

'Bloody generator!'

Carol turns and opens the parrafin lamp beside her desk. She adjusts the wick and lights it. The flame flickers slowly. She looks up and almost jumps back in fright.

A ghost in the doorway, slowly floating towards her. His pale skin sallow, almost bloodless, a thin arm shakily extending to her, ravaged by dark scars.

She stands, transfixed. Jimmy Fenton hands her the photo, his breathing a racking wheeze.

'Eddy . . . Eddy. I remember.'

The next morning, Jimmy, supported by two soldiers, limps with a renewed strength as Cooper and Corbett follow his lead. Carol is at his side, her eyes fixed on him. In front of them, Talbot and another soldier hack a path through the overgrown jungle.

Behind them, Ikeuchi and three Japanese are brought along by Keenan and another guard.

Fenton stops, breath wheezing, gazing around, unsure. The group stops.

'This way?'

Cooper places a hand on his shoulder.

'Easy, Jimmy. There's no rush.'

He looks at Carol who nods her appreciation. Fenton looks in another direction and hobbles towards a wall of foliage.

'This way!'

Keenan steps up to Cooper.

'He doesn't know where he is.'

Cooper glances at Ikeuchi, sensing his unease.

'We keep going.'

He steps past Fenton, takes a machete from one of the soldiers and hacks through the foliage with some effort. It gives way, to a clearing on a rise beyond. The ruins of an old Dutch battlement.

Fenton moves in front of Cooper, his eyes alight with certainty.

'There! Eddy's there!'

Cooper and Carol assist him now, as he hobbles forward urgently. Ikeuchi remains motionless. Keenan gives him a forceful shove.

'Get the lead out of your pants, Tojo!'

Fenton reaches the perimeter of the ruins, gazing around anxiously. He drops to his knees in anguish.

'Eddy!'

The cry echoes around the overgrown walls, birds bursting from the canopy of trees above it.

Cooper and Carol kneel to either side of Fenton who leans forward and touches the earth in an almost reverent way.

'Here. He's here.'.

Cooper stands, takes a shovel from a soldier and places himself before Ikeuchi, dropping the shovel at his feet.

'Dig.'

Ikeuchi considers the shovel, and looks directly at Cooper. A thin smile.

'Geneva Convention say: "Officers not do manual work".'

Cooper looks at the shovel then at Ikeuchi and smiles back.

'Cooper's Convention say: "Ikeuchi dig. Or shovel come in contact with head". Now dig!'

Ikeuchi glances to the three Japanese then takes the shovel. The group make way for him to dig where Cooper kicks the soft soil with his boot. He turns and helps Carol bring Jimmy to his feet, and walk him gently to a log at the edge of the clearing. Cooper passes a grim but appreciative look to her.

It doesn't take long. Cooper stands above the grave as Corbett hands him a rusted ID tag with his rubber gloves. Cooper uses another glove to wipe away the mud. The name is barely visible, but legible. 'Fenton E. RAAF.'.

Roberts looks up from his desk as Cooper enters. He

throws the four tags on to his desk and glares at him.

'Phantoms, Frank! One to four!'

The following morning, Cooper rises and gazes at Roberts and the Bench with a sense of real satisfaction.

'The prosecution calls Private James Fenton to the stand as chief witness in the case against Captain Ikeuchi and others.'

Fenton is assisted to the stand by Littell and two soldiers. Roberts watches their every move, aware of Cooper's challenging look. Cooper watches Ikeuchi closely as Fenton is brought up the passage between the two sides of the dock.

The orderly steps up to Fenton as he is lowered to the chair, Littell taking a seat close by. The orderly places Fenton's shaking hand on the Bible. Littell smiles reassuringly at him as he repeats the oath.

'I solemnly swear to tell the truth, the whole truth and nothing but the truth.'

Talbot, a guard for the Bench, stands to attention, noting the swaggering satsifaction on Keenan's face and feeling his own sense of triumph. His prayers for Cooper's success had been answered.

Cooper steps up to Fenton, gazes around then looks with deliberate admiration at Fenton, dressed in uniform, painfully weak, but with fire in the eyes. Determined to see it through.

'Private Fenton, how long were you a prisoner on Ambon?'

Fenton considers, unsure of himself.

'How long?'

Roberts pounces.

'Sister Littell, are you sure that Private Fenton is capable of testifying?'

Littell glances to Cooper as she stands to reply. But Fenton shakes his head, his voice clear but racked with a wheezing cough.

'Over three years.'

'Were you ever beaten during that time?'

Fenton holds up his bare, scarred arms. He returns Roberts' stern gaze.

'I was beaten.'

'Who carried out the beatings?'

'Ikeuchi. The one we called "The Black Bastard", "Horse Face", "Gold Tooth", "Creeping Jesus", take your pick.'

Cooper steps aside, giving Fenton an unrestricted view of the Japanese.

'Who gave the orders for the beatings?'

Fenton raises his shaky hand, moving in an arc to Ikeuchi, as if drawn by some irresistible force.

'That bastard.'

Reid rises immediately.

'Objection.'

Cooper smiles grimly.

'The witness will refrain from the use of "colourful" language.'

Reid has a parting shot.

'I would have said "emotive".'

Reid sits. Cooper turns back to Fenton.

'What was the nature of these beatings, Private?'

Fenton suppresses a tear as he feels that wave of agony returning.

'Broke eight of my ribs. Split my skull! Almost bloody crippled me.'

He shakes his head at the defendants.

'Into every bit of bastardry going, those blokes.'

Cooper glances to Reid, eyebrow raised. But it is Matsugae who seems totally engrossed in the account.

'Private, do you recall one particular mass beating around July, 1944?'

Fenton thinks for a few moments.

'Yeah, there were thirty of us.'

His breath comes in bursts as his eyes widen. A flood of memories, as he looks at the exhibit table laid out with the instruments of his beating.

He is scampering like a dog, yelping wildly, blood pouring from his face, pursued by a Japanese soldier belting him repeatedly across the back with an axe handle. All around him, the deafening screams and shouts of fellow prisoners being attacked with pick handles, piping, whips of wire and pieces of wood.

He looks up as three prisoners are dragged to a section of the barbed wire fence as another two guards beat back prisoners standing on the inside of the fence, trying to assist their mates. The three prisoners were tied to the fence with wire, arms stretched into a cross, forcing them to stare straight into the blinding sun. The Japanese guards pick up steel piping and commence beating them again.

Then a loud whistle blast. The Japanese guards, breathing heavily, stand back from the fence.

Fenton, lost in memory, gazes right through Ikeuchi.

'And Ikeuchi, Ikeuchi blew that bloody whistle. He blew it to stop the beating. And he blew it to start it. All over again.'

He can see Ikeuchi strolling amongst the POWs writhing in agony on the ground, his whistle at the ready. He gives a loud blast. The guards recommence the beating.

The sound of the beatings builds to a crescendo for Fenton. He holds his ears, trying to block it out, face contorting in pain. Roberts is anxious.

'Captain . . .'

Cooper lays a calming hand on Fenton, noting

Littell's silent instruction. Fenton gradually lowers his hands, shaking, but determined to control himself.

'We lost some good mates that day. The rest of us . . .'

He gazes with hatred at Ikeuchi.

'No one has the right to do that to us! We were soldiers!'

Cooper sees the real concern in Matsugae's face. A similar look from Hideo, seated just behind Ikeuchi.

'Did you manage to escape from the beating?'

'Yeah, sunset. I rolled under one of the huts when the guards walked away from me for a minute. A few hours went by but the beating was still going on.'

'Private, apart from the beating, what else did you see from where you were hiding?'

'What else?'

Cooper remains silent, willing him to remember. Suddenly, the sound of a grinding engine wells up in him.

'The truck. Yeah. The truck driving in . . .'

Fenton is back again, tying a piece of tattered shirt around the wounds on his arm, watching the prisoners lying across the grounds, the evening falling on a chorus of moaning agony.

The truck pulls up beside the camp HQ. Four prisoners are dragged from the rear of the truck, arms tied behind their backs. One of the prisoners stumbles and falls on his face, then is kicked viciously by a Japanese soldier.

As the prisoner is dragged to his feet, Fenton has a clear view of him. His brother, Eddy!

Fenton rises from the chair, wavering, completely lost in events.

'Eddy! You bastards! He's hurt! Stop, you bastards! Don't kick him! Eddy! Eddy!'

Talbot, uncertain about this, finally moves forward and helps Fenton back into the chair with Cooper's assistance. His cries of anguish diminishing to a wheezing whimper.

Roberts pounces again.

'Sister Littell, you assured this court that this man was fit to testify.'

She stands, quietly authoritative.

'That is my professional opinion, Your Honour.'

'It is my advice to this court that he is not!'

A ringing shout.

'I am!'

All eyes are on Fenton. His eyes blazing, his voice clear.

'I am fit to testify!'

He gazes hard at Roberts, willing him to approve. Reluctantly, Roberts nods to Cooper.

'Proceed, Captain.'

Cooper takes three photos from Corbett and steps back to Fenton with a slight hesitation. He hands him the photos.

'Are these the men you saw with your brother?'

Fenton gazes at the photos. No hint of recognition.

'Faces a mess. Impossible to say.'

He hands the photos back to Cooper who studies him carefully.

'Where were your brother and the three men held?'

'Isolation block.'

He is crawling under the wire of the isolation compound, still in pain, but senses alert. He stops short at the sound of laughter from Japanese guards nearby. One guard steps away from the others towards Fenton and urinates in an arc which splashes Fenton, who covers his face. The guard hitches himself up, laughs at another joke and returns to the group.

Fenton crawls along to a spot directly under the isolation block, which is raised from the ground. The cries of pain, of flesh being beaten. He looks up through cracks in the wooden floor.

Eddy, tied to a chair, fully naked, recoiling from Ikeuchi's repeated blows with a piece of pipe. Each blow accompanied by a maniacal shout:

'Your mission was bombing! Bombing! Bombing!'

Eddy can barely speak, his whole body a mass of welts and bruises. Blood dripping to the floor.

'Rec . . . onn . . . sance . . . Gen . . . eva Convention . . .'

This only adds to Ikeuchi's fury. Another rain of blows.

'Geneva Convention dead!'

Jimmy Fenton turns away, biting his hand to stifle his scream. Blood drops from the floor cracks on to his head. He reaches up, tastes it in horror and agony.

Cooper watches Fenton closely, his face wet with tears, tasting them with his quaking hand as if they were Eddy's blood. He hands documents to the orderly who passes them to the Bench.

'I submit records of flight details showing that Flight Officer Eddy Fenton was on a reconnaissance flight over Ambon. This plane was not armed with bombs. Flight Officers O'Donnell, Smith and Rogers were also on board.'

Fenton leans forward in the chair.

'Eddy, can you hear me? The bastard's gone!'

He is reaching through the barbed wire around a window.

'Eddy! Pssst! It's me. Jimmy!'

Eddy is barely conscious, sprawled in a pool of blood near the window.

'Eddy. It's me. Jimmy!'

Eddy, in spastic movements, drags himself across the floor near the window. Jimmy has his head pressed right against it now, his scrawny arm flailing to reach his brother.

Eddy tries to speak but only blood spills from his mouth in a gasping noise. With the last of his strength, he pushes himself up against the wall, arching his hand up to Jimmy's, forcing the words from himself.

'Jibb . . . Jibbbyyy . . .'

Their hands come within inches of each other, then touch. Their fingers interlock tightly.

Cooper lays a hand on Fenton's shoulder, as he is racked with sobs.

'I'd slip out at night . . . give him a smoke . . . try to keep his spirits up . . .'

Cooper studies the faces of the Bench, visibly moved. He looks directly at Matsugae, who hangs his head. Respect or shame?

'When was the last time you saw your brother alive?'

Fenton concentrates for a few moments, frowning.

'It was . . . was . . . the . . . I think, the morning . . . yeah . . . morning . . . Jap guards . . . the truck . . .'

He turns from the window of the isolation block as the truck pulls up. A guard jumps from the rear of the truck where three other guards have three of the flyers, bound with rope. Another guard walks to the isolation block, Jimmy scrambles for cover, from which he has a clear view of the three men.

Fenton looks up at Cooper.

'The photos.'

Corbett hands them to Cooper who gives them to Fenton carefully. Fenton studies them, finally gesturing to one.

'Him. Yes him too!'

He studies the third, uncertain.

'Loaded them onto the back of the truck. Drove out of the camp. Car followed. Japs in the car.'

Cooper takes the photos and looks across to Ikeuchi.

'Was anyone in the court in that party?'

Fenton raises his hand, controlling his anger.

'Him. Ikeuchi. In the car.'

He studies the other Japanese. He does not see Noburo move his head slightly to block his vision. Fenton looks at the sombre face of Hideo but shakes his head.

'No one else I can see.'

Cooper positions himself near Ikeuchi who is seemingly impervious to the damning implications of the evidence.

'What happened next?'

Fenton's words come in quick bursts now.

'Went like blazes under the wire. Followed the truck 'til it turned off near the old ruin . . . running! Got as close . . . as I could. Eddy, the other three guards, Ikeuchi. Japs in the car! Voices too far away . . . almost nabbed by a Jap patrol.'

The tears, the sobs, now a quaking, raging nightmare.

'The rain! Heard Eddy scream as I hid in the jungle!'

He rises from the chair, a wild wraith, arms shivering, sobbing convulsively.

'Murdered him! Killed my brother!'

Talbot steps forward as do Cooper and Littell, grappling with him. Roberts belts down the gavel repeatedly.

'Private Fenton! Control yourself!'

'Animals!'

'Private Fenton!'

Fenton totters on the balls of his feet as if he is about to dive on the Japanese. Ikeuchi suddenly stands, half amused, half anxious about his safety. Matsugae, deeply moved by what he sees, turns to Ikeuchi and whispers savagely for him to sit. Finally, he does. Fenton explodes in a final burst that reverberates out on to the grounds.

'Fucking murdering savages!'

Cooper pulls him back towards the chair as he struggles violently. Suddenly, the life drains from him. He slumps against them. Cooper and Carol share a long anxious look.

They place the wasted, spent Jimmy gently back on the chair. Sheedy surveys the faces of the Australian guards, many with tears welling in their eyes.

Roberts nods to the President who leans over to Littell.

'Have Private Fenton returned to the hospital immediately, Sister Littell.'

'Yes, Your Honour.'

Roberts glares at them.

'This court looks on this incident with grave misgivings. Clearly, Private Fenton should never have been allowed to give evidence. A report will be made to your superiors, Sister Littell.'

She looks at him defiantly.

'Yes, Your Honour. I too will be making a report.'

Fenton, feet dragging, barely conscious, is helped

from the court by Littell, Sheedy and Keenan.

Cooper turns to Roberts.

'Your Honour, responsibility for placing Private Fenton in the witness stand rests entirely with the prosecution.'

Roberts nods gravely.

'The court is well aware of the prosecution's part in this unfortunate incident and that too will be duly noted.'

He looks to the President, who bangs the gavel.

'This court is recessed till further notice.'

Cooper looks at Corbett who sits, stunned.

'Cover for me this afternoon, Jack.'

Corbett nods but his mind is elsewhere.

From deep below the ocean's surface, Cooper ascends. He explodes into the dying light, lungs bursting for air! The sky is tinged with a deep crimson as the sun sets in the distance over the mountains. Finally, Cooper, at breaking point, screams into the empty sky. Then the voice.

You better be getting back.

Cooper swims furiously to the shore, stumbling in the shallow water. Exhausted, lying on the coarse sand, the sea lapping around him. Finally, opening his eyes, he sees a young Ambonese child looking down on him.

The young boy keeps his distance, gazing down at this strange man whom he thought was dead. Another four children appear from a hut on the edge of the beach, giggling and pointing excitedly.

Cooper looks along the beach. Fires are being lit near the *Perahus*, the fishermen cooking their catch. He returns his gaze to the young boy as the four children run off, laughing.

The boy watches Cooper as he slowly rises, his breath now an even tempo. The boy turns, runs to Cooper's clothes and canvas bag on the sand, snatches his cap and shouts to the other children, who fall about as he pulls the cap on, covering his face, running blind.

Cooper smiles wearily, and looks back to the edge of the camp just visible in the distance.

As he approaches his office, a tousled wet figure, towel over his shoulder, bag in hand, he makes out the figure of Sheedy in the shadows. He steps up to the doorway as Cooper approaches. He presents him with a half empty bottle of whisky.

'Been looking all over for you.'

'Skip it, Sheedy. Not tonight.'

He presses past. Sheedy stops him sombrely.

'Fenton died a few minutes ago.'

Cooper stops, turns slowly to the prisoners' compound. The hot filament erupts into life in his chest, then the tight wire uncoiling again.

He leaves Sheedy standing, striding out towards the compound.

CHAPTER ELEVEN

THE RUBICON

Cooper stands inside the closed door of the interrogation hut. He studies Ikeuchi seated on the chair in the middle of the hut. The desk has been pushed to one side. Ikeuchi stares straight ahead, ignoring him. The silence before the storm.

Like lightning, Cooper launches himself at Ikeuchi, kicking the chair out from under him. Ikeuchi hits the floor hard, rolling towards the wall, winded. Cooper grabs him by the back of the shirt, tugs him to his feet, his voice harsh but contained.

'Who executed the flyers?'

'I know nothing.'

'We'll see what you know.'

Cooper pushes him hard against the wall. Ikeuchi bounces, caught by Cooper who uses him like a battering ram, pitched headlong against another wall.

Outside the hut, Keenan stands, drawing quietly on a smoke. Dull thuds reverberate around the walls. Corbett hurries up to the hut but Keenan steps between him and the door.

'You don't want to go in there.'

Inside, Cooper pulls Ikeuchi up from the floor again. His forehead is severely gashed, blood pours from a deep cut above his right eye.

'Who gave the order? Who executed the flyers?'

Ikeuchi goes to spit at Cooper but is blocked by Cooper's hand over his mouth.

'Takahashi's laughing all the way from Tokyo. You're for the bullet!'

His voice now almost hysterical.

'Who gave the order? Who butchered them?'

Ikeuchi grabs Cooper's jacket. As Cooper throws him across the room again, the fob watch and chain tears away, cutting Cooper's arm. The watch flies across the hut, smashing against the wall.

Ikeuchi hits the floor, groaning in pain. He tries to get to his feet with the aid of the upended chair. Cooper strides over, kicks the chair away. He turns Ikeuchi over with his boot, presses down on his chest with it.

'Names!'

Ikeuchi struggles to breathe. Finally it comes with spitting contempt.

'"The . . . Christian!'

'Tanaka?'

A squirming, contorted mask of real hatred.

'Tanaka! The Christian!'

Cooper grimaces in disbelief, pressing harder now on Ikeuchi's throat. He would tear the throat out of this liar. Shred the vocal chords of the bastard who had barked the death sentence and now denied everything. Tear out the windpipe which allowed such a creature to breathe.

'You're going to have to do better than that!'

Ikeuchi almost chokes, gasping and writhing under the pressure, feeling his life ebbing away, desperately pulling on Cooper's boot.

'Tanaka! Tanaka!'

'Tanaka? The Signals Officer?'

184

A last gasp.

'Yes!'

The door swings open. Keenan strides in.

'Jesus Christ!'

He pulls Cooper off with such force that they are pitched backwards. Ikeuchi lies, wide eyed, gasping, certain that he is done for. Keenan steps towards him. Ikeuchi vomits blood, shaking his head in disbelief.

'Tanaka . . . Hide . . . o Tanaka!'

Keenan pulls Ikeuchi to his feet, picks up the chair, thrusts Ikeuchi down on it. Cooper considers his vengeance, ashamed.

'Thanks.'

Keenan glares at him.

'For what?'

'Stopping me.'

He looks down at the shrunken, battered Ikeuchi. Then at his own torn jacket, the fob watch gone. Keenan tugs Ikeuchi to his feet and shoves him towards the door, shaking his head contemptuously.

'Next time, leave it to the experts! Stick to your law books!'

Cooper looks down at the broken pieces of the fob watch. He squats then picks each piece up gently. He does not realise that Corbett is beside him until he holds out a piece of the watch to him, glancing down at his lacerated arm, but avoiding Cooper's eyes.

'You'd better get that seen to, sir.'

Cooper takes the piece from him, looks at the cut then back at Corbett who is already retreating from the room. Cooper raises his arm weakly.

'Jack . . .'

But the fleeting glimpse of Corbett's eyes says it all. This is betrayal, almost unforgivable and certainly unethical. Cooper looks at the watch with remorse, a shattered past in the pieces. And the voice gone also. He was never more alone.

In the hospital, he faces Carol in her office. She dabs antiseptic on the wound. He pulls back instinctively. She is almost fierce in her restraint of him.

'Will you hold still!'

She starts to apply a bandage to the wound, wrapping it tightly, her anger uncoiling in each wind of the roll.

'Did you get something out of that?'

He will not meet her eyes.

'The name of the executioner.'

'Happy with the way you got it?'

He examines the pieces of the fob watch on the table beside him, trying to ignore her.

'This is a side of you I haven't seen. And I don't think I like it.'

Cooper tries to fit the cover back on the crown of the watch but it is too warped. He looks at her, almost helpless.

'I killed Fenton. I could have done it by the book, taken his statement just like the others. But no, I had to push it.'

Carol stares at him, feeling the tension between them easing, seeing their shared grief.

'You didn't kill him, Bob. You couldn't have touched him without my say so. He was holding on for something. You gave it to him.'

He nods, looks back down at the watch. She takes the cover in her hand, looks closely at the photo.

'It's not just about Jimmy Fenton though. Is it?'

Cooper sees her searching look. Finally, he hangs his head, acknowledging her insight.

186

'No. The photo's of my old man and Geoff, my youngest brother. The old man died before the war. Expected a lot of us. Barry's my eldest brother, he's not in it. I was always getting him out of scraps.'

She hands it back to him gently, listening to the halting, pained tone in his voice.

'The battling Cooper clan . . .'

'Not far wrong. Had to be, where we grew up. Took a sharp bloke to talk himself out of a corner. Fists usually settled it. Barry died with a lot of good mates on the Kokoda Trail.'

He looks at the shattered watch, lips trembling. The hard part.

'Geoff. Well he gave me this as a Christmas present, in 1941. Just before Singapore. Then Changi. I tried to get there at the end. But he was dead. He was a tough little blighter, used to run with me to school. But it didn't prepare him for what the Japs did to him.'

She nods, filled with admiration for his candour. Part of her aching to soothe his pain, and for him to assuage her own feelings of guilt.

'Put me through law school, the three of them. Wasn't going to let the brains in the family throw it away.'

He looks up at her. His eyes moist, a new sense of lightness, of relief.

'I should have been with them. Fighting.'

Silence. He starts to rise but she puts her arm gently on his, restraining him. She reaches over the desk and picks up a rolled newspaper.

'Don't underestimate the value of what you're doing here, Bob.'

She holds the paper under the lamp, reads slowly.

'Here on Ambon, three hundred men lost their lives

in a last stand against the Japanese offensive into New Guinea. Some have even called it "Australia's Alamo". Here, a mere handful of men survived horrendous treatment at the hands of the enemy.'

Cooper takes the paper from her, intrigued.

'Sheedy?'

She nods. He picks up the place.

'Now, here, ordinary men try to grapple with issues that are difficult to define, let alone resolve.'

A long silence between them. Could they resolve anything? Would the world really care? How could he prosecute a man who had survived the horror of Nagasaki only to end up here, an 'island in the middle of nowhere'? Was the trial merely a refined form of vengeance? He had only acted to display the true feelings behind it, hadn't he?

She takes up his arm gently again, feels along the wrist and lower arm. Cooper grimaces slightly.

'I wouldn't put any pressure on that for a few days, allow the bruise to heal.'

'That's my writing hand.'

'You should look before you leap.'

He takes the point, chastened.

At dawn, they stand together across an open grave, Fenton's coffin beside it. Roberts and the Bench stand to attention next to them. An Australian flag draped over the coffin, fluttering in the soft breeze from the bay.

Keenan, Talbot and four other soldiers stand ready with rifles on the other side. An Australian Army padre reads from a Bible. The air becomes still as he finishes the reading.

'The Lord is my shepherd.

Blessed be the name of the Lord.'

Sheedy walks quietly up beside a group of

inquisitive Ambonese, standing at a respectful distance beside a group of palms. He brushes the sleep from his eyes, straightens his tie, and looks over at Cooper, intrigued by the bandage.

Littell steps forward, places a single flower on the coffin as a bugler commences 'The Last Post'. Pure, ringing, piercing up through the canopy of trees, notes of farewell meeting the shafts of new sunlight streaming down to the burial site.

The last notes fade away. Keenan snaps to attention and salutes the coffin, then turns to the squad.

'Squuaad! Present arms!'

Rifles are raised as one.

'Salute position!'

Six rifles poised, aimed at an infinite point in space.

'Fire!'

The shot echoes out on to the Bay and back across the grounds. Birds explode in a frightened flock from the trees above. The entire contingent salutes in unison. Littell dabs her tear filled eyes with a handkerchief.

Sheedy has to cover his eyes as the sun bursts over the top of the trees. The coffin is lowered into the grave, slowly, by four soldiers.

Cooper looks over to Sheedy, noting the question in his eyes. Roberts steps across to Cooper as the contingent disperses. He looks at Cooper's hand quizzically.

'Writer's cramp, Bob?'

'No, just a scratch, Frank.'

Roberts seems satisfied with the reply.

'Bob, we'll alter the schedule so you can proceed with Tanaka and Ikeuchi before the rest of them. It's important to get it over with.'

Cooper stares at him, sensing the guilt in Roberts' tone.

'Thanks, Frank. It's a pity we couldn't have "altered the schedule" on Takahashi.'

Roberts turns away, trying to ignore Cooper's barb. Cooper watches as the last of the mound of dirt is packed on to the grave then walks over to Sheedy, waiting patiently.

'We'll have that drink now, Sheedy.'

Back in the office, Sheedy pours generous shots of whisky. He raises his glass in a sombre toast.

'To all the Jimmy Fentons who didn't get their day in court.'

They drink in silence. Sheedy studies Cooper's hand, and puts his glass down slowly. He strains to remember then relaxes as the words flow.

' "The world will very little note . . . nor long remember what we say here . . . but it can never forget what they did here".'

He sees Cooper's puzzled look.

'Abe Lincoln. Gettysburg.'

Sheedy finishes his drink and sighs.

' "It is for us to be here dedicated to the great task remaining before us . . . that from these honoured dead we take increased devotion to the cause for which they here gave . . ." '

Cooper nods, appreciatively.

'Very bloody eloquent.'

Sheedy nods agreement, studying Cooper's bandage.

'So you've got the real culprit now?'

'Tanaka?'

'Yeah. How do you prosecute a bloke who's already survived the atomic bomb and lost his family?'

Cooper looks out across the grounds to the courthouse then turns back to Sheedy, seemingly at a loss.

'Well, Sheedy, we put such things aside in the service of justice.'

'It smells of a set up. Ikeuchi never admits to any executions. Now he tells you that the lone Christian's responsible. Don't you think it stinks?'

'On the face of it. But we'll soon find out.'

Cooper sees the new hostility in Sheedy's face.

'Did Keenan tell you?'

Sheedy is almost noncommittal.

'Oh, I found out.'

'I see.'

Sheedy moves to the door then turns back.

'I've only got a few words of advice, for what they're worth, Captain.'

Cooper waits for the onslaught. But Sheedy's rebuke is edged with disappointment.

'You're only a bloody lawyer. You can't solve the problems of the world on your own. Do your bit and get on with life. Get involved . . . and you're rooted.'

Sheedy exits into the glare. Cooper picks up the file marked 'Tanaka' then drops it, full of mixed feelings. Who had the greater guilt? Tanaka or himself?

At the defence table, Hideo and Ikeuchi stand with Matsugae and Reid as the charge is read out. Hideo stares straight ahead.

Oh, Midori, it is what I have feared. I arrived here as a witness. Now I am accused of murder.

'You are charged under section 3 of the Australian War Crimes Act with unlawfully carrying out the execution of RAAF officers Fenton, Rogers, Smith and O'Donnell. How do you plead?'

Ikeuchi shakes his head, grinning.

'Not guilty.'

Hideo looks to Matsugae who nods slightly.

'Not guilty.'

Hideo notices Talbot's shocked stare then sits slowly.

Cooper stands, holding a file.

'I submit the record of evidence given by the late Private James Fenton, together with photographs of the bodies of the officers, and their identification tags.'

As the orderly steps up and takes them, Cooper observes Corbett dutifully shuffling through files, avoiding his look. He watches the Bench examine the exhibit and then look up expectantly. Roberts nods to the stenographer.

'Let the record show that the prosecution has tendered the evidence as exhibit C.'

'The prosecution calls Captain Ikeuchi to the stand.'

Ikeuchi swaggers over to the stand. The great moment was near.

Matsugae glances glumly to Reid, but Reid also has his head lowered to some documents.

Cooper looks down at his hand, hearing the violent echo of his first question. He had been lucky that Sheedy and Littell had kept his confidence. Otherwise he might not be here to ask it.

'Captain, who gave the order for the execution of these officers?'

'I know nothing of any executions.'

'Private Fenton swore under oath that he saw you "interrogate" Flight Lieutenant Edward Fenton.'

'He is lying.'

'He further stated that he followed a truck carrying the officers and a car in which you were a passenger, along with others, to a place in the jungle.'

Ikeuchi thinks for a few moments then grins.

'I recall Private Fenton. Crazy man. Always causing trouble. Always telling lies.'

Cooper looks at Roberts reprovingly.

'We followed his lies to the spot where you dug up the decapitated bodies of the officers.'

'There was much confusion. Many of my men were poor soldiers. Too long here. Maybe they got out of hand. But I treated the prisoners like a father with disobedient children . . .'

Cooper nods, glad of the description.

'Captain Ikeuchi, the foster father of Ambon!'

He turns to the Bench.

'Bushido tradition demands that officers of the rank of the men in question be executed by officers of equal rank. Not enlisted men!'

He turns back to Ikeuchi who has no answer to this truth.

Ikeuchi stares at Cooper. The ignorant had been doing some study. He would soon see the real bushido. He would be amazed.

Hideo takes Ikeuchi's place. Cooper steps up with the photos.

'Lieutenant Tanaka, do you recognise these men?'

Hideo studies the photos closely.

'Yes.'

Cooper turns to Ikeuchi, impassive as ever.

'When did you first see them?'

'The morning they were brought to the court martial building by Captain Ikeuchi.'

'Captain Ikeuchi . . .'

Cooper lets it hang in the air then turns back to Hideo.

'Where were you at the time?'

'At my desk in the Signals Office. I watched their

arrival through the window.'

'Who was in charge of the court martial?'

'Baron Takahashi presided over them with Captain Ikeuchi and Lieutenant Shimada, the Legal Officer.'

'Baron Takahashi. Were you a witness to the court martial?'

'No, but the main function of the building was for the court martial.'

'Did you see Baron Takahashi or the others enter the building.'

'No.'

'Then what led you to believe that a court martial had actually taken place?'

'Captain Ikeuchi entered the Signals Office later and informed me that I had been honoured by Baron Takahashi, President of the court martial, to lead an execution party of Australian prisoners at dawn.'

'Honoured? Why did they select you, a Signals Officer, to lead an execution party?'

'Bushido tradition requires an officer to be executed by an officer of equal rank.'

'Where are the other officers who accompanied you?'

Hideo looks ahead, gazing momentarily at Noburo, who lowers his eyes.

'I believe that they were killed in bombing raids after I left here.'

'What would have happened, Lieutenant, if you had refused to obey an order?'

'I would have been court martialled. Like any soldier.'

'And what would have been the penalty?'

'Death.'

'What crime had the officers committed to warrant execution?'

194

'They had bombed innocent civilians.'

'The records clearly show that they were on a reconnaissance flight!'

'Our records show it was a bombing raid! According to international law it was a crime! According to Japanese court martial law it was a crime!'

'According to a court martial that we can only assume took place. Isn't that the case, Lieutenant?'

Cooper bores down on him.

'Let's face it, Lieutenant, you are a liar! What did you ever really know? Or care?'

Hideo flares, as if given a great jolt by Cooper's attack.

'Baron Takahashi was in charge! Nothing could be done without his express orders! Nothing! I deplored the conditions of the camp. I protested against orders for the mass beating of prisoners. I made repeated requests to Takahashi! Do something! Prisoners were dying all around us! He did nothing! There was a warehouse full of food! Takahashi let them die of starvation! They were human beings!'

He looks around desperately.

'There was a court martial! Look at the records!'

A loud chuckle, then an explosion of laughter. All eyes turn to Ikeuchi, his laughter uncontrollable. He leaps to his feet.

This is it! The *Shibaraku* scene! Wait a moment! How they will remember this!

'The records! There are no records!'

He pushes Matsugae and an Australian soldier aside as he approaches Hideo. Cooper stands, transfixed.

'Takahashi burnt them! Just like he's burning you! You poor fool!'

Roberts leaps to his feet, furiously banging the gavel, shouting above Ikeuchi.

'Sergeant! Remove him!'

Keenan grapples with Ikeuchi as Talbot grabs his flailing arms.

An explosion of insults at Hideo in Japanese as Ikeuchi is dragged out!

'Shitface! Traitor! Christian liar! Takahashi has sent us to our deaths! *Tenno heika banzai! Tenno heika banzai!*'

The defendants are on their feet, shouting with their superior.

'*Tenno heika banzai! Tenno heika banzai!*'— 'Long live the Emperor!'

Guards move in, pushing them back to their seats. Order returns slowly. Cooper looks across at Matsugae, head bowed, deeply shamed. Between him and Hideo, the vulnerable face of the defeated.

Roberts nods to Cooper.

'Proceed, Captain.'

Cooper steps up to Hideo whose face is full of bewilderment and fear. His hand goes to the fob watch but it is no longer there.

'So, Lieutenant, you say that you took the unusual step for a Japanese officer in protesting orders for mass beating of prisoners?'

'Yes. It was inhuman. It was unchristian.'

'Who ordered the mass beating?'

'As I have already said, nothing like this could happen without the express orders of Baron Takahashi.'

The Bench murmurs amongst itself, the President motioning for silence. Cooper observes with grim satisfaction.

'So Captain Ikeuchi oversaw the beating ordered by Vice Admiral Takahashi?'

'Yes.'

'What was your relationship with Captain Ikeuchi?'

Hideo stares at Ikeuchi's empty seat. Almost as if his threatening eyes could still be felt boring into Hideo, daring him to break their 'unified front'. To tell the 'truth'.

He is standing, filled with anger, watching the camp in the looming darkness. A heavy quiet settles over the prisoners' compound, broken only by the sobbing and fractured cries of the beaten POWs, after the mass beating.

The POW bound to the wire is a stark silhouette against the blood red sky.

Ikeuchi strides up behind Hideo, grabs him and pushes him against the nearest building. Hard up against the wall, shouting into his face.

'Shitface traitor! You dare undermine my authority! I'll have your head! No one goes behind my back! No one!'

He grips Hideo by the front of the uniform, forcing his head repeatedly against the wall.

'Never again! You hear! Never!'

Hideo starts to lose consciousness from the assault. He slumps, Ikeuchi letting him slide down the wall to the ground. He sees the blurred outline of Ikeuchi's raised boot, which suddenly retreats.

Hideo feels behind his head, then brings his hand up slowly to his face. It is covered with sticky red blood. He gets slowly to his feet and stumbles back towards the HQ.

Cooper stands before Hideo, surprised by what he has just heard.

'Lieutenant, how can you be certain that Captain Ikeuchi didn't fabricate this order to avenge himself for your "insubordination"?'

Hideo shakes his head, not wavering.

'Baron Takahashi was the President of the Court Martial! Captain Ikeuchi took the officers into the court martial building!'

Cooper observes him, then looks at Matsugae, bemused.

'Something puzzles me, Lieutenant. You said that the mass beating was "unchristian". So how could you accept an "unchristian" order to execute these officers?'

Talbot and the Bench wait on the answer. Hideo thinks carefully.

'Like an Australian officer, Japanese officers had to obey orders. Are you not here, Captain, because you have been ordered to?'

The irony is not lost on Sheedy who looks down at his notebook. He puts a tick in the 'acquitted' column under 'Tanaka'. The column under 'Ikeuchi' already is full of ticks in the 'guilty' column.

Cooper withdraws to the table.

'No further questions at this time, Your Honour. But I do believe that this case cannot proceed any further without Lieutenant Shimada, the Legal Officer, who may be able to help us.'

Matsugae confers with Reid, then stands slowly.

'Your Honours, we agree with the prosecution's request and we would also like to call an adjournment in this case until the plea of dismissal on the twenty-nine listed defendants is determined.'

Cooper looks over to Reid who shrugs. It was a delaying tactic but legitimate as the plea had been entered before the Tanaka case. Maybe some other evidence would come to light. Perhaps they might get some information as to the whereabouts of Shimada, the Legal Officer. He was now the key. If Ikeuchi didn't crack in the meantime!

Roberts confers with the Bench then turns to Matsugae.

'The court is aware of the defence's existing plea and will grant an adjournment of twenty-four hours while the verdict is considered. As for Lieutenant Shimada, the court will make every effort to locate him as he now seems to be in great demand.'

Cooper mutters under his breath.

'However long it takes, Frank.'

Matsugae bows.

'Thank you, Your Honour.'

The court rises. Cooper turns to Corbett.

'Someone in Tokyo must know about Japanese court martial procedure, Jack. If we can't get Shimada, we'll have to get something!'

Cooper sees the despair in Corbett's eyes. When would they have any joy out of Tokyo? Cooper observes Hideo being escorted from the courtroom along with the others. How could he continue to prosecute after what he had just done? In any civil court, the case would be thrown out. Evidence extracted 'under duress'.

But if he didn't prosecute, someone else would. Would it matter, now that the Emperor, Takahashi and God knows who else were walking around free? And what of the twenty-nine on the list for dismissal here? Was the presumption of innocence being stretched too far? He sees Matsugae staring at him. Was he almost glad that there was some point of common agreement between them? There was no doubt about it. Tanaka had really thrown a cat amongst the pigeons. But did the pigeons know it yet?

Hideo stares out at the courtroom through the wire. An eerie silence hangs over the camp. He washes dishes in an open trough but is preoccupied with the words of the letter he is composing to Midori.

My love.

I am facing their justice. It supposes that a man is innocent until proven guilty. I was an officer. I carried out my orders without questioning them. If that is my crime, then I am guilty. And so is every soldier who ever obeyed the order to take another life in the name of God and country.

You once asked whether the destruction of our city was enough. I fear, it may not be. I remember the words of Dr Nagai on our wedding night. What he said about Nagasaki being the final sacrifice. Perhaps it is like General Miyamoto said to me. We have seen the hell, now we must endure the purgatory of these trials.

It is the thought of returning to you that fills me with hope.

Your loving husband,

Hideo.

He looks up to see Talbot watching him through the wire. Talbot looks around carefully then steps towards him. Hideo stops washing a plate and faces him. Talbot is hesitant, almost frightened.

'Is there anything, I mean, have you got everything you need?'

Hideo looks back to the huts. A group of prisoners are playing cards near the large overhanging tree beside the assembly hut. He looks back to Talbot, uncertain.

'Apart from my freedom? A Bible. Is it possible?'

'I have one. I'll bring it to you.'

Talbot looks around to see Keenan appear from behind a parked jeep. He ambles up, contempt slowly appearing on every feature as he steps out of the early evening shadows.

'Doing a bit of fraternising, are we, Talbot?'

Talbot snaps to attention.

'Sir!'

Keenan stands beside him, hands on hips, sizing it up.

'Haven't you got better things to be doing than chin wagging with these monkeys?'

He looks at Hideo with a malicious leer.

'Or maybe you'd like to be shacked up on the other side of the fence with your mate?'

Hideo steps forward.

'I don't wish to cause any trouble!'

Keenan spits at him.

'Piss off, Tojo!'

Hideo backs off, keeping his eyes on them as Keenan leans forward, a harsh audible whisper burning into Talbot's ear.

'You Jap loving Bible bashers, you turn my stomach! Forgive and forget!'

Keenan pushes Talbot back from the wire and walks off.

Hideo turns to see Reid approaching quickly.

'Lieutenant, Mr Matsugae wishes to see you immediately.'

In the defence's cramped hut, Ikeuchi sits, facing a stern Matsugae.

'There will be no more displays like the one today. Is that clear, Captain?'

Ikeuchi doesn't reply, but draws out a rolled

201

cigarette and lights it, blowing a cloud over Matsugae, who glares back at him.

Reid appears in the door with Hideo who is motioned to a seat beside Ikeuchi. Hideo takes his seat nervously. Matsugae adjusts his glasses, then takes out a fountain pen, placing it next to a blank pad. He looks up at them intently, his eyes searching for the slightest clues.

'I want the truth now from both of you. It is too late for anything less.'

Hideo glances to Ikeuchi. He can see the same contempt that he had just seen on Keenan's face.

Matsugae holds up the photos of the four flyers.

'Captain, Lieutenant Tanaka has sworn under oath that he saw you take these four officers to the court martial building? What happened then, inside the building?'

Ikeuchi ignores the photos, looks over Matsugae's head.

'You expect me to remember four faces from hundreds I saw? I had nothing to do with court martial. Baron Takahashi presided over the court martial. I was not present.'

Hideo shakes his head at Matsugae whose patience is razor thin.

'Again, Lieutenant Tanaka has stated that it was you who gave him the order to carry out the execution, following a court martial presided over by Vice Admiral Takahashi!'

Ikeuchi smiles cynically. Matsugae knits his fingers into a tight ball, face tightening in anger.

'You will please share the joke with us, Captain.'

'This is useless! We know what conclusion they have reached in my case! I do not see why I return to the witness stand to be roasted like a pig when . . .'

Matsugae explodes with unexpected ferocity.

'You are one of the most arrogant and unco-operative defendants I have ever had to deal with! You will do as I say! Is that clear? We all have a commitment to the future survival of Japan!'

Ikeuchi stands, shaking with rage, a savage guttural Japanese.

'No one speaks to an officer like this. Damn you! You believe you can win a war with clever words and colla-boration! That is not our "truth", Mr Smart Lawyer!'

Ikeuchi pushes past Reid who looks very unsettled by the outburst, distinctly feeling the 'foreigner'. Matsugae looks up at Reid, almost in despair. He gazes sympathetically at Hideo, then takes off his glasses and wipes the perspiration from his forehead. He nods to Reid as he rises from the chair.

'Lieutenant, the Major will ask you some further questions. But if you can give us some other piece of evidence, something . . .'

Matsugae suddenly seems very frail, very ancient. Hideo stares at him wide eyed as he turns from the door. In the fading light, very like those old peasants in a woodcut, gnarled, back groaning under the load of wood.

'You must think, Lieutenant. Your life could depend on it.'

Hideo and Reid stare at each other as Matsugae seems to shuffle out into the evening.

On the other side of the wire, Cooper strolls past the open barracks building. Australian soldiers relaxing out on the verandah, playing cards with Sheedy. A shortwave radio crackles on a table with a new song. Cooper stops, listens.

General Macarthur he a god, flowers grow where feet have trod,

Full of fire his speeches burn, tell the world I
  shall return,
Emperor he Macarthur's pet, rising sun begin to
  set,
Now we work for Yankee bum, eating horse and
  chewing gum.

Drinking rum and Coca Cola, rotting every
  molar,
For the rising sun working for the Yankee
  dollar . . .

Sheedy looks up at Cooper standing in profile.
Cooper turns to him. Sheedy grins knowingly at him
as he taps his fingers in time with the song. Cooper
walks on, drawn to the moon over the bay as the
song fades behind him.

Atrocities are all forgot, the General he wipe out
  the lot,
Now he sharpens all our swords, cut the throats
  of the Russian hordes,
Cardinal Gilroy, lovely man, say we quite forgive
  Japan.

As he reaches the edge of the grounds, he becomes
aware of Matsugae approaching with a guard. He
stops a few paces away, and bows to him. The guard
marches off.

'I apologise for the intrusion, Captain.'

Cooper walks along the edge of the bay, Matsugae
falling in with him.

'When I came to these trials, I told my people that
they must tell the truth, hold back nothing, no matter
what their rank.'

Cooper draws on a smoke.

'Good advice.'

They stop to observe a couple of fishing boats skimming across the water, the soft amber light of their naked lamps fusing with the silver shimmer of the moon.

Matsugae cannot look at Cooper but keeps his eyes on the boats.

'I feel a great shame for what happened in court today.'

Cooper turns to him, sees his struggle to admit this.

'I defended Vice Admiral Takahashi to the letter of the law. Now I find myself in a most difficult position.'

A silence. Cooper stubs out his smoke.

'Tell me, did you really believe that Takahashi was innocent?'

Matsugae faces him slowly.

'You must understand, Captain, that my duty was to defend him. But I feel great sympathy for your position.'

'You're not going to tell me that Ikeuchi is innocent?'

Matsugae suppresses an instinctive anger and shakes his head.

'It's Tanaka who's my concern now. There would be a great injustice if the innocent were to be branded with the shame of the guilty.'

'He may not be innocent, Mr Matsugae, but he is the only one who seems hell bent on following your instructions.'

Talbot runs up to them, out of breath.

'Captain, you'd better come quick.'

Cooper and Matsugae follow at a trot as Talbot leads them back into the prisoners' compound. A group of prisoners are gathered around a hut near the perimeter, jostling for a view of something inside.

Cooper and Matsugae make their way through the milling prisoners into the semi darkness of the hut. They approach Ikeuchi, strange patterns on his back becoming visible as intricate tattoos. He squats, facing a picture of the Emperor lit by a lamp, face up on the mat.

Cooper and Matsugae step around him as Talbot and other guards hold back the prisoners. Hideo and Reid enter, Talbot making space for them to squeeze through.

Ikeuchi's hands grip the handle of a crude knife embedded in his stomach. Blood drips through his fingers on to the mat.

His face is a blotchy, almost white mask. No hint of life or death. Around his eyes and down his cheeks, black smudges. His last 'face'. A message to his subordinates. This is the face of Lord Enya Hangan after his suicide in the great *Kabuki* play, *The 47 Loyal Ronin*. Would Ikeuchi's 'loyal *ronin*' now follow him in death?

Keenan pushes his way through the crowd with Sheedy and stares at Ikeuchi, squatting to feel the pulse in his neck.

He shakes his head at Cooper, embittered.

'The bastard. I had a special bullet for him!'

He pulls Ikeuchi down, falling with a thud on to the mat, blood and viscera pouring forth. Matsugae turns to the cowering defendants, his voice breaking with emotion.

'Your superior has defied the Emperor's sacred wishes. You were told. Do not do this. His shame is your shame!'

Hideo stares at Noburo and Matsugae, as if a chasm has just opened before him.

206

Cooper takes one final look at Ikeuchi's death mask then looks up at Keenan and the defendants, many with their heads bowed in respect.

'Get something and cover him. Get them out of here!'

Keenan snaps to it, herding the Japanese out with Talbot and the guards. Hideo leaves reluctantly, perplexed and bewildered.

Sheedy shakes his head at Cooper, a sense of the inexorable in his eyes. He watches Cooper and Matsugae exchange a long look. Where did the interest of both men now differ?

Cooper steps from the hut to find Sheedy waiting. They stand for a few moments, observing a group of Japanese standing off at a distance, all with heads bowed towards Ikeuchi's hut. The other defendants are gathered outside the huts as Talbot and the guards ransack them, upending bunks and belongings in a frantic search for other hidden weapons. Cooper continues on towards the Legal Corps HQ, Matsugae and Reid coming up behind him.

'Where's the honour in taking your own life?'

Sheedy trots after him.

'It was inevitable. His last grand gesture as a true believer. The Emperor. *Bushido*.'

'We can't resolve anything here. We hit them with the law and they strike back with this.'

'He did it as much to get back at what he saw as betrayal by his own people as he did to undermine you.'

Sheedy studies Cooper's face, frustration in every line.

'You've lost the organ grinder. And now, the monkey. Someone's got to get undone here. The brass won't have it any other way.'

'Strange to say, Sheedy, but that smacks of revenge.'

Sheedy shakes his head ruefully.

'It smacks of a big dose of reality, old son. You saw their faces, they've been reminded. Ancient "honour". It'll always triumph when they've got their backs to the wall.'

They reach the door of the offices. Sheedy looks back at Matsugae and Reid approaching quickly.

'We'd all better take a long hard look at those beliefs we hold to be self-evident. How far are you prepared to push them, really push them?'

Cooper's mind is on the compound. He nods to Sheedy and enters the building.

Sheedy stands aside, letting Matsugae and Reid pass.

He looks back to the camp. Whoever the patron saint of justice was in Japanese Christianity, young Hideo Tanaka had better start praying.

CHAPTER TWELVE

SHOWDOWN

Roberts looks up to see a delegation appear before him. He puts down the copy of the *Herald* that he is reading and stands to face Cooper, Matsugae and Reid. Keenan enters with the blood-stained knife wrapped in a cloth and puts it on the desk and salutes. Roberts looks at it darkly.

'Well, gentlemen?'

Cooper nods to Matsugae.

'Major, I am greatly ashamed to report that Captain Ikeuchi has just taken his own life.'

Roberts looks at Cooper. Their trial had just been turned upside down.

'I see. Sergeant, carry out a complete search of all the defendants' quarters. Remove any possible weapons. And I want a full report on how Ikeuchi got his hands on this.'

Keenan salutes.

'I've already started a search, sir.'

He exits quickly. Cooper looks down at the knife. His own blood was on it but he could never admit it. Matsugae wrings his hands in great anguish.

'I must confess, and Major Reid will confirm this, that I had some very strong arguments with Captain Ikeuchi just before his death.'

Reid nods confirmation, looking like he had just

been saddled with the heaviest albatross. Cooper shakes his head.

'I don't think you can take the blame for his death, Mr Matsuage. I believe he'd probably planned this all along. It was only a matter of when.'

His own part in Ikeuchi's demise would remain forever hidden. What price Takahashi now?

'Yes, Captain, but the rest of the defendants will now carry an even heavier burden of shame. I am very concerned about what might happen now.'

Roberts turns to a cabinet, produces a bottle of brandy and a glass, pours a shot for Matsugae and hands it to him.

'This will steady your nerves, Mr Matsugae.'

Matsugae takes it gratefully, downs it in one, licks his parched lips and hands the glass back to Roberts.

'Thank you, Major.'

'Rest assured, Mr Matsugae, that every precaution will be taken to prevent another occurrence like this.'

Matsugae bows, looks to Reid who gets the message.

'If you will excuse us, Major, we must resume our work.'

'Of course.'

They exit. Roberts examines the crude blade fashioned from a piece of jagged steel.

'Probably a fragment from one of our bombs dropped on the camp. A very unpleasant way to go, wouldn't you say, Bob?'

Cooper is pensive, only half listening. Roberts puts the knife down.

'It may be academic now, but Major Beckett is bringing the Legal Officer, Shimada, in tomorrow.'

Cooper is suddenly alert.

'Beckett? What kind of a mug does he take us for,

Frank? Even blind Freddy can see that it's a put up job.'

Roberts is not fazed.

'You wanted him. Now you've got him.'

'No thanks. I'm not putting tainted goods on the stand.'

'Beckett's gone to a lot of trouble . . .'

'I bet he has . . .'

'To get Shimada for us. It'll be the last straw if we throw him back in their face.'

'I want my objection to Shimada's status put on the record.'

'Object all you like, but you are going to cross examine him!'

'And I also want my objection noted for Sister Littell being made the scapegoat for Fenton's death.'

'Objection noted.'

Cooper salutes sharply. Roberts returns it angrily.

Cooper strides past the compound, pausing to look across to Ikeuchi's hut. Two guards stand on duty outside the entrance. It was probably on the verge of becoming a sacred site for the defendants now. Matsugae had said that he felt great sympathy for him after Takahashi's acquittal. He could not help feeling a twinge of the same for Matsugae, whose task now would be doubly difficult.

Yes, the implications of Takahashi's acquittal would soon hit home with full force. Maybe Beckett was handing him the perfect opportunity, thinking that he was going to keep the lid on Takahashi. Now he had to focus his anger, really not let anything past. It was time to hit it right out of the grandstand for six. Maybe even Matsugae would like to see that happen as well.

He turns to see Corbett running towards him with

a sheet of paper, deep in thought.

'Sir, I've got this from Tokyo Naval HQ. It took a bit of doing but it seems correct.'

He switches on a torch so that Cooper can read it. Cooper digests it for a few moments.

'You've really hit the bullseye, Jack!'

Corbett is still puzzled, and wary of Cooper who gazes over to the compound.

'I want you to take this over to Mr Matsugae and see whether he knows anything about it.'

Corbett is astonished by this suggestion.

'Sir?'

'Just deliver it, Jack. Believe me, this is really going to blow the roof off tomorrow.'

Corbett bundles it into his top pocket and walks off, totally bemused. Cooper sees the light burning in the hospital and heads for it.

Littell is carefully packing her files into a large chest, marking them with different coloured inks for ready identification. Cooper stands in the doorway, observing her thoroughness, though her movement is slow and appears reluctant. Cooper steps in, she smiles briefly at him. She continues packing. He glances around with a sense of regret.

'You don't have to take this. Roberts goes by the book. Turn it on him. You don't deserve it on your report.'

She shakes her head wearily.

'My work was almost finished here anyway. And no one's going to give two hoots back home.'

She puts the files on her desk, faces him directly.

'I've made that commitment we talked about, Bob. I'm going back to help those boys. I just can't walk away. Apart from which, there is a mountain of material in these files that has to be looked at by the tropical disease specialists. There'll be no shortage of work for any of us. What about you?'

Cooper produces a couple of smokes from his pocket, lights them, hands one to her. He is uncertain.

'You're surely not thinking of going to Tokyo?'

Cooper exhales slowly.

'If I'm ever going to finish it, really finish it. We've now lost Ikeuchi. Committed suicide. Hara-kiri they call it.'

She sees the anger and the guilt surfacing on his face.

'I'm tempted to make some biblical comment but I won't. Though, I don't think Beckett is going to let you within a mile of Takahashi.'

'I'm going to have a bloody good shot at it!'

There is a long moment as they take each other in. She puts down her cigarette and moves towards him. She puts her hand gently on his arm.

'Bob, there's a time to let go. I know how you must feel about losing those two bastards, but I'm afraid. Afraid that it'll just eat away at you, and even if you wanted to, you won't be able to stop. Ever.'

His eyes soften as he sees the deep feeling in hers.

'I suppose you're right.'

He stubs out the cigarette, feeling awkward and lost.

'Will you be based in Sydney?'

'That's the plan. And you?'

'I'll probably find a little nook in Philip Street. Have to get used to wearing a wig and gown again.'

She could picture him making a forceful point, the judge and the jury impressed with his advocacy. She hands him her cigarette.

'Sydney's not as big as you think. Never know who you'll run into.'

He smiles, although neither of them can wind it up.

'Guess not, when you look at it that way.'

He hands her back the cigarette. She takes one final puff and drops it in the ashtray and smiles at him.

'Well, if you ever need a nurse.'

Cooper nods reluctantly.

'If you ever need a lawyer.'

She smiles, seeing the need in Cooper and feeling her own. Both needs could be met. If ambition didn't get in the way.

She turns back to her files and sighs.

'I'll never get out of here at this rate.'

She resumes packing. Cooper exits, pausing at the door. She looks up but he is gone.

Shimada, in neat uniform, cap and horn rimmed glasses is escorted from a C47 by Beckett. Roberts waits apprehensively beside a jeep with two guards. Roberts sees the simmering explosion and salutes curtly.

'Major.'

Beckett returns it perfunctorily. As they drive off, Beckett doesn't mince words.

'Lieutenant Shimada will confirm that there was no court martial held.'

Roberts nods, choosing his words.

'I don't think Cooper is going to appreciate you turning up with Shimada, Major.'

'I don't give a goddamn what your Mr Cooper appreciates. And where did you find that guy, anyway? First he puts a looney in the dock, followed by a proven liar who's killed himself. Now this!'

'I think that Cooper understands that Takahashi's a closed book.'

Beckett gestures angrily to Shimada in the rear seat, who is apparently disinterested in the argument of the two men.

'This guy's going to make sure it stays shut!'

Roberts wipes perspiration from his forehead. The chills and fevers would soon be impossible to hide. He had been pumping quinine by the bottleful but it still seemed to come in waves, often at the most inconvenient moments.

As they drive up into the camp, they are observed with great interest by Keenan and defendants behind the wire. Corbett is already running to the Legal Corps offices ahead of the jeep.

Beckett leans over to Roberts as they drive slowly through a crowd of milling Ambonese villagers.

'Takahashi's been seconded to highly sensitive duties in the pacification of Japan. Anything upsets that applecart, we're talking civil war! Shimada's due back in Tokyo day after tomorrow. You've got us for twenty-four hours, Frank, and that's it.'

Beckett leaps from the jeep into the Legal Corps offices followed by Roberts and Shimada, escorted by the guard.

Cooper and Corbett watch from the open door of their office as Beckett strides past ignoring them. The trap was set. But who would spring it?

Across the courtroom, Cooper stares at Beckett who fixes his eyes on the President as the court resumes. Johnson takes his time adjusting his glasses, takes a sip of water, then looks up.

'Mr Matsugae. Major Reid?'

They stand. Matsugae very nervous, glances at Ikeuchi's empty chair. Next to it sits Shimada, alert to every action.

'In view of the death of Captain Ikeuchi, we have given new consideration to the defence's plea of dismissal. The court, as advised by the Judge Advocate, has looked at the individual and collective evidence against those defendants listed. The court finds that no prima facie case exists against eleven of the defendants named on this list. These defendants are free to leave this court.'

He hands the list to Matsugae, who appears relieved that he had achieved even this.

'The other eighteen so listed will continue as defendants in these proceedings.'

Matsugae bows.

'Thank you, Your Honour.'

He hands the list to Reid who nods to the eleven. They rise, puzzled, and are escorted out by two guards. The other defendants mutter amongst themselves, very apprehensive. Matsugae raises a hand to them, speaks quietly in Japanese.

'They have no case to answer. There is hope.'

Hideo looks glumly at the eleven marching back across the grounds. Was hope slipping away for him?

Keenan looks at Cooper, his anger naked. Cooper looks away, gazes at Beckett sitting as if bored by the whole proceedings. Cooper looks to Matsugae, who is aware of his gaze, but avoids looking at him.

Cooper was now at the wicket. It was time for revenge.

'The prosecution calls Lieutenant Shimada to the stand.'

Shimada, ramrod straight, takes his place in the chair and is sworn in. He presents Cooper with an amiable expression.

'Lieutenant Shimada, as Chief Legal Officer on Ambon, your duties included advising Vice Admiral

Takahashi on the convening of courts martial of prisoners?'

'That is correct.'

'Were you present at a court martial held for the Australian pilots Fenton, Smith, O'Donnell and Rogers?'

Shimada maintains his composure.

'No such court martial took place to my knowledge. In fact there were no courts martial of any prisoners during my three years on Ambon.'

Cooper looks at Beckett.

'Lieutenant, Vice Admiral Takahashi has stated that if pilots were captured here, they would have been the subject of a court martial. Is that correct?'

'Er, yes. I agree.'

'But how can this be when Japanese Defence Headquarters' policy was for all pilots to be executed without court martial?'

'I know of no such policy.'

'That was your law!'

'Technically perhaps but the Vice Admiral . . .'

Cooper suddenly holds up the rusted ID tags.

'The pilots were executed! An order must have been given by someone in command!'

Shimada's front is crumbling. Beckett's icy detachment is thawing. Sheedy leans forward, tasting blood.

'Perhaps, Captain Ikeuchi . . .'

Cooper smiles thinly.

'Yes. Or Lieutenant Tanaka took it upon himself and organised the whole show without anyone's knowledge or authority! Is that what happened?'

Hideo stands suddenly.

'That is not true. I acted upon the orders of the court martial!'

Roberts bangs his gavel.

'Resume your seat, Lieutenant! Mr Matsugae, if there are any further incidents like this, I will have your client removed from the court!'

'Yes, Your Honour.'

He turns to Hideo, issues a harsh, whispered reprimand. Hideo nods, very embarrassed.

Cooper turns back to Shimada.

'So, Lieutenant, who gave the order?'

'I do not know. But there was no court martial.'

Cooper notices him sneak a glance at Beckett. Cooper seems almost distracted and turns back to Matsugae.

'Your witness.'

Matsugae takes a folder from the table and approaches Shimada carefully, aware that he was about to cross-examine a fellow lawyer.

'Lieutenant, it is my understanding that in British military law, there are two types of court martial. An ordinary court martial and a field general court martial. Is there a similar division in Japanese military law?'

'As far as I am aware, there is not.'

Matsugae maintains his courteous expression.

'Then you have no knowledge of the Emergency Court Martial law?'

Shimada appears genuinely puzzled.

'Emergency Court Martial?'

'Yes. Prisoners could be executed without convening an ordinary court martial. As Chief Legal Officer, surely you must have known of this procedure?'

Shimada smiles noncommittally. Sheedy watches as Beckett leans forward, suddenly very interested in the proceedings. Roberts wipes the profusion of perspiration from his forehead and breaks the silence.

'The witness will answer the question.'

'I was the Legal Officer but Vice Admiral Takahashi . . .'

He catches himself.

'I know of no such procedure.'

Matsugae slides out a document from his file and hands it to Shimada.

'Lieutenant, please tell the court what this document states?'

Shimada adjusts his glasses, his expression now strained. Matsugae is now beside him looking down at the document.

'The heading at the top, Lieutenant?'

'Emergency Court Martial regulations.'

'On behalf of . . .?'

'Imperial Japanese Navy headquarters . . .'

'Tokyo.'

Shimada seems to be shrinking by the second.

'Tokyo.'

Sheedy watches Beckett edge forward, bursting to get his hands on the document.

'And the signature at the bottom of the page?'

Shimada reads nervously, the document shaking visibly.

'Chief Legal Officer, Imperial Navy Headquarters.'

'Your immediate superior?'

Shimada lowers his head, nods curtly. Then suddenly looks up defiantly.

'I have no way of telling whether this document is authentic or not.'

Beckett stands.

'I beg the indulgence of the court.'

Cooper stands instantly.

'Objection! Major Beckett has observer status only in this court!'

Roberts nods to the President.

'Let's hear what the Major has to say. After all, these trials can only proceed by full Allied co-operation.'

'I could be of assistance to the court by having our people in Tokyo verify whether this document is authentic or not.'

Cooper looks at Roberts dismissively.

'Be a shame to take them away from all those elusive boxes of records, wouldn't it, Major?'

Roberts hardens.

'Captain!'

The President looks over to Roberts, obviously annoyed.

'Major Beckett should be reminded that any documents submitted to this court are prima facie valid. If he wishes access to them, he will have to proceed through the proper channels. Once the court has finished with them.'

'But, with all due respect, sir, I believe that what has just occurred here points to collusion between the prosecution and the defence.'

Johnson seethes with anger.

'It is not your place to object, Major Beckett. And your proposition is preposterous!'

Roberts is left with no alternative.

'Please sit down, Major.'

The President makes some notes rapidly.

'Yes. We've wasted enough time on this sideshow.'

Beckett is torn between objecting further and resuming his seat. He returns to it, Sheedy gesturing to it, as if dusting it off for him.

'Please continue, Mr Matsugae.'

Matsugae glances to Cooper and returns the document to his folder.

'There is no need for further questions from the defence, Your Honour.'

He returns to his seat. The overture was over. Cooper would deliver the coup de grace. Cooper rises.

'I do have further questions, your honour.'

He steps across to Shimada. Beckett glares at him, objection written all over his face.

'Who would have drawn up the charges for the Emergency Court Martial?'

Shimada hesitates, eyes darting left and right.

'I do not know of such things.'

'The Legal Officer. Isn't that the case?'

Shimada is mute. Cooper raises his voice an octave sarcastically.

'You're a Japanese Legal Officer. You're under oath! You know what that means.'

Shimada is silent. Cooper stares at Roberts.

'Your Honour. Will you please instruct the witness to answer the question?'

'The witness is so instructed.'

Shimada looks over to Beckett who ignores him.

'I gave myself up voluntarily to the authorities. Where is the justice I expected?'

Keenan leers at him, whispering to a guard.

'Tucked safely where the sun don't shine, Tojo!'

Cooper positions himself between Shimada and Beckett for the final blow.

'I submit that an Emergency Court Martial took place!'

'No! It was legal!'

'Legal? So, there was a court martial?'

Shimada shakes his head vigorously, cast adrift.

'That's not what I meant!'

'There was either a full court martial held or the flyers were tried by Emergency Court Martial!'

'No trial! No trial!'

'As Legal Officer, it was your duty . . .'

'This is not so!'

'To draw up the charges . . .'

'Technically, yes . . . but . . .'

'To carry out either proceeding!'

Beckett leaps to his feet.

'Your Honour!'

Cooper gazes at him pitifully.

'It's no longer a question of written evidence, Major. My evidence is the witness himself!'

The President's voice booms out.

'Sit down, Major! Or I will find you in contempt of court! With a full report back to your superiors of your outrageous conduct!'

Beckett sits, absolutely furious.

Cooper turns back to Shimada, a quivering wreck.

'You and Vice Admiral Takahashi then selected Lieutenant Tanaka . . .'

'I had nothing to do with this! Nothing!'

Cooper isn't listening.

'To carry out the executions!'

'Captain Ikeuchi!'

'As punishment for his insolence in standing up to Takahashi and Ikeuchi!

'No! This was great honour!'

'A great honour? Bestowed on Lieutenant Tanaka by his superior officers?'

'No, you twist my words! I mean if . . . if he had been chosen by Vice Admiral Takahashi. If! A great honour for any officer!'

Cooper stands, gazing at the Bench, Matsugae, Hideo and finally Beckett, observing their sober absorption of what had just happened. Finally, he looks at Roberts, hearing the ironic echo of his words to him—

'I'll break 'em into little bloody pieces if you give me the witnesses on the stand!'

Cooper looks down at Shimada struggling to regain his dignity.

'Thank you, Lieutenant Shimada. I know what you meant to say! And so does this court!'

He turns back to the prosecution table, sees the admiration in Corbett's eyes and the shared understanding in Matsugae's face. He looks at Hideo, considers, then turns back.

'I call Lieutenant Tanaka to the stand.'

Hideo is sworn in, staring at Shimada who averts his eyes. Cooper stands back, observing him.

'Lieutenant, you have heard the evidence of your Legal Officer? What have you to say?'

'I say he is trying to evade his responsibility.'

'In the absence of a full court martial, do you believe the Emergency Court Martial procedure was followed?'

Hideo concentrates hard then nods his head.

'It must have been.'

'How would you know?'

Hideo looks at Cooper, sees the neutral expression on his face, notes the far less harsh tone. Almost as if Cooper was asking for his trust.

'I heard about this procedure at Naval HQ in Tokyo.'

'Do you believe that Ikeuchi acted on his own and gave the order?'

'No.'

'So who would have drawn up the charges for this "emergency court martial"?'

'Lieutenant Shimada. He would then make his recommendations for the death sentence to Vice Admiral Takahashi.'

'Who would then have given the order to Captain Ikeuchi who then gave it to you?'

'Yes.'

'If Captain Ikeuchi had not mentioned that there had been a court martial, would you have still followed the order?'

Hideo thinks carefully.

'Yes, because I believed I was carrying out a lawful order from my superiors.'

'You were dealing with the lives of four men. Surely it warranted something in writing?'

'Captain, we were at war. We had to place our trust in our superiors.'

'Even at the risk of having that trust betrayed by Takahashi when you confronted him over Ikeuchi's mass beating of the prisoners?'

'I respected Vice Admiral Takahashi enough to believe he would listen. I now know that I was wrong. Very few of us are blessed with foresight. We act at the time because we know instinctively that it is right.'

'Instinctively? The taking of these lives? Didn't it cross your mind for a moment . . .'

Hideo shakes his head vigorously.

'Many things went through my mind. Things I cannot understand fully. I was being honoured. But was I also being tested by, a greater power? To which was my greater commitment? To the Emperor or . . .'

Tears form in his eyes.

'I had never killed a man. Could I go through with this and not shame myself? Many, many things, Captain.'

224

Cooper and Hideo stare at each other. For a moment, just two men, not prosecutor and defendant, just two men. Then the voice returns.

'He's guilty under the law, Bob. But he's as innocent as the driven snow.'

Cooper looks around, considering his next question. He no longer wanted to be here. Justice wasn't really attainable here. And his own conduct had brought him to this point. He had to continue but he would find a way out as soon as he could. It was the end of all innocence.

'All those things, Lieutenant, and you never thought: "Am I being set up by Takahashi?" '

Hideo looks down, wipes his eyes, then looks up at Cooper.

'Even if I had, what could I have done? There are many questions that can never be resolved. Not in this court.'

The court is still, almost funereal. Talbot watches Hideo, a turmoil of emotions on his face. Even Keenan's smirk has been wiped off his face. Sheedy looks at Beckett who stares at the floor. Roberts and the Bench exchange a long look. Cooper sees it holding a multitude of emotions under the front of decorum and rectitude. Was it too late for mercy now? Or would 'somebody have to come undone'?

'One final question, Lieutenant. Were you stationed on Ambon in February 1942?'

'Yes.'

'Did Vice Admiral Takahashi order the executions of the three hundred Australian prisoners at Laha airstrip?'

Hideo thinks carefully.

'Vice Admiral Takahashi was here then. He would have to order such executions.'

'Thank you, Lieutenant.'

Cooper stares at Beckett, who avoids his angry eyes, then at Roberts, who looks to the Bench. Cooper steps back to his table, the exhaustion descending again. Sunset was approaching. Another night ahead, and the most difficult speech of his life. His closing address on Lieutenant Hideo Tanaka.

'The prosecution rests its case.'

Matsugae rises, nods to Cooper, then faces the Bench sombrely.

'The defence also rests its case, Your Honour.'

The President bangs the gavel with palpable relief.

'The court is adjourned until 0900 hours tomorrow morning.'

All rise. Cooper watches as Hideo is escorted out by Talbot. Corbett watches Cooper carefully, leans over respectfully.

'You let him off easy, sir.'

Cooper is only half present as he turns to watch Beckett and Roberts walk out together.

'Yeah.'

Matsugae steps over to him.

'Captain, Major Reid and I are very concerned about those who are acquitted. We fear that they might not be welcomed back in Japan. Perhaps you can help?'

Cooper looks at the earnest appeal in Matsugae's face.

'I'll take it up with Major Roberts, Mr Matsugae.'

Matsugae nods, very relieved. Cooper walks out slowly, mind racing.

As darkness falls, the eleven Japanese acquitted dress in Australian Army uniforms by simple lamplight in the interrogation hut. The uniforms are ill-fitting. But each makes the most of what he is given.

Keenan paces outside the hut in front of ten Australian guards including Talbot. He checks his watch, his face taut with anger. He glances at the silhouettes against the blankets drawn across the hut windows.

Hideo watches with other Japanese prisoners. There is a great disquiet amongst them. Talbot looks around, sees Hideo through the wire. His attention is distracted by the soldiers next to him, whispering to each other.

'What's their game?'

'They're shooting through.'

'Where to?'

'Back to Tojo land.'

Talbot turns again. Hideo stares at him. He hadn't given him the Bible. That must be the message. Talbot nods surreptitiously to him, then faces the hut again.

Two trucks appear out of the darkness, rolling up to the hut. They pass Sheedy, who stubs out a cigarette and falls in behind the second truck.

The trucks pull up in front of the hut. Cooper leaps down from one of them. Keenan, anger mounting, watches as Matsugae and Roberts walk towards the hut to confer with Cooper.

The door of the hut opens. Reid looks out at Roberts.

'Ready, Major?'

Roberts nods. Reid gestures inside as the Japanese emerge in single file, dressed in Australian Army uniforms, helped on to the truck by Cooper, Roberts and Matsugae. Beckett watches from the mess verandah.

The guards turn, rifles at the ready. The 'sumo wrestlers', Ikeuchi's former lieutenants, start a chorus of jeering which is picked up by the other defendants.

'Swine! Traitors! Death before dishonour!'

Some of them are worked up into a frenzy, jabbing the air with their fists. Hideo looks on, alarmed. Matsugae, on the other side, is distinctly aware of the insults being directed at him as well as the acquitted prisoners.

Cooper steps up beside Keenan who looks about to explode as the trucks rev their engines.

'A lot of bloody good men died for that khaki! Mates!'

He turns to Cooper, his eyes ablaze.

'You fucking lawyers!'

Cooper steps away towards Sheedy, drawing pensively on a cigarette. A soldier turns to Keenan, perplexed.

'What are they doin', Sarge?'

Keenan shakes his head, almost choked for words.

'I never thought I'd see the day! We're goin' to send 'em home. In our khaki. Just so they can slip past the Jap bully boys back home, just another bunch of *gaijin* white devils!'

The soldier looks to the others, all confused. Keenan roars at them above the jeering prisoners.

'The war never bloody happened, soldier! Tell that to your kids!'

The trucks drive off into the night, leaving behind a fading chorus of insults and invective. Keenan quick marches most of the guards back to the barracks watched by Sheedy, Cooper and Matsugae. Talbot and the two others are left to patrol the fence.

Matsuage turns to Cooper.

'Thank you, Captain.'

He walks off to rejoin Reid who is in earnest conversation with Roberts. Cooper looks across to the verandah where Beckett still stands expectantly.

Sheedy lights Cooper's cigarette cautiously.

'I don't know that you're goin' to win any converts with that stunt.'

Cooper is aware of Beckett's gaze.

'I don't know, Sheedy. But some might say it's a new world. New rules.'

Sheedy glances around to Beckett.

'New. Yes. Different?'

He watches as Cooper walks off and Beckett descends from the verandah to fall in alongside him. Sheedy hums to himself.

Drinking rum and Coca Cola, workin' for the Yankee dollar.

Beckett pulls Cooper up. They face each other.

'That was a pretty bold move, Cooper.'

Cooper draws on his smoke, alert to every nuance in Beckett's voice.

'Yep, you could almost convince yourself that the war never happened, as Keenan said.'

'What do you want, Beckett?'

Beckett gestures to the compound, now quiet.

'You seem to know. You can beat a man to the ground. But you've still gotta live with each other after you've settled your differences. We don't want to break their spirit, we want to shape them in our image.'

Cooper looks at the prisoners now sitting outside their huts, smoking, playing cards, in quiet conversation.

'They're going to throw centuries of tradition over for a hamburger and a Coke?'

Beckett ignores the jibe.

'Cooper, I just want you to see that there's a bigger game, a grander scale than what happened here on Ambon. You think none of this shit happened to our boys?'

Cooper is tempted to walk off but it seemed that

the hidden agenda might now just be revealed.

'Now I'm not saying that Baron Takahashi was innocent. But you should know that he's been given a highly sensitive appointment in the reconstruction of Japan. I can pull the man down from the moon if I wanted to but I can't give you Takahashi. The future of the world has to be worked out right now. We have to use people like Takahashi to serve our purposes.'

At last. Cooper takes a step towards Beckett. The anger is now a sharp beam focused through his eyes at Beckett.

'Yeah, ignore a little incident like the killing of three hundred Australians. Well, I don't have much time for Barons, Major. But let me tell you, the future of the world isn't worked out on a grand scale. It's worked out by ordinary people doing their ordinary bloody jobs. And you're not using Takahashi to serve your interests. You're serving his.'

Beckett sees the total unbending steel in Cooper.

'You really don't understand, do you?'

Cooper throws his cigarette into a ditch.

'All I know is that you're not leaving here with Shimada.'

'We'll see about that.'

'Yeah. We will. And here's a final thought for you, Major. You're not working out the future of the world. You're only preventing it from being different from the past.'

Cooper strides off. Beckett notices Sheedy in the shadows, a witness to the confrontation. If the Australian view prevailed, the world would descend into chaos. Machiavelii had said it so well:

> *Nothing is harder to manage, more risky in the undertaking, or more doubtful of success than to set up as the introducer of a new order.*

230

CHAPTER THIRTEEN

THE LAST STAND

Cooper works under the light of the parrafin lamp, increasingly agitated. He shuffles through a number of notes, feeling the growing futility of his task. He turns to Corbett, sorting through various statements.

'Jack, I don't know whether I'm Arthur or Martha. The more I work on this address, the more I sound like the defence.'

Corbett looks up, sympathetic.

'I wouldn't like to be writing it. Take a breather, sir.'

Cooper puts down his pen, takes a swig of Bintang beer and looks up at the swords, their edges a thin sheaf of gold in the amber light. If Tanaka believed. If the Bench believed Tanaka.

Such thoughts whirling in a diminishing circle. It had to sound like a prosecution's address. But almost plead for his innocence. At least for mercy. Keenan thought he'd never see the day when the Japs would wear Australian Army uniforms. Who would have thought that any of them would be faced with the dilemmas now staring at them?

He had achieved a bridge with Matsugae over Shimada. Beckett had to be put in his place. But with Takahashi apparently beyond reach and Ikeuchi dead, Tanaka's chances were now very slim.

Execution by the sword. A great honour. Did Tanaka really believe that one? Would the Australians believe that the execution of any Japs would be a great honour?

The enemy, the faceless vermin who had to be exterminated now had a face. Could Keenan or anyone else really look Tanaka in the eye and tell him that he deserved to die?

If one believed in the Bible, then Tanaka was not alone in the Garden of Gethsemane. Would his accusers also sweat blood over this one?

Cooper rises, stretches aching limbs, and walks out into the sultry night. He walks slowly across to the compound, drawn by the light outside one of the huts, prisoners gathered around, intent on a hidden figure.

As he approaches, he sees Talbot keeping a close eye on the group. Hideo comes into view, reading from a black book to the six prisoners listening with respectful attention.

Talbot becomes aware of Cooper and snaps to attention.

'At ease, Private.'

Talbot relaxes as Cooper lights a smoke.

'What's going on there, Private?'

'A Bible reading, sir.'

'Yeah?'

Strange how suddenly your thoughts could find an immediate echo in other events. Perhaps they were all caught in some net here, in which the differences could only amplify the common factors.

Talbot looks around nervously and leans over to Cooper conspiratorially.

'I gave them the Bible. At Lieutenant Tanaka's request.'

Cooper studies the ease with which Hideo expounds to the prisoners, some of whom had probably just been shouting insults at their departing comrades.

'I thought they found the answer to everything in their *bushido*, Private.'

'Appears not, sir.'

Cooper turns to him, puzzled.

'What denomination are you, Private?'

'Catholic, sir.'

'Maybe you understand this better than I can.'

'I wish I did, sir. Though Lieutenant Tanaka did say something that seems hard to believe, sir.'

'What's that, Private?'

Talbot keeps one eye on the group, another out for any surprise appearance by Keenan.

'Well, sir, he said that one of the great books on *bushido* was written by a Christian. A samurai he reckoned.'

'Doesn't sound quite right, does it?'

'No. But he seems to know about it all right.'

Cooper walks on, sorely tempted just to go straight over Roberts' head to Johnson and request that the court issue a warrant for Takahashi's re-arrest. That might be jumping the gun, because if Roberts bit the bullet and detained Shimada, it might be the first step to getting Takahashi back.

But he was still back at square one in trying to sound like the prosecution in Tanaka's case. Maybe Talbot had just given him a clue. Were the rigid differences of belief and culture the real issue or was it something more basic?

He looks up at the moon disappearing behind a dark mass of clouds over the bay. If *bushido* and Christianity were similar, as Tanaka claimed, then perhaps he could justify his action and not feel great guilt. Or maybe it was just the rationalisation of a desperate man, looking for any prop to justify himself.

Perhaps, then, he could not rule out Tokyo. If he really believed the arguments about responsibility, then perhaps he could participate in prosecuting Takahashi's own superior there. If the Yanks hadn't done a deal with him as well. Then there was the pull of Carol back in Australia. Which would win out?

Was that the reason that he could really sympathise with Tanaka's position? Both of them had been deserted by their superiors. Both of them had arrived too late at the truth. Both of them might share a burden. One man might die, the other would carry the burden of that death. Till his own death?

He had a job to do. He could always say that. Securing the conviction was the sole reason for which he'd been sent here. He looks around to see Reid taking a stroll at the edge of the bay. Reid notices Cooper and diverts from his path.

Reid offers him a smoke. Cooper accepts, takes a deep drag as Reid lights his own. They might have been adversaries before but that seemed irrelevant now. A long silence between them. Reid breaks it.

'Thanks for your brainwave earlier, with the eleven acquitted.'

'That's okay.'

Cooper sees the genuine appreciation of Reid. A barrier had come down, there was no doubt.

'And for the Emergency Court Martial. I think it proved both our points. And that's pretty bloody rare.'

It certainly was. Another unforeseeable irony of the whole proceeding. Reid becomes glum, looks over to the dark outline of the courthouse.

'I just hope the bastards don't stand on ceremony, Bob.'

'Sheedy reckons that someone's got to get it, Eric.'

'I shouldn't say this, Bob, but I reckon some of the guards here are far more deserving of a bullet than Tanaka. I mean, you read that statement by the Black Bastard and you just have to laugh.'

Reid suddenly adopts a mock sing song Japanese accent.

'I think prisoners not like me because I was always shouting air raid warning at all times.'

Cooper laughs softly then stubs out his smoke.

'Well, if they do stand on ceremony, the Judge Advocate General back in Australia might not agree with their finding.'

'True, but the Army may not feel bound to follow his advice in this case. As you've probably guessed already.'

Another silence. Cooper breaks it.

'What about Tokyo, Eric? Are you going to have the stomach for it after this?'

Reid considers a few moments, then shrugs.

'I don't know any more, Bob. If we've got an Australian President up there, I think we've got to give him all the support we can. But Sheedy's also told me a few things about what Beckett's said to you. It's pretty obvious that the Yanks have their own priorities. I'm no longer sure that justice is what they're all about.'

'Yeah, but somebody's got to keep the bastards honest, Eric.'

Who would it be? They stare at each other, both looking for a commitment that is not immediate. Already, they had both become cautious, guarded, reserved. Cooper looks around at the compound, now totally quiet. He hears the distant echo of Keenan's voice, the day of the mass grave opening. A day now so long ago—'You know what military justice is, Cooper? A bullet!'

'Well, gotta burn the midnight oil, Eric. I imagine Matsugae's not having much fun with this either.'

Reid nods agreement.

'Yeah. Good night, Bob.'

Reid watches him walk off, filled with a sudden regret. They never had much in common. This was the opportunity but it might just drive them apart. Guilt was now not limited to former enemies.

Hideo lies on his bed, pondering his fate. But nagging at him is the memory of his confronting Takahashi with the beatings of the prisoners, Takahashi's almost offhand response and then his outburst in court to Cooper. All that he had said was true. But he had exposed his own fatal weakness. He had accepted the order to execute the pilots. Why?

He had already told Talbot that he believed that *bushido* and Christianity were very similar. The notions of loyalty, maintaining your own integrity and avoiding shame in *bushido* had their equivalents in Christianity. The great book *Bushido: The Soul of Japan* by the famous Christian, Nitobe Inazo, had explained those parallels.

Suddenly, the story of Shimabara comes back to him. In the seventeenth century, 37 000 peasants and Christians in Shimabara and Amakusa had risen up in revolt against the Shogun's brutal repression of Christians and the imposition of heavy taxes. The Christians captured Hara Castle to which the Shogun despatched 125 000 troops to crush the rebellion.

They laid siege to the castle for over eighty days.

Eventually, all the Christians were annihilated along with the peasants. It was very similar to the massacre of the Jews at Masada. Except that the Jews had taken the 'very Japanese' way out. Suicide before the shame of captivity.

Those Japanese Christians had been prepared to die for their beliefs, to avoid shame and maintain their loyalty to Christ, their supreme lord, above any Shogun. Hideo had not. Why? Perhaps the same question could be asked of any Christian soldiers in the Shogun's force who were ordered to execute their fellow Christians. Would they have used the same defence? That they had been given an order by a superior officer? Or would they have become martyrs themselves, just like 'the enemy' in the castle?

Was not the difference in his case the fact that the pilots had violated the law and not that they were condemned because of their religious belief?

Was it his guilt that had driven him to surrender? Or was it the desire to prove his innocence? Perhaps the court would be driven by a 'blood lust', now that Takahashi was beyond reach, and with Ikeuchi dead.

But, Australia was a Christian nation. It had fought the war to defend those values. Surely, it would see in him the same dilemma facing one of their own soldiers. How could an Australian not accept an order like his and not be court martialled, if not shot, himself?

They must see this. Hideo feels for the crucifix beside his bunk. He must pray now very hard, asking God to open the eyes of the Australian court. They had seemed so fair and courteous to Mr Matsugae. They must be men with some feeling, some Christian compassion?

He had a future to return to. His love for Midori and his city to rebuild. A life to put all these horrors behind. He must pray to Our Lady, the patron saint of the Cathedral. She would protect him, she would show the court the mercy in their hearts. Just as he had protected Noburo from any trouble by not admitting his participation in the event.

In another hut, Noburo cannot sleep. He had indeed been very fortunate. First, Matsugae had saved him from the wrath of Ikeuchi and his bullies. Now, Hideo had shielded him from the wrath of the court. Why? He had not stood by Ikeuchi and had told the truth. Ikeuchi had been very cunning and had gotten himself taken out of the court deliberately so that he could not be questioned further.

But Hideo had drawn the line with him. Perhaps he felt quilty for leading the execution party? He was shouldering responsibility entirely. When it should be the Baron and Ikeuchi who should be facing condemnation.

Ikeuchi had known that Hideo had given him some Bible lessons in early 1945. His fanatical hatred of Christians had extended to the local natives, most of whom were Christian. The few Muslims on the island had been the ones who had acted as spies for Ikeuchi, telling him which Christian natives had been smuggling food into the camp.

He had seen the tortures visited upon these poor people for their 'crimes' in helping the dying prisoners. Ikeuchi had threatened Noburo with the same treatment. So he had agreed with Hideo that it would be wise to stop the Bible lessons for a time.

What a relief, now that Ikeuchi was gone, that Hideo could resume the lessons without the shadow of Ikeuchi falling over them. Many of them who had heard Hideo tonight could not help but admire his dedication and honesty. But his honesty? It might cost Hideo his life and it would save his own. Then again, had not Christ said: *greater love hath no man than he should lay down his life for his fellow man?*

Matsugae works by a lamp at the rough hewn desk in his hut. It was clear that his victory for Takahashi had now become a matter of shame.

He had feared for his future if Takahashi had been convicted. But now he feared for his soul if Tanaka could not be exonerated.

He had been plunged into an examination of actions which defied rational explanation. It was as if he were a doctor who had all the equipment and all the training, yet could not find the cause of the illness.

Who could explain the madness that had created the horrors on this island? Perhaps it was a kind of virus, an insidious infection that had entered the very core of Japanese society.

In one way, he was very privileged to be present at this 'post mortem'. Japan had come perilously close to total destruction. It could never afford to choose this road again.

But, if the Takahashis were to be the future rulers of Japan, it could turn out very badly. Presenting an 'acceptable Western face' and yet nurturing all the worst attributes of the 'old way' would only lead finally to international ostracism and, possibly, another war.

Very curious how such an event as this, and the dilemma of his client, Tanaka, should produce such a broad clarity of thoughts. Perhaps, he could be even more systematic with them and give them life in the form of a book about his experiences on Ambon.

Matsugae looks up, his pen poised over the blank paper. Yes, he had a duty to describe these events, both to satisfy his own need and for the information of the Japanese public. Many might be very hostile and it would be a bombshell for the diehards, but there was a 'tide in the affairs of men'. He had to swim with it. He could not drown in his own cowardice.

Forever hidden in that account would be his knowledge of the Prosecutor's 'indiscretion' in extracting the name of Tanaka from Ikeuchi and his own deeply felt guilt in probably pushing Ikeuchi to his final act. Perhaps there was some ancient love in the Japanese for 'truth' revealing something abstract, but a deep unease when it revealed their own selves.

He had thought about this deeply. Perhaps Cooper's sharing of the Emergency Court Martial information was his way of acknowledging the wrong. He could only hope that it wasn't too late.

Matsugae gazes around the faces of the Bench and Roberts with a mixture of apprehension and equanimity. Perhaps after Takahashi, they did not trust him. They might believe that he had concealed information. But such thoughts are a distraction now from his main task.

'The execution of these four officers was a terrible act of war. But it was an act carried out by the order of a superior officer. At no time in this case has Lieutenant Tanaka denied following that order.'

He looks directly at Roberts.

'Who gave that order seems no longer to be in doubt.'

Matsugae returns his gaze to Hideo seated beside him.

'In this respect, he is a true Japanese officer, completely obedient to his superiors and his Emperor. But unlike many Japanese soldiers, he carries an extra burden. He was, and remains, a Christian. As such he had a duty to examine his conscience.'

Hideo looks at the Bench, a sense of calm and detachment surrounding him.

'How many men who have taken on the military uniform to defend their country have been placed in this perplexing position? Where they must fulfil the demands expected of a soldier. Yet, they must also follow the demands of a higher authority?'

He lets the question hang before them. Hideo nods, pleased. His prayers were being answered in the words of his counsel. A sense of displacement suddenly overtakes him. The shock of memory. The smell of a jungle dawn.

He is dressed in full ceremonial uniform, a red sash across his chest. He kneels before a crucifix on the wall next to his bunk. A smaller crucifix hangs from a chain in his hands. He feels his hands tremble as he whispers to himself.

'Father, if it be thy will, let this cup pass from me.'

A sword slides into the chain from beside him, lifting it slowly from his hands. The chain rattles down to the hilt. Hideo looks up. Ikeuchi grins at him.

'Your men are waiting, Lieutenant.'

Ikeuchi lets the rosary fall from the sword, gazing at it, almost considering it like some venomous snake that should be despatched immediately. Hideo picks it up respectfully, brushes off his uniform, straightens himself, then follows Ikeuchi out into the dawn light.

Hideo, almost in a daze, makes his way to the car waiting outside the compound. He grips the sword at his side. Two staff officers bow to Hideo as they open the door for Ikeuchi and Hideo.

The four pilots, ragged and pale, are shoved on to the truck in front of them, their arms bound tightly with rope. They are shadows of their former selves.

Hideo turns to Noburo who gets in beside him. He sees the fear in his eyes. He must not show his own. But both of them had never killed a man before.

The car moves off. Hideo is not aware of their departure being observed by Jimmy Fenton, concealed in foliage nearby.

Matsugae's words are a distant echo as the car leaves the camp, following the truck along a rough jungle track.

'According to the prosecution, international law does not recognise obedience to superior orders as a defence. Nor does it grant immunity from punishment by carrying out such orders.'

Hideo looks up at Matsugae who appeals directly to the Bench.

'But can we expect officers given orders in a time of war to behave like judges? To weigh up the finer legal points? This case must be addressed in this light. Whatever separates us as nations, the responsibility to truth unites us.'

He picks up a Bible from the table.

'On this book, Lieutenant Tanaka has sworn his oath. He has told the truth, the whole truth and nothing but the truth.'

He takes a sip of water, his pulse racing and the

perspiration cascading down his face.

'He believed that the four RAAF officers had been tried by court martial and found guilty of a capital offence.'

He pauses, trying to gauge any response. Nothing.

'If this belief was, in the circumstances, reasonable, then I submit that Lieutenant Tanaka is entitled to an acquittal.'

He bows low to the Bench.

'Thank you, Your Honours.'

He sits, looking at Hideo, who seems locked in his own thoughts. Cooper takes his time, collecting his thoughts as he rises from the prosecution table.

Hideo looks out through an open panel in the court to the mist covered mountain in the distance.

Rays of early morning sunlight penetrate the gloom of the overhanging jungle, investing the old Dutch battlement with a mystical but threatening presence as it looms out of the mist above Hideo and the others.

Hideo stands before the four pilots, with Noburo and the other two staff officers beside him. The pilots muster all the dignity they have, standing before a long shallow grave, two shovels stuck in mounds of dirt at the end of it.

Hideo reads the execution order, very aware of Ikeuchi watching him. Ikeuchi stands next to the pilots, ready for any 'trouble'.

'You have been tried by court martial . . .'

Eddy Fenton, face swollen and contused, snorts loudly.

'That's a bloody lie!'

Ikeuchi swipes him with his gloved hand.

'Silence!'

He turns back to Hideo, but ready to deal with any more insolence.

'Proceed!'

Hideo, very unsettled by Fenton's outburst, looks to Ikeuchi, who nods contemptuously to him. Hideo looks back at the order, reading with great difficulty.

'You have been found guilty under international law and Imperial Japanese Navy regulations. The sentence is death.'

Cooper's voice brings Hideo back into the courtroom.

'It is true that international law doesn't recognise obedience to a superior order as a defence. It is also true that the defendant personally carried out the brutal execution of Flight Lieutenant Edward Fenton.

'This fact is not contested. The question for this tribunal is: Did he know that he was committing a crime? Or was he ignorant of the fact?

'It has also been established that the defendant was deceived by his superior officers. The most senior of those officers has since been acquitted on all charges by this tribunal.

'Through the evidence of Captain Ikeuchi and Lieutenant Shimada, it has now become clear that Vice Admiral Takahashi ordered the summary execution of pilots and destroyed all the records of his command.

'This evidence must be put to better use than to simply convict his junior officers.'

Hideo notices Cooper staring directly at Beckett.

'Officers of insufficient rank, presumably, to play any part in any grand postwar policies.'

Cooper looks back to Hideo and the other defendants.

'And if we were to follow the defence of superior orders back to its logical conclusion, then no one could be held responsible for this act. Except the Emperor himself.'

He looks back at Beckett and then the Bench.

'Is this the justice we seek in this court? No. We must determine the responsibility of his commanding officers here. For actions done in his name.'

He takes a step towards Hideo.

'Lieutenant Tanaka previously questioned the orders of his superiors. This time, he did not. His order to execute a defenceless prisoner was represented to him as a great honour in the Japanese tradition.'

They exchange a brief look. Hideo is pulled back into the past.

He, Noburo and the two staff officers bow to the four pilots. Blindfolds are then applied to each of them. The four pilots commence an emotional, final version of the Lord's Prayer. Hideo silently mouths the words along with them as the blindfolds are tightened.

Hideo is aware of Ikeuchi's scrutiny. Fear grips his stomach as he turns to face his chosen man, Eddy Fenton.

He looks up as Cooper turns towards him.

'The defendant surrendered himself to the judgement of this court, believing that he had been given a lawful order. If the order was not lawful, then the question this court must answer is: At that critical moment, could he have known that it was not lawful?'

Hideo sees Fenton pushed to his knees by a guard. He stands beside him, hand trembling on the sword handle.

'Has it not become clear, Your Honour, that although Japanese culture and military codes are

245

different from our own, it is a wider, more universal issue that we should grasp. It is the way in which the power of a brutal system can make accomplices of those who despise it.'

Hideo slowly draws his sword and gradually brings it up to full stretch, the blade catching the first rays of the sun flickering through the trees. Hideo's breath comes in quick bursts. His hands are burning through his gloves as the wavering sword hangs in the air, just as the sword of judgement was now hanging over him in the courtroom.

'But it is here in this court that we also guard the values that we fought this war to defend. That all men are equal before the law. None above it, none beneath it.'

Hideo's sword sweeps down, decapitating Fenton. Hideo stands back, shaking, sickened, in disbelief at what he had just done to another man. He looks at Noburo, lips trembling, tears flooding his eyes as Noburo takes his position beside the next officer.

Cooper gazes around, notices Talbot's face struggling to conceal his emotions, a struggle noted by Keenan with cynicism.

'We all acknowledge that the world must go on. But if the swift solution to the future of the Pacific and Japan can only be won at the expense of justice, then our grief and our anger at the barbaric treatment of prisoners of war will not be washed away in this century.'

He turns, gazes at Hideo with respect, then turns back to the Bench.

'If this officer is found guilty, I request that mercy be shown to him.'

Again, the court is filled with an uncomfortable silence as Cooper sits. Hideo stares straight ahead.

Tendrils of mist surround him as he throws flowers on the grave of the pilots. He turns and walks back through the jungle.

Roberts clears his throat, addresses the Bench.

'I will remind the Court that there must be a fundamental presumption of innocence uppermost in their minds when they are considering their verdict in the case of Lieutenant Tanaka.'

The President bangs the gavel with a singular gravity.

'This court is adjourned until further notice.'

Hideo looks across at Talbot walking towards him. He sees the smirks of the other guards who regard their contact with contempt.

Talbot ignores them and escorts Hideo out, watched by Matsugae and Cooper. Matsugae nods appreciatively at Cooper. It had been a very effective, if not masterful, final address. It had not avoided the issue of individual responsibility. Nor had it denied the horror of the act. But Cooper had given a context to Tanaka's action which would surely give the court much to think about. In fact the combined efforts of the defence and the prosecution would be likely to provoke some heated debate amongst the members of the Bench.

It also reminded him of some of the ideas in the Western existentialist writers he had been told about by his literary friends in Tokyo. They were said to be the new explorers in the areas of freedom, individual and social responsibility. Perhaps the trials might also throw some light on these issues, a beacon along the road from the darkness of war into the new world.

Cooper watches Beckett looking out at Shimada being escorted into the compound. Beckett turns, sees Cooper's look and meets it with a direct challenge. Cooper could not but allow himself an amused thought. Here was the US Federal Marshal come to take the local boy back to Washington, but the townsfolk and the local sheriffs were not going to surrender him. He was going to face hometown justice. And that was that.

But what of the big landowner? For whom the local boy was just a hired hand? Well, it was high noon for all of them.

Cooper follows a seething Beckett into Roberts' office and closes the door quietly. Beckett pours himself a whisky and takes a sip before facing Cooper and Roberts with an expression of invincibility.

'You guys. You have the chance to be part of something . . . important. And look at you.'

Cooper puts his satchel down, extracts a document and faces Beckett.

'What's the good of your bloody "reconstruction" if you're going to kick the guts out of the law?'

Roberts maintains a neutral expression. Beckett downs his whisky, pours another shot.

'You go after Shimada. You know what'll happen!'

Cooper looks at Roberts. Come on, Frank. Put your chips down. The fence is no longer standing, mate. Roberts takes the document from Cooper, looks at it, then looks up at Beckett reluctantly.

'Our hands are tied. Shimada's condemned himself out of his own mouth.'

Cooper takes a step towards Beckett, restraining his anger.

248

'Didn't count on that one, did you, Major? Fly in here with a trained prize witness we've been hunting for months. Neatly tucked under your arm. Tie up the loose ends. Just so we'd close the file on Takahashi? Nice try!'

Beckett's eyes narrow.

'You're the worst kind of pain-in-the-arse, Cooper. A fuckin' idealist! We've got a whole nation to keep in line, because if we don't, the Soviets will. Is that what you want to see? Face it, this is a whole new ballgame. Like we've never played before.'

Cooper shakes his head, feeling the hot tight ball in his chest glowing again.

'Nothing's changed from where I stand, Major. It's still run by a pack of bastards. You know. I came here to indict a nation but now I can see you can't condemn a whole race for the crimes of individuals. However, someone's got to be responsible. And someone's got to pay the price!'

Beckett looks at Roberts for support but finds no comfort there. Roberts has his head down to the document, concealing his turmoil. The moment of decision.

'Well, you've got your man. Shimada leaves with me in the morning.'

Roberts finally signs the document and hands it, grim faced, to Beckett who scans it, realising the gravity of the contents.

'I must warn you, Major. This island is under Australian jurisdiction, any attempt to remove Shimada will be met with force. And you have in your hand a warrant for the re-arrest of Vice Admiral Takahashi. Please see that it is duly served.'

Beckett throws the warrant back on the desk and leers at both of them, a sense of megalomania rising.

'You guys think you have the muscle to whup me on this? You're looking at the champ!'

Cooper grins. The Marshal was walking out of town empty handed. Very embarrassing.

'Take your word for it, "champ".'

Beckett straightens his coat, looking for a way out of this with some dignity.

'You haven't heard the last of this.'

Cooper lights a cigarette.

'Surprise me.'

Beckett exits, slamming the door behind him. Cooper shakes his head.

'I can't believe we fought a war with those bastards.'

Roberts slumps on the chair behind his desk. Relief and great disappointment as he studies the warrant thrown back by Beckett. His berth in Tokyo was no longer a foregone conclusion. He looks up at Cooper, struggling for the words.

'I think it's going to be a bumpy ride from now on.'

'You and me?'

'Australia.'

Cooper studies him. Roberts had shrunk. He was now like a man who had surfaced too fast and was trying to hide the agony of the 'bends'. The narcosis of power and ambition which he didn't know he was suffering, till he reached the surface, the top. That was the fatal illusion.

Cooper picks up the warrant, returns it to his satchel, stubs out his cigarette.

'Thanks for Takahashi. And Shimada.'

Roberts nods, pale, concealing a trembling hand under the desk.

'I don't guarantee getting Takahashi back here.

But Shimada is all yours. The rules, Bob. They're all we've got.'

Cooper smiles thinly, salutes casually and exits.

Ambon had been Australia's 'Alamo'. Now it was Beckett's.

Cooper emerges into the evidence room, deserted except for Sheedy and Corbett in quiet discussion beside the map. He steps up beside them, produces the warrant for Takahashi. Corbett takes it, studies it with great pride. He hands it to Sheedy, who grins at Cooper.

'Maybe they'll ask him to hand back his DSC, eh Captain?'

Cooper looks at the warrant, then looks out at the compound. He turns back to them, uncertain of his reply. This last 'lap' had been the most gruelling of his career.

'It probably won't help Tanaka.'

Sheedy and Corbett are silent. Sheedy hands the warrant back to Cooper.

'Whatever happens, Captain, I think a few people have learnt some lessons out of this. I'd like to buy you both a beer.'

Cooper smiles sadly.

'Thanks. I don't know what I would have done without you both.'

CHAPTER FOURTEEN

JUDGEMENT

Hideo, stripped to the waist, works with Noburo and a party of four other prisoners, thatching the roof of a new hut. They work in silence, with precise fluid movements, imbued with a common purpose. Hideo is pleased with the progress they are making and reaches down to hammer a nail into a cross beam before signalling for more thatch to be laid over.

As he finishes, he stands and observes the half finished roof. It felt good to be able to use his hands again. How would the reconstruction of Nagasaki cathedral and the city be progressing? It would be emerging from the depths of winter and the work would surely be picking up speed. He longed for some word from Midori. But the postal system in Nagasaki and Tokyo would be like much else— needing to be totally rebuilt.

His drifting thoughts are interrupted by a shout from below. He looks down to see Talbot, in singlet and shorts, standing ready with a rough wooden cross attached to a rudimentary pulley.

'Okay?'

Hideo points his index finger up. He nods to the others who wind up the rope carrying the cross. Hideo smiles at Noburo as the cross reaches roof level. Suddenly he becomes transfixed by the cross. He feels his hands trembling, a cold sweat, the zephyr of memory sweeping across his skin.

It becomes the stone head of Christ, hovering from the pulley under the cobalt blue sky of Nagasaki. The challenging dead eyes. The final, gut wrenching realisation. The head had been decapitated from the statue.

Dr Nagai's words are now closer than his breath.

'This was the *hansai*—the burnt offering, the one pure lamb that had to be sacrificed on His altar, so that millions of lives could be saved.'

Had not Christ sent him a message that day? How he could not avoid his fate? How it was part of that sacrifice?

That was the meaning, the personal meaning hidden deep within those words, which seemed so astonishing and so incomprehensible on his wedding night.

He turns back to see Noburo and the others staring at him as the cross dangles beside him. He takes it, unties the rope and places the cross firmly on the mounting at the roof's edge. He looks down at Talbot, gives the thumbs up and shakes hands with his comrades.

Suddenly, shouting from the compound. All eyes turn to a Japanese prisoner and two Australian guards trying to break up a fight between two Japanese swinging fists and screaming abuse at one another. Hideo shouts down to Talbot.

'Jim, it is the sun. It turns them, how do you say?'

Talbot considers a few moments, then grins.

'Troppo.'

Hideo is highly amused by this description.

'Troppo! Troppo!'

He does a little singsong jig on the roof.

Talbot is not amused.

'Stop it, Hideo! It's not funny!'

Hideo loses his balance and slips off the edge of the hut. He lands on Talbot with a thud, who falls sideways with him, landing hard up against a small sago palm.

They get to their feet, slightly shaken, dusting themselves off. The others watch with concern. Hideo bows to Talbot.

'Are you all right, Jim?'

Talbot feels a tender spot on his leg, winces.

'Yeah, I'm okay. You?'

'Yes, I am okay.'

Talbot shakes his head, looks over to the fight now broken up then back to Hideo.

'None of it's funny. Don't you see?'

Hideo is suddenly serious. He looks up at the cross on the hut.

'Yes, Jim. It isn't. And it is maybe too late for me now. It was even too late when Ikeuchi told me that I had been honoured with the execution. Was I the instrument of God? Or only the Emperor?'

Talbot shakes his head, suddenly distraught.

'I don't want to see you die.'

Hideo sees the deep feeling in Talbot's face. He turns away, absorbed in his thoughts.

'We're all sworn to obey orders, Jim.'

Talbot feels a great apprehension, as if Hideo and himself were being drawn to something final together. Would there be any choice? Or would it be decided for them? He nods.

'Yeah. I don't know what I would have done.'

The gong is rung loudly. The Japanese head for a line leading to a table where Australian guards serve soup and vegetables from a large pot. Talbot

254

nods to Hideo and makes his way back through the milling prisoners to the mess.

In the mess, soldiers eat at tables, their conversation muted. Keenan is seated at one table, dunking bread into gravy and talking at the same time with two soldiers.

Talbot enters, walks up to the serving table, passing Keenan's table. Keenan leans over to the two soldiers, whispering. They burst into laughter.

Cooper, at a table by himself, picks up on it. Talbot, instinctively aware of the laughter being directed at him, steps up to the servery. He takes a tray and stands before the serving soldiers.

One of them grins to his mate then sniggers at Talbot.

'Sorry, Private. No "fish" on today.'

Talbot stares at them, picks up a bread roll and some fruit and heads for a table, which is almost fully occupied by guards. He sits. Without a word, the soldiers seated next to him rise and walk away. The 'isolation' of Talbot is carried out with perfect army precision.

Keenan stares across from his table, with the knowing look of one who has orchestrated the move. Keenan looks to Cooper for tacit support. In return, an icy stare.

Cooper turns to see Roberts enter and take up a vacant table away from the others. They were both in suspended animation. The trial of the others would proceed. But the result almost didn't matter now. The Tanaka case had tipped the scales.

Cooper rises, steps across to Talbot.

'I hear that you're helping build a chapel for the prisoners?'

Talbot looks up, surprised.

'Yes, sir.'

Cooper fixes Keenan with a challenging look.

'Any problems with supplies, let me know.'

Talbot gazes reluctantly at Keenan, nods nervously.

'Yes, sir.'

Cooper glares at Keenan then exits. Talbot returns to his food, pleased with this unexpected alliance.

In the special hut allocated for the Bench, the President paces agitatedly. Trays of food remain untouched, as the other three glumly review the transcripts of evidence.

Major Graham shakes his head despondently.

'It all comes back to Takahashi. Shouldn't we wait and see what happens with the Americans again?'

The President is grim faced.

'Raking over the coals of Takahashi isn't getting us anywhere. And from the behaviour of Beckett in court, I'd say that the Americans 'll do anything they can to keep their hands on Takahashi. No, I'm afraid we've got to look at Tanaka closely. Whether he could have done something to verify that a court martial had been held.'

Captain Patterson studies his notes, shakes his head, puzzled.

'Cooper did bring the house down with that "Emergency Court Martial" evidence. And Tanaka did say he'd questioned Takahashi's orders before.'

Johnson takes a sip from a mug of tea, stops pacing.

'Precisely. So if he knew Takahashi was in charge of the court martial, why couldn't he have verified its decision?'

Graham considers a few moments.

'Perhaps he'd burnt the written orders immediately. He was covering his tracks all along.'

Johnson nods, sighs heavily.

'We're all at fault here. He's the biggest con man this side of Tokyo. And we gave him the benefit of the doubt.'

An uncomfortable silence. Graham breaks it.

'I don't think we'll be alone in decisions like that. There'll be tribunals from here to Tokyo who'll be acquitting blokes who should be going to the wall. But I think Cooper made a very important point . . .'

Johnson cuts across him, anticipating him.

'That one about "the brutal system making accomplices of those who despise it"? Yes, it's one that really does apply to Tanaka. But we're still operating with international law and superior orders are no defence.'

Graham stares out at the gathering dusk. The Army and the public wanted scalps. Of that, no doubt. But whose conscience would be satisfied with this 'guilty' verdict? Such thoughts could run riot, poisoning the legal process. He turns to Johnson who puts down his mug of tea, his neatly combed silver hair now splitting into sweat soaked strands, the dishevelment of real anxiety.

'Ted, we have to face one undeniable fact. Four of our officers were executed—and someone has to be brought to book for that.'

They stare at each other. Nothing finally resolved.

In his hut, Hideo writes by candlelight, imagining Midori walking by the cathedral, the reconstruction well advanced. The flowers blooming again.

Even a young Australian guard, Talbot, who has been friendly to me, believes this is so. If there has been any wrong doing in this matter, Takahashi is the one who must answer for it.
I had to tell you this, finally, as I could not bear the shame of hiding it from you. I know that

you will understand. I put my trust in God. He
will protect me.

He looks down at the photo of Midori, with a
sudden sense of foreboding.

I have only your photo. But soon, I will see
those real eyes, shining with love, again.

Hideo puts down his pen, rereads the letter to
himself. He looks up, realises he is not alone. Talbot
is in the doorway.

'I thought . . . maybe . . . you'd like to talk . . .'
Hideo folds the letter slowly.

'I was writing home.'

Talbot turns to leave. Hideo stands, gestures to
a chair. Talbot looks back out the door nervously.

'I can't stay long. Sergeant Keenan . . .'

Talbot steps in, takes the seat. He looks down at
the Bible with the letter to Midori on it. Her photo
beside it. Talbot picks it up.

'She is very beautiful.'

'Yes. Her name is Midori. My wife.'

'And you are both from Nagasaki?'

'Yes.'

Talbot puts it down, sombre.

'I heard that the city was totally destroyed . . .'

Hideo is very quiet.

'Almost, yes. I keep asking myself, Jim, how a
Christian people could justify . . .'

He looks at Talbot, whose young face is so
innocent. Could anyone remain so in this world now?

'It is strange, Jim. I am here, charged with
executing men who bombed civilians. But no one
is charged with the bombing of my people . . .
civilians. Tens of thousands. Shadows on the ground.
My parents and sisters . . . turned to ash in an instant.

One moment laughing happy people . . . the next . . .'

Talbot cannot face him, lowers his eyes. Hideo lowers his voice to a whisper.

'Your people say that this Ambon camp was hell. They have no idea what hell really is.'

Talbot sits, as if in a trance, then picks up the letter.

'They open all your mail before it leaves here . . .'

Hideo takes the letter gently.

'Good. We were soldiers doing our job under impossible conditions. Your superiors should know how we feel.'

Talbot rises slowly, scanning the grounds through the small window.

'Right through this, I kept asking myself what I would have done if I'd been in your shoes.'

'How did you answer yourself?'

Talbot shakes his head, struggling.

'I haven't. I mean, I swore to serve God, King and country. So, I don't know what I would have done.'

He hovers for a moment, touches the Bible with a faint smile and exits, more disturbed than Hideo.

The work on the roof of the 'chapel' hut is almost complete. Hideo and Noburo survey the attap thatching with satisfaction. Talbot climbs a ladder, checks the firmness of the attap layers and gives them the thumbs up.

A shout from below. Keenan.

'Hey, Tanaka, the headmaster wants to see you. On the double.'

He jerks his head towards the courtroom. Talbot sees the calm in Hideo's eyes, feels his own heart racing suddenly. The moment of truth. Or travesty?

Hideo is escorted by Talbot into the court. They stop before the empty Tribunal bench. Johnson and the others enter. Cooper looks across to Matsugae and Reid, who catch his glance. A look of shared hope, watched by Sheedy, pen and notebook ready.

Johnson sits. The court is still. Talbot feels the sweat pouring down his arms, moistening his grip on the rifle butt. Johnson looks up, adjusting his glasses as he reads from a single sheet.

'The court has given lengthy consideration to the case of Lieutenant Tanaka. Particularly in respect of possible mitigating factors surrounding the question of whether or not a court martial of the four officers was held. And whether or not he was aware that he might be committing a crime.'

Matsugae feels the knot tightening in his stomach. It is too much, this tension. How calm Tanaka seems. He is a true officer.

'This issue aside, there can be no doubt that the defendant carried out the execution of Flight Lieutenant Fenton.'

A pause as he looks down at Hideo. Cooper feels that galvanic current on his skin. This is it.

'It should have been the responsibility of the defendant to confirm that a legal court martial had been convened and that a legal order had been given pursuant to its decision.'

An eye cocked towards Hideo, who lowers his, feeling the path of the decision.

'Clearly, the defendant did not so inquire. The Emergency Court Martial as submitted is not recognised in any form by international law nor is it in accord with natural justice.'

Matsugae glances to Cooper who shakes his head slightly. Sheedy's pen is at the ready. Keenan glances to Talbot, a knowing grin.

'Accordingly, this court has no alternative but to

find the accused guilty as charged.'

The pen ticks. Cooper lowers his head. Matsugae feels a wave of grief rising up from his stomach. Talbot's hand trembles on the butt.

Johnson takes off his glasses, glances at the other judges then looks back to Hideo, seeming to struggle for the words.

'This is a capital offence. The sentence is death.'

Hideo closes his eyes momentarily. The Christ head appears from out of the darkness—*Thy will be done.*

Talbot looks to Keenan who smirks trimphantly. It was not over yet.

Noburo hangs his head. The shame. When he was equally guilty.

Cooper looks across to Corbett and then to Matsugae who rises with difficulty, as if the weight of the entire world had just been thrust on him.

'The defence will lodge a petition against the findings and the sentence, Your Honour.'

Roberts confers briefly with the Bench. Hideo feels the anguish of Talbot next to him. Roberts turns back to Matsugae.

'A petition is so granted.'

A curt bow.

'Thank you, Your Honour.'

Hideo bows and is escorted out by Talbot. Johnson looks over to Cooper.

'The trial of the other defendants will proceed. Captain Cooper?'

Cooper rises, looks over some documents and hands them to the orderly.

'The prosecution calls Lieutenant Noburo Yamazaki to the stand.'

Matsugae looks around and nods to Noburo who

rises, suppressing his panic. Would he now be found out?

Talbot stops at Hideo's hut, the anguish paralysing his face. He turns away, watched by Hideo as he heads back to the courtroom. It seemed as if he had just lost any sense of his role as guard to the condemned man.

Cooper sits alone in his office, pondering a blank piece of paper. He takes up a pen suddenly, writes quickly.

Dear Carol,
I had hoped to get a longer letter off to you but you well know the pressure I'm under.

I'd like to say, firstly, my thanks again for Jimmy Fenton's presence in court. Now that the mass trial is in full swing, his statement is of great value in indentifying the leading Japs involved in the atrocities.

We've had one death sentence; Tanaka, the young Christian. It's on appeal but Eric Reid and I don't like his chances. Ikeuchi is the one who should have got it. But he'll probably be condemned posthumously. Cold comfort.

This is a roundabout way of telling you that I will be going to Tokyo. We've got Roberts to sign a warrant for the re-arrest of Takahashi. I'll have to see it served up there, just to make sure that Beckett doesn't interfere again.

I probably won't stay for the major trials but will head back to Sydney as soon as possible.

Let me know where you'll be. My thoughts have been with you and I hope you're well and adjusting to life in 'civvy street'.

Please write if you have a moment.

All the best (and a kiss!)
Bob Cooper.

Cooper re-reads it carefully. Maybe a little too dry but then again he had had his share of 'confessional' moments with Carol. She would understand. He signs it quickly and then returns to the mountain of files before him.

The following morning, Talbot and Hideo work with the four prisoners in assembling some rough benches and an altar of planks inside the hut. The Army chaplain, Reverend Martin, had agreed to hold a ceremony in the hut that afternoon.

Hideo keeps glancing nervously to the empty courtroom. Noburo had kept very silent about what had been happening. Probably waiting to ride it out. He might even be acquitted.

Matsugae and Reid appear in the door of the chapel. Hideo looks up, bows to them. Matsugae steps inside the door, admiring the carpentry work, then faces Hideo.

'Major Roberts wishes to see us, Lieutenant.'

Hideo looks back to Talbot who immediately picks up his rifle from a wall and follows them out. Hideo sees Noburo watching them as he is escorted out of the compound. He is standing in a line with the other defendants about to be escorted into the court. Hideo whispers to him as they pass.

'*Inotte kudasai.*' (Please pray.)

Noburo looks away, bewildered.

In the office, Hideo salutes Roberts who stands before his desk, grim faced. Talbot watches as Roberts picks up a document, coughs officiously and reads.

'In the case of Lieutenant Tanaka, the Confirming Authority, after studying the advice from the Judge Advocate General and the defence's petition, has

263

decided that both the finding and the sentence should be confirmed.'

Roberts looks up.

'The sentence will be carried out tomorrow at first light. I'm sorry, Lieutenant. Mr Matsugae. There is nothing further I can do.'

Hideo looks to Matsugae, who bows, his face ashen. Hideo salutes and walks out with Talbot, averting his eyes from Talbot's stricken gaze.

Matsugae stands as if transfixed. Roberts hands the sheet to Reid who passes it to Matsugae, who reads it slowly. Reid shakes his head.

'It's a bloody travesty, Frank. They haven't followed the Judge Advocate General's advice. That's unheard of.'

Roberts looks at them, trying not to appear as the Pontius Pilate of the moment.

'I agree, Eric. But there's nothing I can do.'

Matsugae takes the paper, places it in a file, turns to walk out, then turns back.

'Major, I would like permission to be present tomorrow along with Captain Cooper.'

Roberts looks at Reid, caught on the hop.

'There's no precedent for that, Mr Matsugae, but I have no objection to your request. I don't believe Sergeant Keenan will have any objection.'

Matsugae bows then leaves. Reid lingers a few moments, his ruddy face now a deeper shade of red.

'I don't know that Bob or I will be up for Tokyo, Frank.'

Roberts nods, then resumes his seat. So much gained, yet so much lost. Reid exits, slamming the door. Roberts picks up his pen. The letter to the Army Minister lies before him. He had couched it in his best diplomatic legalese. He just hoped that the Tanaka case did not cause any further waves. Damage control was now imperative.

Matsugae catches Cooper as he walks from his office with Corbett, laden with files. He hands him the sheet of paper. Cooper reads it then hands it to Corbett slowly who uses his free arm to read. Cooper senses the utter desolation in Matsugae's halting voice.

'I want to thank you, Captain. For your fairness and your sense of justice in Lieutenant Tanaka's case.'

They stare at each other. Cooper shakes his head, almost at a loss for words.

'We both did our best, Mr Matsugae. I'm sorry it's turned out this way.'

'I have asked Major Roberts whether I can attend tomorrow morning and whether you could accompany me, Captain. He was agreeable . . . would you?'

He trails off, choked with emotion.

'Of course!'

Matsugae holds out his hand to him. They shake. Matsugae turns and walks out into the light.

Sheedy steps across from his desk in the office and takes the sheet from Corbett, studies it, drawing deeply on a kretek.

'The sacrificial lamb.'

Cooper strides out the door, Corbett in tow. Sheedy grabs his jacket and notebook. He stops, looks over at the photos of Takahashi and Ikeuchi, repeating to himself bitterly.

'*Musi*. Not guilty.'

As night falls, Talbot paces on duty outside the wire surrounding the chapel hut. He is in a great state of agitation. He watches anxiously for Keenan but there is no sign. He turns suddenly. Hideo is at the door, letter in hand. He approaches Talbot, hands it through the wire to him.

'Here is that letter to Midori.'

Talbot slips it into his jacket.

'It won't be opened, I promise.'

A long awkward silence. Hideo sees his avoidance of eye contact.

'You have been ordered to join the firing squad, Jim?'

Talbot faces him, distraught.

'How did you know?'

'Sergeant Keenan, he made certain I knew.'

Talbot's face is a sudden mask of fury.

'He can order me on to the squad. Nothing in the world's going to make me pull that trigger!'

Hideo closes to within a couple of feet of him. An almost consoling tone.

'You are a soldier, Jim. You have to obey the order.'

Talbot's shaking hands are on the wire. Hideo lays his hands over them, willing him strength.

'No evil will I fear.'

Talbot nods slowly, remembering.

'Though I walk through the valley of the shadow of death . . .'

Hideo and Talbot lock eyes.

'No evil will I fear.'

Hideo looks across to Cooper, standing off at a distance, then smiles sadly at Talbot.

'I will have a new church, Jim. Its roof will be the sky, its floor will be the fields and flowers and I will be with God in his new church.'

Talbot looks around to see Cooper approaching, then turns back to Hideo, his face now a continual tremor of emotion. Cooper appears beside him.

'Private, could I talk to the Lieutenant alone?'

'Sir.'

Talbot walks off slowly, glancing back to Hideo who throws him an encouraging smile. Cooper stands, feeling an awkward silence descending. Finally, the words come.

'Maybe it's too late for this. But I want you to know . . . the Bench's decision. It wasn't . . .'

Would he say it? Could he admit it? He had set out on a voyage, the passage would be clear and swift. He hadn't counted on meeting the dark, treacherous waters within. Where was the compass for him? Where was it for any of them, now?

Hideo sees Cooper's turmoil, looks him straight in the eye.

'Your people must have their sacrifice. We are only accomplices, Captain. That's all we ever are.'

Cooper hears the echo of his closing address, the words that fell on deaf ears. Hideo pauses, smiles gently.

'When I am gone, put this behind you. I do not want my death to destroy another man.'

Cooper has no answer to this. Hideo holds out his hand. Cooper takes it through the barbed wire. They shake firmly.

CHAPTER FIFTEEN

BROTHERS IN ARMS

Hideo reads Talbot's Bible by the failing light of a candle. The last candle flickering in a soft breeze through the window of the chapel hut. Streaming on to him is the powerful silver beam of a full moon. The last moon.

'The Gospel According to Matthew', it was always his favourite. Now it would be his last comfort. The Christ who appeared on those pages was a man of great courage, of compassion and a warrior in the name of his Father. There was no hint of compromise or weakness in him. Had he not predicted many of the things that Hideo had seen? The *wars and rumours of war*?

Could it be that Nagasaki was the sign of the last of days? *When the Son of Man comes, it will be like the lightning that springs up from the east and flashes across to the west.*

When the bomb had fallen, had not the *sun darkened, the moon refused her light, and the stars fallen from heaven*?

Could it be that Dr Nagai and Father Shirato saw this as the great sign of hope, *that the Kingdom of God was at hand*, that it was an occasion for great joy?

It all seemed to describe a pattern. It had all been

predicted. It would seem that now the only triumph would be the love of God, not just the love of the Emperor, family or country.

But I tell you, love your enemies, do good to those who hate you, pray for those who persecute you and insult you, so that you may be true sons of your Father in heaven, who makes his sun rise equally on the evil and the good, his rain fall on the just and on the unjust . . .

This was God's final challenge to him. He had been found guilty under man's law. But in the eyes of God, he was untainted by this, by any alleged 'crime', by this 'sin'. But only on one condition.

If he was about to be with God, then he must pray that no corner of his heart be filled with recrimination against any of his 'persecutors'. And if this was the 'last of days', then he had to feel, to see his God, even in the eyes of those who hated him.

For heaven and earth will pass away. But my words will never pass away.

He would face them with that knowledge. Only then would he be ready.

The full moon over Nagasaki. Is Midori awake, pining for him, the husband who would never return? Another empty page lay beside him. Although Talbot had his last letter, he had written too hastily, in a state of fear. He did not have the new words, but clarity was now coming through those words of St Matthew. She was to be tested too.

His journey on earth would end before hers. But they would be united in the love which no man could 'put asunder'.

A cold shiver of fear. Was he strong enough? Who could be? How was he to write, to know the right prayer for this moment? Fear would blind, paralyse and diminish him. He turns a page, searching desperately. It did not take long.

This, then, is to be your prayer . . .
Our Father, who art in heaven . . .

The very first prayer he had learnt from his parents. He would honour them by reciting it as his last words. A rush of great joy. He would be joining them as well and all those who had disappeared when the sun fell on the earth, the moment of total sacrifice.

Doubt. Could it be that those taken by the bomb were the only ones ready to face God? Was he brought back to Ambon to face this final test, to make him ready? Was his marriage to Midori in the ruins of Nagasaki only a symbol of the marriage with Christ that he must now face?

He had not had time to enjoy the pleasures of an earthly marriage. So, perhaps this was the case.

Do not lay up treasure for yourselves on earth,
where there is moth and rust to consume it,
where there are thieves to break in and steal it; lay
up treasure for yourselves in heaven, where there
is no moth or rust to consume it, no thieves to
break in and steal it. Where your treasure house
is, there your heart is too.

Christ had foreseen all he had experienced. Then, he must now be aware of all his thoughts, his every breath until that last moment in his body. He would find the key in his heart. That was the last refuge, the great simple secret, that final solution to the puzzle of this existence.

All men, when they are about to die, need a sense

of their divinity. Even Ikeuchi, in his last moments, focused on a symbol of his divinity, became united with the Emperor.

One could laugh at this as utter foolishness. Yet the total destruction that he had witnessed could only affirm this need, this unquenchable craving to reach beyond mere human limitations to the exalted state, the *peace that surpasses understanding*.

The unbearable light radiating from the bomb had shown that. God's knowledge had arrived on earth through the most evil of inventions. It was God's light, not man's. Then perhaps, he could see it as perfect that God could call his people to join him in that light. Christ had taught in the form of parables, so tellingly described in Matthew. So, God his father had revealed his teaching with the paradox of total destruction.

I am the abomination of desolation. That was the statement of the Old Testament God. But now Christ called him.

I am the way, the truth and the life.

Hideo puts down the Bible. He could now write the letter. The first streaks of pink dawn now visible, like veins in a rock of black quartz. Soon they would spread into the light of his last day.

He looks out at the dark shapes of the courtroom, the huts and other buildings. How would Noburo and the others fare after him? Perhaps the court would be satisfied with him as their sacrifice and would be lenient with the others?

He picks up the pen, commences to write. Fluent and clear.

Cooper sits on the edge of his bunk. He fumbles for a cigarette from his pocket, his head swimming in the pool of images near the edge of sleep. A very strange dream.

It was a clear, cold morning, the mist rolling along the high ridges of the Great Dividing Range outside Goulburn. He and Geoff, armed with 303 rifles, were stalking a mob of kangaroos that they had chased up a ridge. They had lost them in a cloud of mist near the top of the ridge.

They then separated to execute a pincer movement on opposite ends of the ridge. Then the roos would have no place to run. Easy pickings as they descended down the ridge to his uncle's fence.

He took off at a jog, trying to tiptoe as lightly as he could and to control the sound of his breath. Roos had very powerful hearing. He was just nearing the edge of the ridge when his foot caught some loose stones and sent them tumbling down.

At that very moment, he saw the old man roo. Barely twenty yards away now, he sat up on his hind legs, smelling the danger, listening with ears pricked. The mob had moved further down the ridge. But he was waiting. He was their protector, the last line of defence.

Cooper nestled his rifle in the bough of a young sapling. He took aim, steadying himself, drawing in his breath slowly. Suddenly, the old man was facing him. Cooper was looking straight into his eyes.

Suddenly, the roo's face had changed. It became the face of Hideo, staring at him calmly. He felt his finger tightening on the trigger. But those eyes, challenging him. Daring him to destroy their light.

He released his finger, stood up, shouldering the rifle. In a couple of bounds the roo was gone, vanished into the mist.

Those eyes. They were to end his hunting from that day. Did it mean that now he would be finished with this 'hunt' when Tanaka was gone?

It now made sense. It had been the same look that he had seen in his eyes when they were facing each other at the wire only hours ago. A knowing, fearless, look. Maybe even tinged with pity. Or was it a yearning for the end of all the agony in both of them?

He could not carry the anger now. Perhaps Tanaka had seen it and forgave it. Unlike Ikeuchi who carried his own anger and which, colliding with his, could only produce the inevitable explosion.

He stands, his body dripping perspiration. He would walk out into the dawn soon to witness the ritual of death. He had been forgiven by the victim. But those eyes might go with him to the grave just as Geoff's innocent, larrikin smile would always haunt him.

Hideo puts on his freshly pressed shirt and uniform, carefully adjusting his belt. He polishes his boots then slips them on. He takes the photo of Midori and places it in his top pocket. He picks up his rosary and slips it into his trouser pocket, making sure that it is within reach.

He looks around the chapel hut then kneels before the altar. Soon the Australian priest would arrive and they would pray together.

Like a machine, Talbot rises at the piercing sounds of reveille. His uniform and rifle are ready, his brass buckles polished and slouch hat cleaned. He suppresses a dry retch, feeling an awful paralysing fear spreading up from his stomach.

Keenan appears in the barracks, walking silently past, but with an air of expectation. He turns at the end of the room, observing the soldiers as they dress. He smiles as he produces a cartridge from his pocket and holds it up.

'Righto, who'll have the blank?'

Everyone stands to attention. Talbot dropping his belt to the floor. Keenan walks along the line of men, the cartridge extended. No one reacts. Keenan reaches Talbot, takes a couple of paces towards him, holding the cartridge before his eyes.

'You want it, don't you, Talbot?'

Talbot stares at it. Keenan's taunting face now a mask of contempt, his thin lips taut with sarcastic delight.

'Wasn't it Jesus who said: *Do unto others as you would have them . . .?*'

He leans over to Talbot, his ear cocked for a response. Talbot's lips tremble as he feels for his voice. Dry, cracked.

'Do unto you. Sir.'

Keenan leans back, grins, nodding.

'Yeah. Do unto you.'

He looks at the others, some of whom lower their eyes, not sure how to respond. Others exchange a knowing look with Keenan. He turns back to Talbot, his voice a savage hiss.

'You think the Japs'd give you one of these, Talbot?'

He thrusts the blank cartridge into his face. Talbot feels his face burning with rage and embarrassment. He shakes his head.

'No, sir.'

Keenan steps back, pockets the cartridge, satisfied.

'No. But we're going to give them one. Because we're not savages. And we believe in justice, don't we?'

The bitterness and the upward nasal inflection. Talbot yearned to strike out at Keenan. But the man was full of fury and would beat him to a pulp. Keenan turns suddenly and marches towards the door, turning as he reaches it.

'This'll be quick and clean. Understood?'

He exits, leaving Talbot staring at the others. Some of them give a brief sympathetic look, then turn away. Talbot stares at his rifle. How could he look into Hideo's eyes as he stood ready?

Cooper is alone on the empty grounds. Sheedy appears, then Matsugae. A heavy silence between them. A handful of Ambonese hover nearby. Cooper looks into the faces of a couple of children who observe him intently. The children from the beach on the night of Fenton's death.

The Australian and Dutch flags are raised as the first rays of sun drive the shadows back along the base.

Hideo steps from the hut, now in full uniform. He carries Talbot's Bible. He bows to Reverend Martin then turns to face the two lines of assembled Japanese prisoners, all in uniform, at rigid attention. They form a parade of honour between the hut and the waiting truck.

Hideo bows to them then walks down the parade. Most of the prisoners bow to him, others salute. Noburo is the last on one line. Hideo stops before him. Noburo bows low, unable to face him, his head bowed in shame.

Hideo lifts his face, smiles at him. Noburo offers his hand. Hideo feels Noburo's emotional grip and shakes his hand firmly. He proceeds on, watched by Cooper, Matsugae and Sheedy. He stops before

Talbot and hands him the Bible. Keenan watches them closely.

'Thank you, Jim. My final letter to Midori is in the cover.'

Talbot nods, puts it shakily inside his trouser pocket. Hideo climbs up on to the rear of the truck, the five other soldiers climb up beside him. Keenan faces Talbot who reluctantly climbs aboard. When the back of the truck is secured, he climbs into the cabin with the driver. The truck revs its engines, then drives off slowly, followed by the children. Two jeeps follow, with an Army doctor and two M.P.s aboard.

Cooper and Matsugae walk to a waiting jeep. Sheedy stays rooted to the spot. Cooper turns at the jeep.

'Coming?'

Sheedy shakes his head.

'I did say they wanted blood back home. But how do I write Tanaka's story?'

Cooper climbs into the front and takes the wheel. Matsugae slides in beside him. He starts the engine and drives off, but stops a moment, looking back to Sheedy, a solitary figure against the morning stillness of the base.

As the truck winds its way along a jungle track, Hideo looks back down on the town below. The distant sound of a choir borne on the breeze from the bay. He pictures Midori receiving his letter, walking along the water in Nagasaki.

My love,
It is difficult to understand what forces have
shaped this trial. My accusers themselves seem
puzzled. They look for the answer amidst their
law books and procedure but they are looking in
the wrong place.

The answer they seek is buried in the depths of the human heart. But they are afraid to seek it there.

It seems that they need a key with which to unlock their souls so that they can emerge from the darkness.

Is this key a last ritual, a sacrifice of blood on the altar of peace?

I am always with you, Midori, even until the end of the world, as Christ said.
Your husband,
Hideo.

The truck pulls up at a long avenue of palms. Hideo looks down his last walk to the execution post, mist drifting across the path. He looks at Talbot, nods encouragingly, then jumps down from the truck. The two M.P.s escort him down the track, followed by Keenan, Talbot and the squad, the doctor, the priest then Matsugae and Cooper.

Hideo looks up as the rays of sunlight descend, illuminating each side of the track.

They are the shafts of light pouring in from the windows of Nagasaki Cathedral.

The palms are the slender columns of his last church. The mist wafting up like the gossamer wisps of incense ascendng from the altar, the fragrance now the pungent smell of spice hanging in the humid air.

Then the crypt with its altar. The post.

Hideo is bound to it tightly by the M.P.s who step aside for the Reverend Martin, who blesses Hideo.

The firing party is at attention. Keenan walks up to Talbot, hands him the black blindfold and jerks his head towards Hideo, a thin smile.

'So you can't look at your mate, Private.'

Keenan then hands him the white target triumphantly.

'So you can't miss.'

Talbot, repulsed, slings his rifle, takes the blindfold and target then approaches Hideo. Keenan throws Cooper one last look of satisfaction. Cooper looks across at a couple of children peering through the bushes, alert to every move. He glances at Matsugae, who takes off his hat in respect, then back to Hideo.

Talbot stands before him, trembling with the blindfold. Hideo looks him in the eyes.

'I forgive you, Jim.'

Talbot brings up the blindfold. Hideo shakes his head.

'I don't want the blindfold. I'm not frightened of death.'

Talbot shakes his head, his voice a cracked whisper.

'I'm sorry. It's regulations.'

As he applies the blindfold, Hideo recites softly:
Forgive us our trespasses.

Talbot joins him, his voice now a burning fire.
As we forgive them who trespass against us. And lead us not into temptation but deliver us from evil. Amen.

Talbot applies the small white target over Hideo's heart, glimpsing the photo of Midori in his pocket. He turns to face the firing squad, his hand reaching behind to squeeze Hideo's for the last time.

'Goodbye, my friend.'

Choking back his tears, Talbot steps back to join the squad. Hideo feels for the rosary at the edge of his pocket and grasps hold of it tightly.

Keenan snaps to attention.

'Firing party! Port arms!'

Talbot raises the rifle, tears blurring his vision.

'Load!'

Five breech bolts slammed in unison. Talbot's a second behind.

'Present!'

Talbot struggles desperately to control his shaking arms. Finally the sight settles on the target.

'Fire!'

The flash of the muzzles. The brilliant light of the bomb's explosion. The screams of frightened birds. A shattered body slumped at the post.

Talbot opens his tear soaked eyes. It was over. His first and last killing.

Keenan waits, letting the moment sink in for all.

'Firing party! Port arms!'

Talbot shoulders his rifle, his body numb, his lips trembling with an incoherent prayer.

The doctor steps up to Hideo, checks that he is dead then nods to two soldiers. Cooper and Matsugae exchange a long look.

In Matsugae's eyes, a grief and feeling of futility. In Cooper's eyes, a gentle acknowledgement of this. Matsugae walks off, leaving Cooper to watch Hideo taken down from the post.

Rain descends, a sudden downpour. Cooper turns, walks towards the track, disappearing back into the thickening, swirling mist.

Back to a new life.

SUGGESTED READING

Beaumont, Joan, *Gull Force*, Allen & Unwin, Australia, 1988. The story of Gull Force's captivity on Ambon.

Brackman, Arnold C., *The Other Nuremberg*, Collins, UK, 1989. The previously untold story of the Tokyo War Crimes Trials.

Dower, John, *War Without Mercy – Racism and Power in the Pacific War*, Faber & Faber, UK, 1986.

Dubro, Alec and Kaplan, David E., *Yakuza*, Futura, UK, 1987.

Glynn, Father Paul, *A Song for Nagasaki*, Catholic Book Club, 3 Mary Street, Hunters Hill, NSW, 2110, Australia, 1988.

Halberstam, David, *The Reckoning*, Morrow, USA, 1986.

Hidaka, Rokuro, *The Price of Affluence – Dilemmas of Contemporary Japan*, Penguin, Australia, 1985.

Ibuse, Masuji, *Black Rain*, Kodansha International/John Martin, UK, 1989. The most acclaimed account of the bombing of Hiroshima.

Macarthur, General Douglas, *Reminiscences*, Da Capo, USA, 1988.

Maruyama, Masao, *Thought and Behaviour in Modern Japanese Politics*, Oxford University Press, UK, 1979.

Moffitt, Athol, *Project Kingfisher*, Angus & Robertson, Australia, 1989. The story of the Sandakan death marches and the war crimes trials in 1946.

Nelson, Hank, *Prisoners of War – Australians under Nippon*, ABC Books, Australia, 1985.